THE
TRUTH
ABOUT
MARTIANS

THE TRUTH ABOUT MARTIANS

MELISSA SAVAGE

A YEARLING BOOK

For Tobin. No one braver.

Text copyright © 2018 by Melissa Savage
Cover art copyright © 2018 by Lydia Nichols

All rights reserved. Published in the United States by Yearling, an imprint of Random House Children's Books, a division of Penguin Random House LLC, New York. Originally published in hardcover in the United States by Crown Books for Young Readers, an imprint of Random House Children's Books, a division of Penguin Random House LLC, New York, in 2018.

Yearling and the jumping horse design are registered trademarks of Penguin Random House LLC.

Visit us on the Web! rhcbooks.com

Educators and librarians, for a variety of teaching tools, visit us at RHTeachersLibrarians.com

The Library of Congress has cataloged the hardcover edition of this work as follows:
Names: Savage, Melissa, author.
Title: The truth about Martians / Melissa Savage.
Description: First edition. | New York: Crown Books for Young Readers, [2018] |
Summary: When a flying saucer crash-lands next to Mylo's Roswell, New Mexico, ranch in 1947, he and his friends Dibs and Gracie set out to find and help the Martians.
Identifiers: LCCN 2018010157 | ISBN 978-1-5247-0016-4 (hardback) |
ISBN 978-1-5247-0017-1 (glb) | ISBN 978-1-5247-0018-8 (epub)
Subjects: CYAC: Extraterrestrial beings—Fiction. | Unidentified flying objects—Fiction. | Adventure and adventurers—Fiction. | Friendship—Fiction. | Family life—New Mexico—Fiction. | Roswell (N.M.)—History—20th century—Fiction. |
BISAC: JUVENILE FICTION / Social Issues / Friendship. |
JUVENILE FICTION / Family / General (see also headings under Social Issues.) |
JUVENILE FICTION / Action & Adventure / General.
Classification: LCC PZ7.1.S2713 Tru 2018 | DD [Fic]—dc23

ISBN 978-1-5247-0019-5 (pbk.)

Printed in the United States of America
10 9 8 7 6 5 4 3 2 1
First Yearling Edition 2020

Random House Children's Books
supports the First Amendment and celebrates the right to read.

CONTENTS

1. The Crash	1
2. A Man of Steel	12
3. A Spit-Shake Promise	23
4. Fried Attic Bats	34
5. Interstellar Warfare Readiness	41
6. A Martian Holdup	45
7. My Very Own Lois Lane	57
8. A Cracker Jack Superhero	66
9. Batter Up	74
10. Tomato Guts	79
11. Martian Mind-Control Caps	87
12. Heavenly Chili Cheese Dogs	90
13. The Purple Spot of Death	99
14. Chicken Liver	106
15. Brave	111

16. Shortstop 118

17. Telepathic Superpowers 126

18. A Martian Prayer and a Promise 138

19. The Wrong Boy 143

20. Leave It Be 156

21. In the Shadow of the Moon 164

22. Martians Don't Eat Ice Cream 170

23. A Flying Disk Captured 180

24. Superhero Sidekick 184

25. Zucchini Squash 198

26. A Moontian Cover-Up 207

27. Fried Attic Bats with a Side of Ham 215

28. A Real-Life Lex Luthor 227

29. Faraway Stars 238

30. Nabbed 246

31. The Moontian Rescue 256

32. Krypton's Heavenly Stars 265

33. Stealing Our Thunder 268

34. The Mother Ship 272

35. Out of Time 277

36. That Horrible Day 280

37. Good-Bye 283

38. Broder 291

39. A Champion for the Underdog 304

40. New Beginnings 310

Author's Note 319

The true courage is in facing danger
when you are afraid.

—L. FRANK BAUM

1

THE CRASH

July 4, 1947—11:53 p.m.

In a fiery blaze.

That's how they show themselves for the very first time.

It's not like a Martian invasion is the first thing I think of when I see it, because I'm not crazy.

But it's *definitely* the second.

Not because I'm crazy, though. It's because that's exactly how Superman arrived.

In a fiery blaze.

His parents, Jor-El and Lara, sent him to Earth in a little space vessel to escape the annihilation of the planet Krypton.

You could say I'm sort of a Superman expert.

Well, both me and my best friend, Dibs, are. Except he's got this weird obsession with Martians, too. Mostly the Planet Comics series. It's his favorite, even over Superman.

Which is why Martians are the second thing I think of.

Because it's all he talks about some days. Martians this

and Martians that. It's hard not to think of them even when you're trying not to because he's always jabbering on about them.

Whatever it is that I'm seeing now streaks a blaze of fire through the black, thrashing thunderclouds on the hottest night of the summer in the middle of a monsoon and turns the small town of Corona, New Mexico, into a real-life comic book. The only difference is that no one's shouting *This looks like a job for Superman!* And Kal-El, the Last Son of Krypton, is a no-show.

It's just me.

Mylo Affinito.

And I'm no superhero. Not even close.

Neither is Dibs, who sleeps through the whole darned thing.

"Dibs!" I whisper. "You see that?"

He's sawing logs and sucking his middle knuckle.

"Dibs!"

That kid wouldn't wake up if the vessel landed on the roof and Superman himself stepped out and started dancing a jig to "The Boogie Woogie Bugle Boy."

Downstairs the baby is too busy crying and Momma too busy rocking and hushing in the creaky chair to notice any difference between that fiery flash of light and plain old lightning.

But *I* do.

I mean, I think I do . . . it just happened so fast.

Baby Kay doesn't like summer monsoons. Especially the loud ones. The ones that crash and crack and light up the nighttime sky in an angry battle of cloudy wills. I think maybe in her tiny brain she thinks if she wails the loudest she'll win and send all the clapping thunderclouds running. At least that's what it seems like, because she can howl real good sometimes.

It's when the brilliant flash of light dashes a second time across the bedroom ceiling from one corner to the other in less than one blink that I sit straight up. It's a flash so bright and so fast that it makes me wonder if I really saw anything at all.

Dibs and I are in my bed lying toes to nose, sweating under a single white sheet even though there's another perfectly good bed sitting on the other side of the night table. Which he reminds me of just about every single time he sleeps over. And that's a lot of nights since his momma left.

The bed on the other side of the night table with the blue quilt pulled straight and tight stays empty, though.

Empty for one year, one month, and eight days.

I look down at Dibs, watching him saw logs loud and steady. His mouth wide open now, sucking air in and out like the sky hasn't just caught fire for a moment. His face peaceful and totally unaware of his impending doom.

A dirty-foot-in-the-face alarm clock.

And since he doesn't see it coming, I get him real good, too. This time with my toes rubbed up right under his nose.

He sits straight up.

"Aw, that's just foul!" he cries.

"How could you sleep through all that?" I whisper.

"Through what?" He holds his hand up to his nose. "Don't you ever wash them things?"

"You only missed the whole darned thing," I tell him.

"The scum under your toenails?" He sticks his pointer finger inside his left nose hole, knuckle-deep. "Seen it. And smelt it, too. You shoved your pinky toe in, you know. *In*."

I stretch my neck to get a better look out the window as Grammy Hildago's old lace curtains billow in the wind like two white ghosts scrambling in from the rain.

Momma and Daddy took over Grammy and Pappy Hildago's ranch five years ago after Pappy Hildago died. Daddy left the Army Air Force and we moved to New Mexico from the Bronx, where he grew up. I was six and Obie was eight and Baby Kay wasn't even born yet. But I hardly remember life before Corona.

"It was like the sky turned to daytime and back to night again in a single blink," I whisper down at Dibs.

He's not even listening to me, holding one nose hole closed and snuffing in and out of the other. "I hope you're happy, because that funk is probably stuck up in my nose hairs for life."

"Dibs!" I sit up. "I'm trying to tell you something important here."

"About the light?"

"Yeah," I say.

He hoists himself up on one pointy elbow and holds his head in his hand, blinking at me. "What's the big deal about lightning?"

"That's what I'm trying to tell you," I say. "I don't think that's what it was. At least it didn't look like lightning. It looked like . . . like the sky caught fire or something."

"So . . . *lightning*."

"I told you it wasn't, didn't I?"

He yawns a long, bored yawn. "If it wasn't lightning, then what was it?" he asks.

"That's the question," I tell him.

He clicks his tongue at me, rolls his eyes real big, and flops back down on the bed. "Good night," he tells me, sliding a flat pillow with a yellowing case over his head. "And if I get another toe in the snoot, you're going to get this knuckle sandwich right in the kisser." He pushes a single skinny duke out from under the pillow.

I snort at that one and hear his muffled giggle against the mattress.

That's because we both well know that his sandwiches couldn't make a dent in *anyone's* kisser. Knuckle or otherwise. He's a skeleton with the skin still on and he knows it, too.

And then another fiery streak lights up the room, this time with a *whoosh*ing noise that sounds like it's blowing the green shutters clear off the windows as it blazes on by.

I know he sees something this time, too, because his head pops straight up from underneath the pillow. Baby Kay howls her loudest wail yet. And I rush to the window, clinging to the wet sill with wide eyes peering out into the blackness.

Sloppy raindrops soak the cows soggy out in the field and pummel the roof of the front porch and the barn, too. Small lakes form in the dirt drive and the large drops drench the chicken coop and Daddy's tractor parked out front.

"What is it?" Dibs asks, holding the sheet tight under his chin like a threadbare protective shield. "What do you see out there? Is it Martians? It is, isn't it? Martians landing to take over the planet. Just like a real live *War of the Worlds*. It is, isn't it?"

"Why don't you just come over here and look for yourself," I say.

"I'm not going anywhere until I know for sure there isn't any Martian out there waiting to beam me up to the mother ship," he says. "You check first."

"I'm not your Martian checker."

"You know they'll harvest your brains out your ears as soon as look at you," he goes on. "That's how they are."

I blow air out of my mouth. "You read way too many comic books," I say.

"On *The Whistler* last week," he goes on, "they had a whole episode about this guy who was abducted by Martians and they probed his brain and he became a mindless, soulless shell of a human to further the Martian agenda here on Earth and no one even knew it because he still kept his same human form."

I scoff. *"Probed his brain?"*

He looks at me real serious. "Yep, Martian mind control."

I shake my head at him but he keeps on anyway, just like he does when he blabs on with his Martian stories.

"Maybe they already probed 'em and we don't know it because they already took our brains for experimentation and they're gone now," he says.

I turn to face him. "Maybe yours is." I smile.

He smiles back at me with his big beaver teeth that don't all fit in his mouth yet. "Well, they do tend to prefer geniuses." He puts his chin in the air and puffs his skinny chest out.

"Will you stop being a chicken and just get over here already?" I order, pointing at the floor next to me.

He sighs heavy and slides his leathery bare feet across the worn floorboards until he's kneeling on his knobby knees right beside me. His feet are tougher than the finest leathers in all the land on account of never wearing boots. He says they pinch his toes, but I think it's really because he doesn't have ones that fit him right. Not since his momma left him and Mr. Butte two summers ago.

We stare out the window together, leaning against the sill, chins resting on our forearms.

Waiting.

Mist from the heavy drops sprays into our eyes and sprinkles our skin, cooling us from the sweltering night. The rusted-up tin windmill out past the chicken coop gripes a high-pitched metal wail, complaining to the wind for pushing it around. My heartbeat pounds in my ears and Dibs's heavy breaths are short and fast, going in and out of his bony chest.

"Maybe it was a ghostly spirit from H-E double hockey sticks," he finally whispers after a good long while. "I heard this story one time about an evil demon stuck in Purgatory who blasted right out and snatched this kid down in Albuquerque and they never seen him again. Not ever. Stole his soul right out from under him. You *know* something like that's got to be true. People don't make that stuff up. You believe in ghosts, Mylo?"

I shrug. "Depends," I say.

"How about Martians?" he asks. "You believe in them?"

This time I don't answer.

Things to know about Dibson Tiberius Butte:

1. The only things bigger than his tall tales are his beaver teeth and those ears.
2. His toes stink way worse than mine no matter what he says.
3. He's my very best friend in the whole entire universe.

We wait.

Thunder rolls.

Lightning flashes.

Downstairs, Baby Kay is finally quieting and the creaking of Momma's chair slows some.

And then in a single second comes the loudest thunderclap I've ever heard. It shakes the earth and shatters the desert silence. It's a clap so loud it sounds like it cracked a million-mile crater deep into the center of the whole wide world, and that's when we see a colossal explosion, out in the direction of Foster Ranch. The blast sprays brilliant bits of fire out in a dazzling burst of light toward the heavens.

When I see all that, I duck under the windowsill and Dibs scrambles for cover in the bed under the safety of his sweaty white shield.

"Did you see that?" he says from behind his cotton armor. "Did you?"

"Yeah," I say, peeking back up over the sill.

"That"—Dibs points a single skinny finger out from under the sheet—"wasn't lightning."

I roll my eyes at him. "Didn't I tell you so?"

I watch in amazement as the explosion turns to small specks of light spraying back toward the earth. It's like the fireworks display we saw tonight at the Fourth of July parade in town, but instead of bits of light bursting up high and then falling down, this explosion happens on the ground and shoots straight up in a blazing bouquet.

"Think it's Martians?" Dibs peeks one eye out.

"Nah," I say. "Has to be something else. Maybe someone just goofing off with leftover firecrackers."

"*Firecrackers?*" He gives me a look. "Are you kidding me?"

A cow out in a nearby pasture moans.

Another one answers her.

"Even the *cows* are talking about it," Dibs tells me.

I watch the lights in silence for a long while, seeing the fiery bits burn out in slow motion toward the ground until it's almost all dark again.

"One of us better go and check things out," Dibs says. "And when you do . . . make sure and tell 'em you come in peace."

I snort again and point a thumb out toward the field. "You're off your rocker if you think I'm going out there," I inform him.

"Well, *I'm* sure not doing it."

I watch the light storm until each of the fiery flickers goes mostly all dark and the desert and the ranch and all the fields around us grow quiet again.

Too quiet.

Even the sloppy drops have stopped shearing the grasses and filling the puddles in the muddy drive, the cows have given up and gone back to sleep, and Momma has shushed and rocked just enough until both the sky and the baby have settled.

All the lights have finally flickered out . . . except one.

But it isn't just any light.

It's . . . *green.*

One single green beam.

My fingers stay glued to the rain-soaked sill as I stare out the window, unable to breathe or move or speak, watching as the far-off green light glows dim and then bright, dim and then bright.

Like an eyeball . . . blinking at me.

Watching me like I'm watching it.

Dibs slides his leathery feet across the floorboards again, until I feel him standing right behind me.

"Will you look at that?" he whispers. "That's a Martian ship sure as I'm standing here."

"You don't know that," I tell him. "We're more likely under attack from the Russians than men from Mars."

I wipe a mixture of sloppy mist and sweat off my chin with the back of my hand and finally let in the air I didn't realize my lungs were aching for. Outside the window, it smells like wet grass and smoke and something burnt up real bad.

"Don't even try and tell me that you're not thinking the very same thing, Mylo, because I know you too well," Dibs says. "Look at that thing out there."

Our stares stay fixed on that blinking green eyeball. Glowing dim and then bright. Dim and then bright.

"There has to be another explanation for it," I whisper into the darkness. "Maybe a meteorite or asteroid."

"*Krypton burns like a green star in the endless heavens,*" Dibs says in an announcer voice just like the narrator from *The Adventures of Superman* program that we listen to on the radio in the evening after supper.

As he slides his bare feet back to the bed, I stay stuck on the sill, my head resting on my arm, watching the sky. Bright stars push and peek their way out between the dark, swirling storm clouds as the monsoon blows its way east. And I wonder which star is yours.

Obie? I whisper to the night. *Did you see it, too?*

2

A MAN OF STEEL

July 5, 1947—6:15 a.m.

Nightmares are dark and gray and deep and scary.

They take all of you when you're not even looking, until you're sweating and running and praying to get away.

And then you wake up.

That's when the nightmares are supposed to creep back into the dark crevices of the world with the rise of the sun. But sometimes . . . they stay.

Even in the light.

It's not Martians that wake me the next morning. Or a space vessel blasting through the sky and crash-landing on Earth, either.

It's Jor-El McRoostershire the Third, crowing his morning wake-up song, that opens my eyelids, and it's Momma's churro hotcakes frying up in the pan downstairs that wake my stomach.

Dibs is gone.

He doesn't need any rooster to wake him up. Birds, either.

He has an automatic alarm clock inside his brain to make sure he gets up and off on time to do morning chores on his daddy's farm, Butte Rise and Swine Pig and Poultry.

Nothing different than every other single normal day.

That nightmare of Martians landing out in the desert and blinking green eye is long gone with the sun and the normal noises of the yard down below my window.

I stretch and yawn and rub my eyes awake with my knuckles. But when I look over to see if you're up, too, all I see is an empty bed.

The one with the blue quilt pulled straight and tight.

And I remember that you're gone all over again.

I remember that even though nightmares are supposed to creep back into the dark crevices of the world with the rise of the sun . . . sometimes they stay.

The billowing curtains lie still now, without even a hint of breeze to blow them. I stretch my neck to see out the window. The sun is already scorching the soggy earth back into dust and cracking the mud puddles dry again.

The yard is alive with sound just like any other morning.

Daddy's tractor roars in the field.

Chickens cluck and peck in the coop.

Cows moan in the pasture.

I pull Shortstop out from under my pillow and hug him close to me, breathing him in at the top of his head, between the ears where the fur has been loved almost clean off.

The tiny bear smells of Obie's freshly oiled leather catcher's mitt and the dirt from the pitcher's mound that we built together out back . . . but mostly of him.

And of his courage.

There's no one braver.

Not even the Man of Steel himself. Obie was a Man of Steel and then some.

Shortstop looks back at me with his one good eye. The other hangs by a single thread. I know if that hanging eye could cry from missing Obie, it would cry real tears just like mine still do at night when I know no one else can see me.

"I know you miss him, too," I say, hugging Shortstop close. "Not as much as me, but a lot still, I bet."

I feel the tears.

Pricking behind my eyes and clutching my throat.

And then the gray.

The deep dark gray that threatens to snatch me when I think too long about everything that happened.

So I just keep running.

To make sure it can't ever catch me and swallow me whole.

"Mylo!" Momma calls from the kitchen. "Time for breakfast!"

Momma's churro hotcakes smell like sweetness and vanilla and cinnamon and toasted oil from the skillet on the stove. And today there's the smoky smell of bacon, too, making my stomach rumble. I take a deep breath in and stretch.

"Mylo?" she calls again. "You up?"

"Coming, Momma!" I holler back, peeling the white sheet off me and swinging my legs over the side of the bed.

Martians.

I shake my head in the safety of the light.

If it were still night and Dibs were prattling on with his stories, he might still have me believing in his stupid theories about Martian mind control. Not because they think he's a genius, though. I don't think any Martian would care two hoots about harvesting a brain that only makes Cs in arithmetic.

The absolute truth about Martians:

1. They can't really harvest brains (I'm pretty sure).
2. Only God has the power to take a soul, and that's the real truth of it.
3. And this is the most true thing: there isn't any such thing as Martians.

Jor-El McRoostershire the Third is still crowing, Baby Kay is downstairs talking her goo-goo gibberish in her high chair, and our old springer spaniel, Clark Kent, is barking on the front porch.

It's a whole lot of nothing.

Which is how it is in Corona, New Mexico. A whole lot of nothing.

Until . . . there's something.

Help.

I sit straight up in my bed.

I stretch my neck out and look past the curtains.

A word.

Just one word.

Help.

It's like a whisper and a scream all at once.

I hold my breath still inside me and listen again.

Daddy's tractor putt-puttering.

Chickens clucking.

Baby Kay gibbering.

I breathe out.

Nothing.

And then another something . . .

Help.

I scramble down out of the bed, my bare knees against the worn floorboards, and place my cheek against the cool surface, peering underneath the mattress.

When I was a little kid you couldn't have paid me a million dollars to do something like that. I used to think the Boogieman lived under there. And in the nighttime, he stalked children's ankles, ready to strike for his nightly meal. So I'd hold it all night, even if I really had to go bad. But if it was an emergency, I would call to Obie and he would stand guard for me until I jumped safely back between the sheets.

He wasn't ever scared to stand up to the Boogieman.

He was too brave for that, too.

Of course, now I don't believe in the Boogieman anymore. In the daytime I don't. But when it's dark, anything is possible.

Obie's catcher's mitt with a baseball tucked inside it is still between the mattress and the box spring. The best way to break in a glove. He used to keep it under his mattress, but now I keep it under mine.

Underneath the bed are one rusted pair of old metal roller skates, a chipped World War II model plane, an old tiddlywinks game with the cover missing, and a tangled mess of a Slinky that Baby Kay got her sticky fingers on and twisted up into a wiry knot.

No monsters, though.

If Dibs were here, he'd tell me a story about some kind of creature with the ability to go invisible and whisper and scream and hide in the depths of darkness under the bed ready to grab little boys' feet on their way back from the bathroom.

And if it were dark enough, I might just believe him.

But not in the light.

In the light it's supposed to be safe.

Help.

I jolt up and scramble to the closet, flinging the door open. Obie's clothes are still inside, mixed in with mine. Momma thinks I'll grow into them by next year. His Yankees cap sits on the top shelf. The one we got when Daddy took us back to New York to visit Granddaddy Affinito in the Bronx and see a game at Yankee Stadium. We took the same Lexington line as Daddy did growing up, transferring at 125th. Obie and I had brought our gloves with us that day and prayed for a fly ball. But neither one of us caught one. After that, Obie always said he was going to be the next Yogi Berra.

And he would have been, too.

He was the best catcher I've ever known. He never missed a ball, even when I threw him a curve now and again when he wasn't expecting one.

I push the hangers aside and look beneath the folded T-shirts and piles of itchy winter sweaters on the shelves.

Nothing.

I stand still, holding all my breath inside me again, and listen real hard, waiting to hear it one more time.

"Mylo!" Momma calls again. "Breakfast is ready!"

"Yes, ma'am!" I call back.

"Dibs is on his way up the drive," she says. "No comic books until chores are done. And make sure you scrub all the way to Z with the bar of Ivory."

Before Obie got sick, Momma was happy if my hands saw plain old water after chores. But now there's a bar of Ivory at every sink and even extras in the kitchen cabinet in case we run out. And she makes both me and Daddy scrub the whole entire alphabet before we can rinse.

I can hear Dibs's horse, True Belle, gallop up the long dirt drive out front, pounding her hooves deep in the dirt.

Pound. Pound. Pound.

Clark Kent barks from the front porch.

Dibs's daddy doesn't seem to care to get what a growing boy needs to eat. Not since Dibs's momma left two years ago, leaving nothing but a note. Dibs never told me what the note said, but I didn't need to see it to know it was bad.

Because she never came back.

I grab my crumpled overalls from the floor, pulling the straps over my shoulders and fastening the bronze buckles to the bib. I lick my hand and try to rub some mud off the knees from yesterday's chores. Just below my window, Clark Kent's nails scrape against the porch floorboards as he scrambles down the front steps to meet up with Dibs.

From underneath the sheet, I pull the crumpled Superman comic book that Daddy brought me from town and try to smooth the corners flat again. I read it three times by the light of the crashing sky last night after I crawled back under the white sheet and Dibs went back to sawing his logs. When I smooth out the creases, best I can, I pull the drawer open on the night table between our beds and carefully set the number forty-five issue on top of number forty-four, glancing at the stack of my homemade comics in the pile next to the Supermans.

The very top one—

THE DEFEAT OF THE MARTIAN SUPERVIRUS
Volume Sixteen of
THE AFFINITO BROTHERS' SUPERHERO DUO
COMIC BOOK SERIES

—is still missing its ending.

I push the drawer closed again and a metal picture frame on top wobbles. It's the one of us smiling together in our matching caps and mitts that day at Yankee Stadium. Smiling like a couple of dummies who had no idea that bad things really happen.

Like the endings to stories are always good ones.

My throat starts to feel tight and my stomach twisted up and it feels like I'm slipping. Slipping into the gray. A deep dark place that always seems to be chasing me.

Chasing me for one year, one month, and nine days.

It lies in wait, ready to pull me in and never let me go. But I figure if I run fast enough, it won't ever catch me.

"Mylo!" Dibs calls from outside.

I hear his bare feet hit the dirt on the drive and the sound of a rope being thrown over the wood post out front as he ties up True Belle to drink from the trough.

"Mylo!"

I push the curtains aside and shield my eyes from the hot sun already drying and cracking the mud puddles from last night.

"What are you hollering about?" I call down to him.

Dibs is standing just below my window, a deeply tanned hand shading his eyes as he squints up at me. He's in his same baggy overalls ripped at the knees with no shirt, dirty bare feet, and the same old sweaty Yankees cap that he always wears backward on his head covering up his crooked blond buzz cut. The one I brought back for him when Daddy took us. He only takes it off in church, at meals, and when a lady's present.

"I'm hollering 'cause I seen it, that's why!" he calls back, his bare, bony chest pumping up and down.

Clark Kent lies at Dibs's feet, his tongue dripping and his tail swinging up a dusty red cloud.

"You saw what exactly?" I ask.

Dibs hocks a thick, juicy loogie from way down deep and spits in the dirt. "That explosion! Out at Foster Ranch! I seen where it hit!"

I stare down at him. "Military, right?"

The screen door creaks open and Momma steps out onto the porch, wiping her hands on her apron. "Dibs?" she asks. "I've got churro hotcakes ready. Is everything okay?"

"Ma'am." Dibs removes his cap for Momma and nods

her a proper hello. "Yes, ma'am. I just seen something out at Foster Ranch this morning. Something crashed out that way. Last night. In the storm. Mac Brazel says he's going to call out the fire department today to take care of things."

"Lord have mercy," Momma says, and crosses herself.

Momma always crosses herself when she says that.

She shields her eyes with her palm and stares off in the direction of Foster Ranch and then out toward where Daddy is working in the field.

"Well, you'd better leave it for them to handle. Have you had any breakfast at all yet today?" she asks.

"Yes, ma'am," Dibs tells her. "Mrs. Brazel made Daddy and me chorizo and eggs early this morning, but with all this excitement, my stomach is hungry all over again."

Momma gives him a warm smile. "Come on in and get washed up," she says, then calls up to me, "Hey, little man? You coming down? After chores, I've got some fresh-baked jalapeño corn bread I need you to get over to Mordecai Lord's place."

"Yes, Momma," I answer.

"Thank you, ma'am," Dibs says.

"Not at all," she says, letting the screen door bang behind her.

"Do you know if she made the Mexican chocolate sauce to go on top?" Dibs calls up to me. "I mean, it's good either way, but I love your momma's Mexican chocolate sauce."

"So what was it that you think you saw out there?" I ask.

"I told you it was a Martian ship last night, didn't I? Didn't I tell you that?" He lowers his voice.

"So?"

"So I was right," he says.

"No, you weren't."

"How do *you* know?" he demands.

"Because I *know* there isn't any Martian ship sitting out there," I say.

"And how can you be so sure?" He puts his hands on his hips.

"Because," I tell him. "There isn't any such thing as Martians."

He shrugs and heads toward the house. "Don't believe me then," he calls over his shoulder. "But if that isn't a space ship from Mars crunched up in that field, I'll eat it up without salt or pepper."

"Well, I hope you're hungry."

3

A SPIT-SHAKE PROMISE

July 5, 1947—6:40 a.m.

I'm pretty sure God hates me.

And I can prove it, too.

As far as I see it, when He was drafting my human image up in Heaven, He left out some very important parts.

Very important.

Parts that most boys in my class already have (with the exception of Dibs, of course) and even one girl, too.

Eunice Snodgrass.

Maybe God hadn't had His morning coffee yet or maybe it's just a horrible joke for a good heavenly laugh. But my bet is . . . He just plain hates me.

My missing parts, thanks to God:

1. Not one single, solitary muscle yet.
2. A bare-naked upper lip without even a hint of a wisp.

3. And this is the biggest one—my courage
   part is missing.

Even Eunice Snodgrass has all three

Last year she punched me behind Corona General and took my box of Cracker Jacks and I had a bruise for a whole week. Now I just steer clear of her altogether.

But that's not even the worst of it all, with God I mean.

The worst of it is, He doesn't listen.

Not to me, He doesn't. Not even when it's real important.

Not even when I prayed and begged and pleaded and promised.

He just took Obie away from us and didn't even care that it broke our family into so many pieces that it will never be whole again.

Never.

So I say fine by me. If He's not going to listen to me, then I'm done listening to Him. That's why we don't talk anymore. Not even in church on Sundays.

But I fake it for Momma's sake. If she knew I wasn't speaking to God, I'd be saying Hail Marys until she was good and sure my soul was back on track toward heavenly salvation.

I wash up with the sloppy bar of Ivory soap that's in the dish next to the bathroom sink. Only sudsing up through J today. I figure I'll have to wash to Z after chores anyway, so J seems good enough for churro hotcakes.

I stare at myself in the mirror above the sink and flex both arms like a tall, proud, skinny saguaro cactus. I stand up on my tiptoes and examine my arms carefully, searching for any evidence of divine muscular intervention during the night.

But all I see are string beans.

Two spindly, sunburnt string beans.

Obie had 'em. He had them when *he* was eleven. He had muscles, wisps, and the biggest courage part of anyone I've ever known. Obie could do ten pull-ups without stopping even once. And not cheating by raising his chin high, either. He did 'em with his chin straight.

Straight.

And when he got sick I never once saw him cry. Not once.

That's how brave he was.

I brush my teeth and wet down all the cowlicks before I head downstairs.

When I pull open the bathroom door, I hear Dibs still running his mouth in the kitchen.

"It wasn't like nothing I've ever seen before, Mrs. Affinito," he's going on over his shoulder while he scrubs with the Ivory at the sink.

"Anything you've ever seen," Momma corrects him.

"Right, nothing like it," he says. "Silver pieces of this metal that was as light as if you're holding nothing at all . . . and they have these weird purple markings across 'em. But they're not like words or letters or nothing like that, either, more like shapes, symbols . . . that kind of thing. . . ."

The kitchen is scorching. Even hotter than the upstairs.

The black metal fan in the corner buzzes as the blades go around, pushing the sweltering air in hot circles. A small wooden radio on the bookshelf in the sitting room plays music on low. Bing Crosby is Momma's favorite. She used to play it loud and sing and dance in the mornings while she was cooking, but I haven't seen her do that in a long while.

Baby Kay is talking to herself in her high chair, her wispy dark curls wet against her forehead. She's giving a baby-gibberish play-by-play about the soggy hunks of chocolate-soaked churro hotcakes she's chucking off the side of the tray and how they're still there when she peeks over the edge.

"Lolo!" she screeches when she sees me, throwing her chocolatey hands up in the air.

"Hi, Baby Kay," I tell her, kissing the top of her sweaty head.

"Mo woc lat?"

"Momma," I say. "She wants more chocolate sauce."

"Bibby Boo!" Baby Kay squeals to Dibs, holding out a mushy hunk of hotcake in his direction.

"The thinner pieces crumple right up in your hand just like paper and then straighten back out again like they were ironed with heavy starch," Dibs keeps on while he wipes his hands on Grammy Hildago's kitchen towel with an embroidered rooster on it.

Grammy Hildago had an obsession with roosters same as Dibs and his Martians. Even the kitchen clock above the sink has a rooster on it. And the black iron weather vane on the top of the barn is a rooster, too.

"And they are so strong," Dibs blabs on. "I mean, you can't tear it no matter how hard you try. Mac Brazel even tried to shoot a hole in one of them thicker pieces this morning and it didn't even make a single dent. Not one single dent." Dibs wide-eyes me. "*Invulnerable* . . . just like the fabric from Krypton that made up Superman's suit."

"Bibby Boo!" Baby Kay calls again, waving the churro mush in the air.

Dibs gobbles it up, pretending to eat her fingers, too. She squeals again, this time a high-pitched giggle.

There's a round burn on his palm that wasn't there last night. It's the exact size of a hot tobacco pipe. But I don't ask him questions anymore. This one time, I did say something and his cheeks turned fire-engine red and his eyes got narrow and he snapped real good at me. So now I just leave it be.

While he's still going on about whatever fell out of the sky at Foster Ranch, he pulls out a chair from the table.

Obie's chair.

I put my hand on top of his without saying anything. He pushes the chair back into its place and slips into the spot across from mine. He sets his Yankees cap on the table and licks his palm to slick down his crooked buzz cut. I sit down then, too, and give him a good hard stare.

"Roswell Fire's going out there today, then?" I ask him.

His tongue reaches out over his gigantic white teeth to wet his cracking lips. "That's right, and you want to know what else?" he whispers to me, glancing back at Momma.

"The only thing I should be hearing over there is some thanking of the Lord for the bounty of this breakfast," she tells us, sliding hotcakes off the griddle.

"Yes, ma'am," Dibs says, closing his eyes and folding his hands in his lap.

His lips move while he talks to Him.

I know that because my eyes are cracked open. I don't have anything to say to Him about this breakfast or anything else.

I wonder if God strikes people down who are mad at Him. I don't remember ever hearing anything about it in the Bible, but it's a pretty thick book. There's probably something in there about it.

"Amen," Dibs says, crossing himself.

"Min!" Baby Kay shouts, clapping her hands high above her head in a baby hallelujah.

I just clear my throat and sputter out a fake cough before giving my front a fake Father, Son, and Holy Ghost cross. Dibs catches me this time and eyes me suspiciously from across the table, but before he can open up his big mouth, I let him know exactly what I think of those pieces he's going on about. "I bet you anything it turns out to be a meteorite."

Dibs sits up taller in his seat and puffs his chest out at me even though it's all bone and no meat. "You don't know nothing," he says. "You weren't even there."

"Anything," Momma corrects him.

"See, your momma even agrees with me," he says. "You don't know nothing about anything."

Momma smiles. "That's enough now." She sets a plate of hotcakes in front of each of us. "I don't want to hear another word about it. I want you both to stay away from whatever is out on that ranch, do you hear me? You don't need to be bothering with it. The fire department will handle what needs to be handled."

"Yes, Momma," I say.

"Dibs, same thing goes for you," she says.

"Yes, ma'am," Dibs says with a full fork already in his mouth.

I look up at her.

Her eyes are puffier underneath than they normally are

and the white is more red, too. But Momma's got her courage part. I know it because of that horrible day. The worst day that ever was, while me and Daddy couldn't even see straight, Momma stood strong for us all. It never seems like she's got the gray chasing her.

"All right then," she says with a sigh. "Plates in the sink when you're done, then out to do chores."

"Yes, Momma."

"I want you to come straight inside afterward. Hear me?" she asks, pulling Baby Kay out of her high chair.

"No. No. No!" Baby Kay protests. "Mo woc lat!"

"The loaf of jalapeño corn bread is on the counter there wrapped up for Mordecai Lord," Momma tells me, bobbing and weaving like a prizefighter between the baby's messy fingers.

"Yes, ma'am," I say, watching Baby Kay bounce over Momma's shoulder on the way out of the room for her morning nap.

"That isn't all I seen, either," Dibs whispers across the table after Momma's gone. "But Mac Brazel and my daddy told me it's best I don't tell nobody about that until they get someone out there to get a good look at it. So I'm not going to tell one single person. Not one single one. And that includes you."

Suddenly the hotcake sweetness and the bacon smokiness make my stomach feel more sick than hungry. "Fine by me." I push my plate away. "I don't believe you anyhow."

"You not eating those?" He points to my plate and sticks a fork in.

I shake my head and watch him pile my churro hotcakes and bacon on top of his own. He takes another big bite and stares at me while he chews.

"It's too bad I can't tell you, either. Because this secret is a doozy. A *dooooozy!*"

"Yep, too bad." I bite at the cuticle around my pinky nail where it's already tearing to show him I don't give two hoots about his doozy.

"I mean, I'd tell you if I could, 'cause you're my best friend and all, but I can't. And you want to know what else? I can't even tell you why I can't tell you."

I look at him. "You can't even tell me why you can't tell me?"

"That's right." He stabs a fork into another hotcake and tries to shove the entire thing in his mouth. And it almost fits, too. "That's how big the secret is," he says with his mouth stuffed and hotcake pieces flying.

I keep biting until the cuticle part stings me and blood squeezes out from under my skin, making my mouth taste more like a pocketful of nickels than churro hotcake with Mexican chocolate sauce.

He whistles then and a chewed-up chunk slips from between his pucker and flies across the table. "Woo-hoo, it's even more than a doozy. It's like . . . it's like it's a double doozy. A double double doozy, really."

"Uh-huh." I suck the blood.

Dibs stares at me for a long time and when his mouth is all done chewing, he peeks over his shoulder in the direction that Momma disappeared to and then leans in real close again. "If I do tell you, do you promise you won't tell another living soul?"

"Sure." I shrug. "I promise."

"Swear it?"

I roll my eyes to the ceiling. "Will you just tell me already? You know you're going to eventually. You can't keep a secret and you know it."

He checks over his shoulder one more time. "Okay, but only because you're making me do it, not because I can't keep a secret, 'cause I can keep one just fine." He leans in close again and starts to whisper, his voice so quiet that his words barely make it across the table. "There's another place. Out past old, crazy Mordecai Lord's place and Richards's farm, too."

"What do you mean, another place?"

"Mac Brazel thinks the thing hit on Foster Ranch, went back up, and then crashed in a spot that's more than a mile out . . . and it's still sitting out there."

"Did he see it?"

"Doesn't need to," Dibs says. "He knows it's there. Just like me."

"Knows *what's* there?"

He leans in even closer this time.

"A real live flying saucer full of Martians," he whispers.

My stomach lurches again. I want to go back upstairs and hide under the white sheet and pretend everything is still the same as it used to be.

Before the sky caught fire. Before the blinking green eye. Before the whisper and the scream all at once.

Before God took Obie away from us.

I sit still, blinking at Dibs.

No one says anything for a real long time while the clock ticktocks above the kitchen sink, the low hum of the fan blades buzzes in the corner, and Baby Kay is still demanding her chocolate from the back bedroom.

"Well?" Dibs asks me.

"Well what?" I say.

"Well . . . I just told you something that could change the course of planetary history." He waves his hands in the air. "The status of our entire universe as we know it and maybe even the future of the human race on the planet Earth. Don't you have one single thing to say about all that?"

"You're telling me that out there on Foster Ranch there is a flying saucer with real live Martians inside it?"

"I didn't say they were alive," he says. "They're probably all burnt up. You know . . . *dead*."

I swallow hard.

I hate that word.

It's the worst word in the whole entire universe.

"You want to go and look for our own selves?" he asks. "We could ride out after you get the bread out to Mr. Lord's place."

"Do *you* want to?"

"I asked you first," he tells me.

Obie wouldn't think twice about it.

And he wouldn't have to search for his courage part to do it, either. He would go on a flying saucer hunt in the desert without even thinking twice about it.

"Okay," I tell Dibs. "After Mr. Lord's house. But you have to go drop the bread off with me."

He thinks about it.

The one thing that Dibs is more scared of than a real live Martian invasion is old Mordecai Lord.

"Fine," he says. "But we can't tell another single solitary soul. Promise?"

"You're the one with the big mouth, not me."

"It's a pact, then," he says, spitting into the middle of his palm and holding out his hand.

I stare at it, chewing on my bottom lip. There's no going back on a pact sealed with a spit shake.

Dibs stares at me. "Are we shaking on it or what?" he wants to know.

I take a deep breath and gather up all the spit in my mouth. Then I hock a good one in the center of my palm and slap my sloppy hand against his.

4

FRIED ATTIC BATS

July 5, 1947—9:40 a.m.

"**H**-hello?" I call, peering through a long, jagged rip in the screen door. "Mr. Lord? You in there?"

Dibs is standing so close to me that I hear the spit croaking down his skinny throat every time he swallows.

"I don't know how you talked me into coming out here with you," he says, his hot breath against my cheek. "This guy is off his rocker. Everyone knows he traps the bats from his attic and fries them up on the stove. And once those bats run out, I'll give you one guess what he'll be frying up next."

I push him back. "Will you quit breathing your churro breath on me?" I tell him. "And he doesn't eat any bats and you know it. Now hush up before he hears you."

"Do you ever see him go to town?" Dibs whispers. "No, you don't. Not even for church on Sundays. What do you think he eats stuck up in this place all by himself?"

"You know Superman's Secret Citadel?" I say. "Where he goes to be alone and think hard about important stuff, like how he's going to save the world from evil? Maybe that's what Mr. Lord is doing in there. Maybe this is his very own Super Secret Citadel. Or like the Temple of Wisdom for the governing council on the planet Krypton."

Dibs squeezes one eye closed and squints through the screen with the other. "Spuds told me the guy chopped up his whole family with a pickax," he whispers. "What if he's sharpening up his ax in there for us?"

"Will you stop?" I say.

"Diego Ramos said he was a military spy in World War One who lost his mind, went AWOL, and came home and killed his whole family. Thought they were the enemy, like he was still out there fighting."

"That's not true, either."

"Sure is," he whispers. "People don't make this kind of stuff up."

"Sounds made up to me," I tell him.

"They're dead, right?"

"It doesn't mean he killed them, and stop saying that word already."

"What word?" he asks.

"Just hush up before he hears you."

Dibs blows air out of his mouth. "Look at this place," he keeps on. "It gives me the creeps."

"Shhh!" I give him a good, hard elbow straight to his rib cage.

He's right, though.

Mordecai Lord's house looks more like a shack than a home. But you can tell it used to mean something to someone a long time ago. Old flowered curtains hang dirty and torn in an open window upstairs, and the house used to be painted white, but now it's weathered wood with just a few stubborn patches of white stuck to the graying boards that refuse to let go. If the house were a person, he'd be a sad, rickety hundred-and-eleven-year-old man.

Momma makes Mr. Lord a loaf of bread every week and wraps it in a brown paper bag, and I'm the one who has to bring it out to him. Most of the time Mr. Lord just juts a chin in my direction and I do the same and that's all that needs to be said.

He isn't crazy. I can tell. It's in the eyes.

But I have to admit, I do wonder what he eats in there, besides Momma's weekly bread, I mean.

I give the door another good knock. Harder this time, and I peek through the rips in the screen.

"What is that?" I whisper to Dibs, leaning my ear toward a hole in the screen. "Do you hear that? What is it?"

He listens. "Is that . . . is it radio static?"

"Who is it?" A voice barks from deep inside the house.

We both jump and Dibs inches backward.

"If he comes to this door with his pickax and makes a good summer stew out of us it's going to be all your fault!" Dibs jams his hands into his armpits and his chin into his chest.

"Ah . . . it's me, Mr. Lord . . . M-Mylo Affinito. My momma made you some jalapeño corn bread this morning."

"Just leave it." Dibs points to the ragged mat in front of the door that used to say WELCOME, but now the E, L, C, and M are worn off and it only says W O E.

Heavy footsteps on floorboards inside the house shake the front porch under our feet outside. And then he's peering out at us from behind the large gashes in the screen.

No ax.

Just one chipped blue cup in his hand, a tablet under his arm, and a pencil tucked behind his ear.

"Hi . . . hello, Mr., ah, Mr. Lord. It's Mylo Affinito, sir, and Dibson Tiberius Butte, too . . . I, ah, I mean to say my momma made another loaf for you." I hold out the bread. "Jalapeño corn bread this time."

He stares at me under deep wrinkles that rest heavy over his top lashes. He's wearing a dirty undershirt with a hole in the front, boxer shorts, and a battered plaid bathrobe, untied and barely hanging on to his shoulders. His wild white hair could use more than just a dab of Brylcreem to tame unruly tufts like Momma makes us do on Sundays. He coughs without putting a hand over his mouth and then scratches at the whiskers on his chin. The tops of his hands are like a road map with twisted purple veins for the roads and brown patches for the land. There's an Army Air Force tattoo sticking out from the top of his undershirt, with a picture of an eagle and the initials *AAF* written underneath.

And on the tablet tucked under his arm is a whole page of numbers. Except they aren't all the numbers.

Only ones and zeroes in all kinds of different patterns.

Mordecai Lord pushes open the screen door and a waft

of strong coffee, peanut butter sandwiches, and man sweat fills my nose.

"You can come in," he barks. "If you want to."

I hear another loud swallow squeeze down Dibs's skinny neck.

"No—no, thank you, sir . . . we just, ah . . . came to bring you the, ah, the bread here," I say, still holding it out for him.

He doesn't take it. He just stands there, leaning against the doorframe and taking long sips from the mug in his hand.

He squints us over real good for a long while.

"Well." I start to inch backward now, too. "We'll be seeing you, then—"

"Hope you aren't thinking of going out there," he booms.

Dibs and I look at each other and then look back at him.

"Sir?" I ask.

"Out there." He juts his chin in the direction of Foster Ranch.

"I—I don't know what you mean," I say, shaking my head slowly.

He snorts. "Is that so?"

Dibs stretches his chapped lips over his giant teeth and shakes his sweaty Yankees cap back and forth.

"No, sir," I say.

"Nope." Dibs's voice comes out in a high-pitched squeak. "Don't even know anything about what's laying in that field out there."

Mr. Lord holds out his hand.

I stare at it.

His long, jagged fingernails have black underneath them

and there's something dark caked in the cracks of his palm, too.

Attic bat blood?

"The bread," he says.

"Oh . . . right." I take a step forward and set it in his hand.

"Tell your momma I said thank you kindly," he says, in a quiet voice this time with a nod like he really means it.

I stare into his eyes.

They're not crazy. They're drowning. Drowning in the gray . . . it took every part of him and now he is suffocated by it. Overpowered by it.

Dying from it.

It stalks me, too, but I keep on running. Running scared that one day it will catch me and, like Mr. Lord, I'll live in a graying house of WOE.

"Yes, sir." I elbow Dibs to get moving. "I'll let Momma know you said so."

We scuttle down the porch steps, but just as the tip of my boot hits the very last one, Mr. Lord's voice cuts through the scorching desert air again.

"You should know," he calls after us. "You boys need to stay away from there."

I stop and turn back to face him.

"What?"

"Just keep walking," Dibs hisses, tugging hard on my arm.

"I'm giving you a warning," Mr. Lord says. "Best to stay away, they'll be out there soon enough."

"Who's that?" I squint back at him and then shield my eyes from the blazing sun with both hands against my forehead.

He scratches at his whiskers again. "I got a 32V-1 ham radio transmitter in here and I hear it all," he says. "They're on their way, so if you think you're going to go out there and mess with things . . . I'd think again. It's not safe for you boys. And if they catch you out there—"

"Come on!" Dibs whispers, louder this time and pulling even harder.

"Mr. Lord," I call. "What are all those ones and zeroes written on that tablet?"

He glares at me harder. "Didn't you hear me?" he shouts. "I know it was you," he adds, slipping back inside his Secret Citadel, letting the door slam behind him. He peers one more time through the ripped screen. "And they do, too," he says.

I watch him through the holes until the sad house swallows him up again.

"What was that supposed to mean?" Dibs asks me.

"Don't know," I say.

Dibs blows air out of his mouth and shakes his head slowly. "Doesn't sound good," he says.

"Sure doesn't," I agree.

"Think he's crazy?" he asks.

"Nope," I say.

"Still want to go out there?"

I turn to face him. "Do you?"

He squints back at me, his hand shielding the sun. "I asked you first."

5

INTERSTELLAR WARFARE READINESS

July 5, 1947—11:05 a.m.

Pig stink.

That's how you can tell you are exactly at the halfway mark between our ranch and Dibs's daddy's pig farm, because that's when the stink of pig hits you smack-dab between the eyes like a fat, smelly bullet.

After collecting all my Martian hunt necessities and saddling up Pitch, I meet Dibs at his daddy's farm just like we planned.

Things to bring on a Martian hunt:
1. One slingshot. Check.
2. A token of peace and goodwill—
   one small American flag. Check.
3. Shortstop. Check.

Dibs is already there waiting on top of True Belle, posing like a slick character in a cowboy movie, chewing on the end of a piece of long grass like he's trying to be Roy Rogers or something. Except he doesn't look like the King of the Cowboys to me. To me, he just looks like a scared, skinny kid pretending he's not.

There's dried blood on the side of his mouth.

"You're late," he tells me.

"You got . . . there's blood." I point to the corner of my own lip.

A red wave rolls over his cheeks as he quickly licks his palm and scrubs the stain clean. Then he leans in my direction, puckering up his lips to show me. "Gone?" he asks.

"Still looks kind of red," I tell him.

He rubs at it again.

"Maybe you should let Momma—"

"Why are you so late?" he snaps, readjusting the canteen that's strapped across his chest. "Thought you might have chickened out. We said eleven o'clock, didn't we?"

I point to his canteen. "Good idea. I forgot about water," I say. "What else you got with you?"

"A box of Red Hots, a pocketful of marbles, and this." He pulls out his metal Buck Rogers Atomic Disintegrator Pistol.

"What are the marbles for?" I ask.

He shrugs. "Sometimes you need marbles."

"For a flying saucer hunt?"

"Well, what do you think you're going to do with that?" He points to Shortstop peeking his one hanging eye out of the bib of my overalls.

I push Shortstop's head back deeper inside the pocket.

"He's not all I brought," I tell Dibs. "I brought an American flag and a slingshot, too."

Dibs closes one eye tight and aims his Buck Rogers Atomic Disintegrator Pistol in the direction of Foster Ranch. "Yep, we have to be ready in case we find ourselves on the front lines of interstellar warfare," he says. "If something's still alive out there and they're not friendly, we need to be prepared. I hope you know that it might be up to us to defend our Earth from planetary invasion."

"And you're going to do it with that?" I point to his stupid toy gun.

"Yep." He pulls the trigger and blows on the end of the gun before he holsters it in the back pocket of his overalls.

"At least my weapon's real," I say.

He snorts. "What's a slingshot going to do?"

"A slingshot is way better than some toy gun," I inform him. "Momma says it can cause a real mean skin irritation or poke an eye right out."

He shrugs. "I suppose." He pulls a stained, used-to-be-white hanky out of his pocket. "I also brought this. So they know we come in peace, and if they know the rules of warfare, they won't fire on us if we wave a white flag. You think Martians know the rules of warfare? Oh, and this came today." He holds out his fist.

"You got the Kix Atomic Bomb Ring?"

"Yep." He huffs hot air on it and rubs it against his dirty pants leg. "It'll detect anything radiating out there."

"I don't think it *detects* radiation," I tell him.

"Sure does."

"It doesn't say it detects radiation on the Kix cereal box," I say.

"Kix can't charge fifteen cents and a box top for nothing," he informs me.

"Do you really think things might be radiating out there?" I look off into the distance. "I guess if it's a misfired atom bomb or something they're experimenting with that got away from them. Even a meteorite could be radiating from space. Or if it's some kind of new Russian technology."

"Or a Martian ship," Dibs adds.

"How do you know Martian ships radiate?"

"*Everybody* knows," he tells me.

"Come on," I say. "We've got to get going or we aren't going to make it back in time to finish our chores."

"*Tune in tomorrow, boys and girls,*" Dibs says in his radio announcer voice, "*and watch Mylo and Dibs search for a real live flying saucer out in the middle of the desert. This episode brought to you by Kellogg's Pep, the buildup wheat cereal. With fruit, sugar, and milk, maaaaan, it sure is delicious!*"

"Will you just come on?" I say to Dibs, snapping Pitch's reins.

We start out through the hot desert.

Me and Pitch are out front and Dibs on True Belle trudges up behind. Horseshoes clomp the dry ground and crunch over stone, low brush, and tumbleweeds loosened by last night's storm.

We're on our way to find a flying saucer.

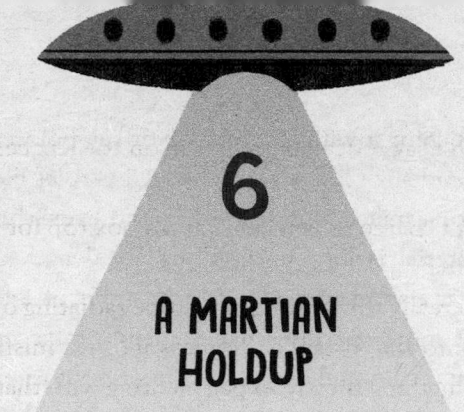

6

A MARTIAN HOLDUP

July 5, 1947—12:55 p.m.

Those pieces Dibs was going on about were right where he said they'd be.

About a billion of them.

Scattered across the tall grass and tangled in trees and brush for a mile easy. Earth scorched as far as you can see, trees scabbed and some even blackened by fire.

Torn.

Broken.

Jagged.

Ripped from something that used to be whole.

"I told you so! Didn't I tell you so? No way these are from this planet, there ain't no way! And it's no meteorite, neither. This isn't natural. Someone or something made these things. And they're silver, for crying out loud. Meteorites are dull rock."

I kneel down in the dirt and examine one of the pieces

up close, touching it with the very tip of my pointer finger. It feels warm and slick like a shiny new Chevrolet Fleetmaster. Polished like a metal, but smoother and even shinier. This strip of material is long and skinny, the length of a ruler and as thin as a sheet of paper. It's the color of a brand-new quarter, but more sparkly—like someone mixed specks of diamonds in a coin and then made it smooth as glass. With raised purple symbols down the edge, just like Dibs went on about at breakfast.

"This one looks like a girder or I beam or something," I say, running my finger over the pictures and wondering what those symbols could mean.

"Look at this one." Dibs picks up a different piece that's paper-thin and looks like the foil on the inside of a Hershey chocolate bar. "These thinner pieces will straighten back up in your hand. Go on, try and crumple it up."

I take it from him with just two fingers and give it a sniff.

"What're you smelling it for?" he asks me.

"I don't know," I say.

He gives it a sniff then, too. "What's it smell like?" he asks me.

I think about his question. "Smells iffy," I say.

"What does that mean?"

"It means it might smell like it's radiating or it might not." He sniffs it again. "Smells Martian to me," he says.

I roll my eyes. "What do Martians smell like?" I ask him.

He points to the material. "That," he says. "Go on and try to crumple it up."

I wrap my fingers around the thin metal and squeeze my hand tight, crunching it up in a ball like a piece of paper.

"*Watch Mylo Affinito rend solid steel in his bare hand as if it were paper,*" Dibs calls into his fist like he's holding a microphone.

I stare at the ball of metal in my hand.

"See that? Not a sound!" Dibs exclaims. "Isn't that the most amazing thing you've ever seen? Now let it go."

I loosen my grip on the crumpled ball and watch as it pops right back to the same smooth, flat shape it was before, right there in the palm of my hand without a single crease. Smooth as glass.

I gaze up at Dibs.

"What'd I tell you?" he says. "Strong as Kryptonite."

"Still doesn't prove it's Martian," I say, but he's not paying attention anymore.

"*We're in the money! The skies are sunny!*" Dibs starts to dance and sing a goofy old song while he grabs pieces off the ground and shoves what he can into his pockets and the leather pouch attached to True Belle's saddle. "I'm taking as many back with me as I can fit," he says, leaning down to grab another. "You think we'll get a reward for finding these? I bet people would pay big bucks for a piece of a real flying saucer."

"Leave it," I tell him.

"But we need it," he says.

"For what?"

"My daddy needs it to pay Mr. Funk at the bank," he tells me. "Mr. Funk's been to the farm three times already since school's been out, looking for money, but we don't got any to give him. He wants a lot of it and we don't have even a little. He might take these pieces instead."

"If you think that ring actually works, let's do a radiation sweep on this stuff first. You know, check it with the ring, make sure nothing's radioactive."

"Good thinking," he says, setting pieces of metal back down on the ground.

He crouches over them and slowly moves his ring up and down over the pile while I take cover behind him, peeking over his shoulder.

Nothing happens.

He looks up at me.

"What's it supposed to do?" I ask him.

He shrugs. "Maybe beep or something?" He shakes his hand and then holds it up to his ear. "You think it's busted?"

"Try again with that one." I point to a larger piece on the ground.

He slowly moves his hand up and down the metal.

Nothing.

I blow a blast of air out of my mouth. "I told you it doesn't detect the radiation, didn't I?"

I pick up a smaller scrap this time and look it over front and back.

"See the burnt-up earth?" Dibs points along the ground. "Mac Brazel says it's at least a mile or even longer."

I slip the small scrap into my front pocket. "Let's keep going." I shield my eyes with my hand, staring off in the direction of Foster Ranch.

Dibs frantically grabs a few more crumpled-up chunks and stuffs them in his overalls and then we climb back up on Pitch and True Belle and continue on, clomping over rugged ground and bypassing hundreds more of the broken pieces.

"There's got to be an explanation for this," I finally say to Dibs.

"Yeah . . . it's Martians," he says. "I told you already."

"It's got to be something else." I shake my head.

"Like what?"

"I don't know," I say. "Maybe it's one of those Army Air Force weather balloons that are always coming down in pieces."

"Who wouldn't know if it was one of those weather balloons? Those dumb things are always falling out of the sky. The Roswell water tower has got 'em stuck all over it. Mac Brazel and me are always picking up after the Army Air Force in the field, even. You think I'm stupid or something? And how could a weather balloon made of balsa wood, tape, and tinfoil leave the earth burnt up like that?"

"Maybe it was some kind of burnt-out star or pieces of an exploding planet . . . you know, like Krypton exploded right after they sent Superman hurtling through space in a rocket ship toward Earth."

"The dirt on the ground is burnt up into almost coal," Dibs tells me.

"A piece of Krypton could've done that," I say. "After it exploded, it could've."

"What exploded planet would have purple symbols printed on it?"

A big blast of wind whips up, tossing loose dirt and gravel across the ground. But that's not all that blows in. With the breeze, a wicked stench suffocates us. A stink that smells so bad it makes me gag and cover my mouth with my hand. A smell that's even worse than when Dibs gets the toots under the white sheet at night after eating onions for supper, or the pig-stink cloud that hangs over Butte Rise and Swine Pig and Poultry.

Dibs's eyes meet mine.

"Was that you?" I ask him behind my palm.

"Are you kidding me?" He pinches his nose with his thumb and pointer finger.

"What is it, then?"

"Beats me." Dibs spits into the dirt. "I didn't smell anything like this before."

"Where's it coming from?" I look all around me.

"I don't know."

"My eyes are burning," I say.

"Mine too." Dibs farmer-blows toward the ground and a bunch of runny snot shoots out of his nose.

"Try the ring again," I tell him, wiping at my forehead with my arm. "Wave it up in the air this time."

Dibs holds his ring high in the air, moving it slowly back and forth above his head. "Nothing. If it's not flashing or beeping some kind of warning, then there's probably nothing to worry about. I'm pretty sure I remember that now from the back of the Kix box. We should be okay."

"That stink doesn't smell like we're okay to me," I tell him.

"Hey," he says, studying the ring closely. "What if the radiation is so bad that the ring just plain quit working on account of the levels being too high?"

"Yeah," I agree. "Maybe we should go back, huh?"

"Want to?" he asks.

"Do you?"

"Asked you first," he answers, pulling a red bandanna

from his back pocket, carefully folding it in a triangle over his face, and tying the corners behind his head.

"To catch the snot," he informs me.

"You look like Billy the Kid."

"I got another one if you want it." He pulls a blue one out of his back pocket.

"You want me to put your nasty snot-rag on my face?"

"It's only got sweat on it. And it helps with that stink."

My eyes are watering from the smell now, too, and my throat feels like I swallowed a lit match. "Fine." I reach out and grab the bandanna.

I fold it in a triangle just like he did, put it over my nose, and tie it in a knot behind my head. Now we both look like Old West bandits ready for a holdup.

"Let's keep on," he says, adjusting his bandanna so high over his nose that it's almost covering his eyes, too. "We've come this far, let's just keep going a little longer, and if it gets any worse, we'll head back. Deal?"

Everything in me wants to say no.

Everything in me wants to get on my horse and keep on galloping until I'm back home and in my bed under the white sheet, where the world seems safest these days. But I don't want Dibs to think I'm a chicken.

I swallow hard. "Deal," I say.

We start moving forward again, the stench getting thicker with every step. Dibs lifts the bottom corner of the bandanna and spits down into the dirt about every five seconds as the horses scuffle over brush and climb over jutting rocks and crumbling dead tree trunks dry and rotting on the ground.

I reach into the bib of my overalls and rub Shortstop's

head with my free hand, wishing Obie were here with us. He'd be out front leading us like he wasn't scared at all.

That's how much courage he had.

He was the closest thing to a human superhero I've ever known.

"Take a break?" I call out to Dibs when I see a tall yucca tree up ahead.

"Yep."

"That ring of yours doing anything?" I ask him, climbing down off Pitch.

"Nuh-uh." His voice is muffled behind the bandanna.

The inside of my mouth and throat are tingling something awful from the stench now, and there's a funny taste in there, too. I still can't see anything and I'm so hot, it feels like I could catch fire without a match.

And there's something else, too.

"Mylo," Dibs says, his voice quivering as he slips down off True Belle. "Something's . . . something is happening. . . ."

"What is it?" I say, feeling a tugging from the deepest part of my body that pulls me in every direction and lifts my arms straight out from my sides.

Dibs holds out his forearm. "Look at that! All the hairs are standing straight up. Look at it! Look at it! And my lips itch, too! Do yours? Do your lips feel itchy?"

"It's like there's electricity in the air," I say.

"It's those Martians trying to harvest our brains right out our ears, just like I told you they would," Dibs says. "I know it."

"It is not," I tell him.

That's when he points a finger out toward a large arroyo in the distance and breathes in real hard, choking on the fumes and then gagging. "Oh, my good God!" He lifts the bandanna against his forehead, spitting into the dirt. "I see it!" He shouts. "That's it! I can see the edge of it! A disk! There!" He points harder this time. "See it now? Right there!"

I squint, holding my hand over my eyes to shield them from the sun. "I don't see anything," I tell him.

"No! It's there!" he insists. "I can see it! Dead ahead!"

I squint again. "You're crazy," I tell him. "There's nothing out there."

"Then you need glasses, because it's a real live flying saucer!"

I squeeze my eyes shut real tight and then open them again, inching my boots forward one more step, then another. The ground's uneven and the whole entire world feels so unsteady that one wrong step will send me spiraling into the abyss of nothingness.

I strain my eyes, peering through the haze of the heat mixed with fumes, taking another slow and careful step, sliding my boot forward. The left one, then the right one. Left, then right. Left—

And then . . . there's something.

My boots inch closer as a shape forms in front of me. A shape that doesn't belong out in the desert. Or anywhere on Earth, either.

It can't be.

It's a bad dream.

It has to be.

Wake up, I tell myself. *It's only a dream! That's all it is!*

My lashes separate.

No sweaty sheet . . . No toes to nose . . . Just one silvery disk wedged and crumpled, tight against an arroyo in the desert.

Its final resting place.

I stand frozen, blinking at it.

A real live flying saucer.

"Come on!" Dibs starts to run.

I watch him sprint toward the disk, my feet frozen to the dirt and electricity buzzing all around me.

"Mylo?" Dibs stops, shouting back at me. "What are you waiting for?"

I drag my boots after him, watching him pull ahead of me as he runs full blast toward the thing.

When I finally catch up to him, we stand there staring at the thing. A broken flying saucer right in front of us.

"So." Dibs smiles big. "You believe me now?"

I don't say anything.

"You think it's full of dead Martians?" he asks.

"Why can't you stop saying that word!" I demand.

"Martians?"

"No," I snap.

"Oh," he says.

He's quiet then, while I inch forward.

"You can go and check to see if any of 'em might still be alive if you want," he says, pulling out his toy gun. "I'll cover you."

"I'm not going in there!" I tell him.

"Well, *I'm* sure not doing it!"

I take another few steps forward until I'm so close I could reach out and touch it. Most of it is smooth and sleek and silvery with no edges or wings or windows like they have on an airplane. Just a glassy round disk with a raised center. The other part is all scratched up and crunched up against the jagged side of the arroyo. It's bigger than Daddy's old Ford pickup truck but not much.

"Look at this thing," I whisper. "Look at the underbelly." I point. "It's a million tiny individual cells, like the thing itself is a living, breathing animal."

"Or used to be," Dibs says. "Touch it," he tells me.

"You touch it!" I snap back at him.

"Not with a ten-foot pole!"

"I can't believe it's true," I whisper.

A real live flying saucer.

Broken and silent in the desert. Nothing but a coffin now. A coffin for Martians. I wonder what their tombstone would read.

HERE LIES THESE MARTIANS
WHO KNOWS WHEN–JULY 5, 1947
FAMILY.
FRIENDS.
PILOTS THROUGH THE STARS.

Maybe even . . . loved?

They had to be, right? Loved by someone. Somebody real far away. Families who are waiting for them to come home for supper from their mission to Earth. Do they pray, too?

Or refuse, too, when God doesn't care enough to listen? Do they eat spaceman hotcakes and moon dust corn bread? Do they watch the Mars Meteorites beat the Saturn Star Hoppers in spaceball and read comic books about Earthlings from another world with endings the way they should be?

Endings where they come home.

And then I hear it again.

Just one word.

Help.

Like a whisper and a scream all at once. The very same one I heard before.

I grab Dibs by his bony elbow when I hear it. "What was that?" I ask him.

"What was what?"

I hold my breath, searching the desert in every direction and waiting to hear it one more time. But the desert stays silent.

No birds chirping.

No bugs buzzing.

No swishing winds through the branches.

Nothing.

"I don't hear anything," Dibs says. "What is it?"

I turn to look at him. "I—I don't know," I say.

7

MY VERY OWN LOIS LANE

July 6, 1947—2:07 p.m.

If Dibs is the Jimmy Olsen to my Superman, Graciela Maria Delgado is my Lois Lane.

"Is she looking now?" I ask Dibs, slicking my cowlicks down with as much spit as I can muster.

Dibs stretches his neck. "Nope."

"How 'bout now?"

Dibs stretches his neck. "Nope."

After lunch, Dibs and I head to Corona General for a cold pop. Well, *he's* there for the Coke. I had another mission in mind.

I sneak a peek, eyeing her between the cans of Campbell's Tomato Soup and Bush's Best Pork and Beans. The Corona General Store smells sweet from fresh baked goods and a little bit tart from fruits ripening in the heat. She's perfect.

Graciela Maria Delgado.

I watch her over the cans. She's reading a book on a stool

next to the cash register while her aunt Beatrice rings up Mrs. Manuela. Gracie's dark hair is pulled back with a barrette but there is one long strand by her ear that she twists and untwists around her pointer finger, her lips moving as she reads. She's wearing a sky-blue button-down shirt and jeans with bobby socks and saddle shoes that have a sprinkling of mud on the toes.

I know what book it is without even seeing the cover.

I know it because every Saturday night Dibs and I go to the Roswell library on Third Street while Momma, Daddy, and Baby Kay go visiting in town. My most favorite librarian, Mrs. Bishop, works on Saturdays and always has a very special book ready for me. And each Saturday, I carefully print my name on the card under *Gracie Delgado* and Mrs. Bishop stamps it with her date stamp and I go on my way.

"She's reading L. Frank Baum's Oz series," she told me weeks ago.

That's how I know what book it is without even looking. She's reading number eleven, *The Lost Princess of Oz.* And I'm on number ten, *Rinkitink in Oz.*

Gracie's daddy is a general at the Army Air Force Base in Roswell and they live in a big brick house three blocks off Main on Kentucky Avenue, but she spends her summers at her aunt and uncle's farm to care for her horse, Betsy Bobbin.

Dibs puts a cheek next to mine, trying to get a look between the cans, and then shakes his head.

"What's so great about her, anyway?" he asks me.

"What's *not* so great about her?" I say.

"Well . . ." He thinks about it. "I bet she can't even field a baseball."

"So?"

He shrugs. "So we need a shortstop."

"Did you know she has a horse named Betsy Bobbin after a character in a book by her favorite author?"

"What's the big deal about that?"

"She's smart." I shrug. "I like that about her."

"I'm hungry," he says. "You think we have enough for a snack? I don't know if I'm going to make it all the way to dinnertime without some sort of snack."

"What do you think it'd be like to kiss her?" I wonder out loud.

He turns to me with an ugly scowl stuck on. "Are we getting the Cokes or what? And did you hear what I said? I'm starving."

I put my hands on my hips. "You had two breakfasts and a lunch already today," I tell him. "How can you still be hungry?"

He shrugs. "My stomach has a mind of its own and it's decided it needs more in there to be happy."

I check my pockets for coins, and he does the same.

"How much do you have?" I ask.

"Let's see . . . I've got two, four, six, seven cents," he says, fishing out coins. "And . . . these, too." He reaches into the bib of his overalls and pulls out two marbles, an Eddie Stanky baseball card, and an empty Wrigley's spearmint gum wrapper. "What've you got?"

"One nickel and five pennies." I count from my palm.

I add it up in my head. "I think that's enough for two Cokes and one pack of chocolate Neccos to share," I tell him.

"Yeah, except my tongue is tired of chocolate Neccos."

"How about Cracker Jacks?" I ask. "Your tongue okay with Cracker Jacks?"

He smacks his lips, considering. "Yep, I think both my tongue and my stomach would be happy with Cracker Jacks," he tells me. "Here." He pushes the hand with the marbles closer to me. "You can have these and the prize at the bottom, since you're paying three cents more. Even Steven, okay?"

It's a solid green one and a real cool clear one with sky-blue swirls.

I start to reach for them and then stop. "Keep 'em," I say.

"Really?" he asks. "Even Steven?"

"Yep."

We grab two frosty Cokes from the way back of the cooler and pop the caps off with the opener on the side, grab the box of Cracker Jacks, and head up to the front counter, where Mrs. Delgado is standing in a crisp, flowery dress, fanning herself with a fancy lace hanky. Gracie doesn't even look up.

"That was some monsoon we had last night," Mrs. Delgado is saying, smoothing a loose black hair back into place with the others that are already slicked close to her head and twisted tight in a bun that sits right at the back of her neck. "We lost some pieces of roof off our barn from the winds. Mr. Delgado is out there today, nailing up new boards."

Mrs. Manuela shakes her head. "You know what some people are saying, don't you?" she asks.

"No, what?" Mrs. Delgado asks.

"*Flying saucers*," Mrs. Manuela says.

I drop my Cracker Jacks.

Gracie peers up over the top of her book.

Mrs. Delgado snorts. She smiles like Mrs. Manuela just gave a punch line to a knock-knock joke. "Nonsense," she says, shaking her head and loading a bag of Gold Medal Flour into a paper sack.

"You know me." Mrs. Manuela waves a hand in the air. "I'm never one to gossip, but that's what I'm hearing. The papers have been reporting an increase in sightings around the U.S. this summer. It's got people wondering, is all I'm saying."

Dibs gives me a pointy elbow in my side and raises his eyebrows at me.

"Oh, yes, I've read about the sightings," Mrs. Delgado says.

"You're not a believer in those Mars men, I gather?" Mrs. Manuela asks her.

"A Martian invasion?" Mrs. Delgado smiles. "I most certainly am not."

"Uh-huh," Mrs. Manuela says, and then turns to Dibs and me. "Has your daddy said anything about it?" she asks, staring right at me.

I look at Dibs and then back at her. "Me?" I ask, pointing to my chest.

"Yes. . . . Well, you know it's none of my business, but I've heard your daddy was involved in that incident in California a few years back. Right before he left the military. The Battle of Los Angeles, I think the papers called it?"

"What was that?" Dibs asks.

"It happened February 25 in 1942," Mrs. Manuela starts. "In the early-morning hours over Redondo Beach, California, everyone awoke to the air raid sirens going off. People fled from their beds to see what was happening."

"A Martian invasion?" Dibs asks.

"Well, first came a complete blackout over the city," Mrs. Manuela says. "And then . . . everyone saw it."

I swallow. "Saw what?" I ask.

"The lights in the sky," she says.

"Were they green and blinking like a big fat eyeball?" Dibs asks.

Everyone looks at Dibs.

His cheeks flush and he stares at his bare dirty toes. "I— I was just . . . I mean, I didn't know . . . sorry," he says. "Go on with your story."

"Well." Mrs. Manuela begins again. "You know at that time it hadn't been three months since the attack on Pearl Harbor, and of course the United States had just joined the fight in Europe, so I imagine that was the first thought . . . that we were under attack. So the military sent their planes to circle whatever it was that was flying up there, and they responded by land, too, shooting some fourteen hundred anti-aircraft rounds into the air at whatever it was flying overhead. At least, that's what the papers reported."

"Did they hit it?" Gracie asks.

"Not a one of those bullets could penetrate it," Mrs. Manuela answers. "Then whatever it was just shot out of the sky faster than any of our planes could fly. It just disappeared"— she flicks her wrist in the air—"into the stars as fast as it came."

Mrs. Delgado shakes her head, adding canned beans and a bundle of fresh green beans to Mrs. Manuela's paper sack.

"Did they ever figure out who it was?" Gracie says.

"That"—Mrs. Manuela points a finger at Gracie—"depends on whom you believe, young lady."

"What does that mean?" I ask.

"Well, my sister Thelma and her husband, Roger, live in El Segundo, right near there, and she says everyone was talking flying saucers. Why, the next morning there was shrapnel everywhere you could see. It had hit homes and cars and landed in backyards and in the middle of the streets. In fact, six people died that night from all those rounds we shot up in the sky."

Dibs pokes me in the side. *"Agents from a strange and foreign planet,"* he whispers.

Mrs. Manuela's eyes meet Dibs's again. "Exactly, but that's not what the military said. No, sir." She shakes her head.

"What did they say?" I ask.

"The military came out with a statement telling the public it was just a weather balloon." She picks up her sack of groceries and sets it carefully in her wire shopping cart. "You can read it for yourselves and see it, too. There was even a picture of it on the front page of the *Los Angeles Times.* And I'll tell you what, that was no weather balloon. Anyone who has eyes can see that."

"You mean those dumb balloons the Army Air Force is always sending up and they're always falling down and getting stuck on the water tower in town?" Dibs asks. *"Those* weather balloons?"

"One and the same." She nods.

"Fourteen hundred rounds and we couldn't take down . . .

a weather balloon?" Dibs looks at me. "It's balsa wood and tinfoil. Who in the world would believe something so dumb?"

Mrs. Manuela scoffs. "Everyone, dear." She grabs the handle of her cart. "Especially if it's in the newspaper. No one is going to question it."

"But what if it isn't true?" I say.

"The military doesn't lie," Mrs. Delgado snaps at me. "If the military says it was a weather balloon, then that's what it was."

We all stand in silence for a moment.

"Well then, you all have yourselves a nice day now," Mrs. Manuela says over her shoulder as we all stand and watch her pull her cart toward the door.

"Good-bye, Mrs. Manuela," Mrs. Delgado calls after her, shaking her head again. "Is this all for you boys?"

"Yes, ma'am." I lay our coins out on the counter for the Cokes and the Cracker Jacks.

Mrs. Delgado pushes buttons on the register until it dings and the drawer flies open. "Don't you two let her fill your heads with crazy stories," she tells us, dropping our seventeen cents into the proper compartments.

Gracie's eyes meet mine.

"You want a sack for that?" Mrs. Delgado points to the box of Cracker Jacks, pushing the register drawer closed.

"No, thanks," I tell her.

"Don't you go dropping kernels in the back while you're reading those comics. Mr. Delgado doesn't like having to sweep up popcorn kernels after you kids."

"Yes, ma'am," I promise her. "We won't open it until we're headed on home."

"All right then." She smiles.

Dibs and I head toward the back, past the boxed pastries and the store-bought breads where there are tall wooden shelves and round wire racks of magazines, books, and comics.

"Is she looking?" I whisper to Dibs.

He stretches his neck. "Nope. How about what Mrs. Manuela was saying?"

"Yeah," I say.

"Why would she think your daddy knows anything about it? He's not even in the military anymore."

I shrug.

"Has he ever talked about that thing in California?"

"He never talks about anything he did when he was in the Army Air Force," I say, leaning back to catch another glimpse of Gracie.

She's back to reading and twirling and untwirling her hair around her finger.

"You know Mrs. Manuela," I say. "She's always gossiping about something. She's probably got it wrong. Did you see the way Gracie looked at me?"

He shrugs. "You think they have the new Planet Comic yet?" he says.

"She has the prettiest eyes I've ever seen."

"They look like plain old brown ones to me," Dibs says, scanning the shelves of comic books.

"They're not *just brown*," I tell him. "They're the color of Hershey's Kisses with flecks of Bit-O-Honey mixed in."

He rolls his eyes. "That's the most disgusting thing I've ever heard of. . . . Ooh." He reaches for the latest Planet Comic from the shelf. "They got the new one."

8

A
CRACKER JACK
SUPERHERO

July 6, 1947—3:45 p.m.

After Mr. Delgado shows up and tells us the Corona General Store isn't a library and we'd better buy something or be on our way, Dibs and I head out.

Gracie is still on her stool reading. She doesn't even look up as we pass by.

When we make it out the door, Dibs turns to me. "She wasn't looking," he tells me.

"I didn't ask you if she was looking."

"Yeah, but you were gonna." He smiles.

"Hey, Affinito!"

I turn to see Diego Ramos and Spuds Whitaker heading in our direction.

"Great," Dibs mutters under his breath.

Diego and Spuds are two years older, same as Obie. Diego is at least a head taller than me and two taller than Dibs, and about last December he started sprouting so many wisps on his upper lip that he carries a tiny-toothed plastic comb in his back pocket. I'm pretty sure God gave my share to him, because he's got a lot more than any other boy in Corona. So many that he's constantly checking his upper-lip locks with his fingertips to make sure they're straight and if they're not, he pulls his tiny comb out of his back pocket.

Spuds is round and dimpled just like a baking potato, and he isn't completely lip bald, but it's not enough to run a comb through. Plus, he thinks he's so funny. He's always telling the dumbest jokes. No one even laughs at them. Except for him. He laughs at every single one even though he already knows the punch line.

"Butts!" Diego slaps Dibs's shoulder three times like his hand is a hammer and he's hammering Dibs deep into the sidewalk.

"It's Butte, and you know it!" Dibs snaps at him.

Diego just laughs and takes his stupid comb out of his back pocket to pull through the lip hair. "You hear about that flying saucer?" he asks.

"Nope," I say, before Dibs can run his big mouth.

"Hey, Mylo, why did the Martian throw beef on the asteroid?" Spuds throws his hands out. "He wanted it a little meaty-or." He laughs his head off and slaps his knee. "Get it?" he asks. "Meaty-or! Like meteor with meat. Meaty-or."

Diego ignores him. "Out in Mac Brazel's field," he goes on.

"I told you. I bet it turns out to be military," Spuds says.

"Or a meteorite." I jump in, eyeing Dibs a warning to keep his big mouth shut.

But he misses it completely. "Oh, it's Martian all right,"

he tells them. "Mac Brazel is going to call Roswell Fire out to look at it."

"What do you know about it, Butts?" Diego demands.

"I bet I know more than you do about it." Dibs puffs up his bony chest. "And you better stop calling me that if you know what's good for you."

"Is that right?" Diego laughs. "And what are you going to do if I don't?"

Dibs squeezes his fingers into two skinny dukes and holds them up high to show Diego. "How about I knock your block off?"

Diego laughs.

"You're right, Spuds. It's probably military." I grab Dibs by the rear of his overalls and pull him back to my side. "I thought we weren't telling anyone," I remind him.

"Even Mrs. Manuela knows it's the Mars men, Affinito," Diego says. "Get a clue, why don't you." Then he stretches his neck to peek in the door of Corona General. "You guys see if Gracie's here today?"

Diego and Spuds push each other aside while they sneak a peek in the doorway of Corona General and wave.

"Hi, Gracie," Diego calls.

"Did you see that?" he asks us, feeling his lip hairs to see if they're straight. "She looked right at me. Probably noticed my 'stache."

I roll my eyes at Dibs.

"Yeah, right." Spuds punches his arm. "That thing is so thin, from a distance it looks like you forgot to wash the dirt off your lip. She was looking at me."

"You? Please! She wouldn't spit on you if your hair was on fire." Diego punches him back.

"Oh, she sure was looking at me." Spuds smirks, licking his pointer finger and thumb and sliding them over his dark eyebrows. "Those brown-with-a-fleck-of-gold eyes were taking all this in." He waves a hand up and down his dimpled middle.

I poke Dibs. "See? They're not just plain old brown," I tell him.

"Come on." Dibs pulls on my arm.

"Well, we'll see you guys later, then," I say.

"Wait," Diego says. "You guys really know something about what's going on out there?"

I look at Dibs.

He's gnawing at his bottom lip, his eyes darting from Diego to Spuds to me and back again, and I know he's about to blow.

"Dibs—" I warn.

"We know more than you about it," he bursts out.

"Dibs!" I punch him in the arm.

"We saw it, okay? We went out there and we saw it!"

I throw my hands up in the air.

"Well?" he says to me. "It ain't no secret now that Mrs. Manuela is going on about it. The whole town probably knows by now. She has lips *faster than a speeding bullet, more powerful than a locomotive—*"

"You saw an actual ship?" Spuds asks.

Dibs points a thumb out at me. "We both did," he says. "Him and me, we went out there and we saw it for our own selves. It's crunched up real good against the side of an arroyo. Tell 'em," he says to me. "Tell 'em what we seen."

"You really went out there?" a soft voice calls from the doorway.

Dibs sucks air.

Gracie Delgado.

She is standing in the doorway, her book in her hand. But it isn't an Oz book after all; it's *Comet in Moominland* by Tove Jansson. On the cover is a red sky over a pasture with a blazing ball of fire hurtling toward Earth.

"I—I don't . . . I mean, I—" Dibs starts. "Mylo?"

"What'd you see, Affinito? Spit it out already." Diego combs his wisps, looking down at Gracie like he's a coyote and she's an unsuspecting rabbit. "You either seen it or you didn't. Which is it?"

I sigh.

"Yes," I say. "We saw it."

They're standing in a circle now, surrounding me, breathing in my air.

Their eyes are burrowing into me.

I lick the salty sweat off my lips. My cheeks feel hot and my tongue is swelling and my brain can't find the words I'm searching for.

"Did you see a real live Martian?" asks Spuds.

"I'm not all that sure . . . I mean, ah . . . I really . . . ," I mutter. "I, ah—"

"What's he saying?" Diego asks Spuds, leaning in closer.

"I, ah . . . I said I don't know what it was, or, ah . . . what I heard. I just don't really know—"

"Well, *I* know," Dibs spouts. "It was an army of Martians. Some say they have quadruple the brains we do. Fat-brained green Martians. Me and Mylo went out there prepared for interstellar battle just in case they had any Martian funny business in mind." He pulls his Buck Rogers Atomic Disintegrator Pistol out of his back pocket to show them. "There was an electromagnetic field all around and it took all our muscles to stay connected to the Earth and not be beamed up to the mother ship. I bet they were just up there waiting to vacuum us up while they sharpened their probes and charged their phasers. Not to mention the radioactivity all around the area. Mylo and me are sure to be radioactive after being out there yesterday. I'm surprised we aren't glowing."

"What Martian hunt were *you* on?" I ask him.

"You should've sent in for one of those Atomic Bomb Rings. They detect radioactive material," Spuds informs Dibs.

"I don't think it *detects* the radiation," Diego says.

"Sure does," Dibs pipes up. "The air was so thick with radiation, the ring couldn't even read it. That's how I know it was working."

"Are you done yet?" I ask Dibs.

"Well, then *you* tell us what happened out there," Gracie says to me. "What exactly did you see?"

"Yeah, how close did you get?" Spuds asks.

"You see any bodies?" Diego says.

"All we saw was the ship," I tell them. "That's it."

"I'm going!" Diego announces.

"Me too," Spuds pipes up.

"Gracie." Diego leans against the shop window like some smooth character. "You want to come out with us? I'll protect *you* from the Martians."

This time Gracie rolls her eyes all the way to the sky and back again. "And who's going to protect you?" she wants to know.

I snicker behind my hand.

What's so great about Graciela Maria Delgado?

1. Only everything.

On the way home Dibs and I break into the box of Cracker Jacks.

"Kind of neat that Gracie is coming with us tomorrow, huh?"

Dibs is picking the peanuts out of his handful of caramel corn and chucking them into the field for the birds.

"I can take her or leave her," he says.

"What's that supposed to mean?"

"She'll probably just scream the whole time."

"Why would she do that?" I pop another kernel in my mouth.

"'Cause she's a girl. That's what girls do. You know, like in the movies. Whenever something scary happens the girls are always screaming their heads off and the men have to slap them or shake them right again."

"I don't know any girls like that," I say. "Momma certainly isn't like that."

"People don't make that kind of thing up," he tells me.

"Movies *are* made up." I pop another kernel.

"Are you going to hog them *all* or what?" Dibs complains, holding out his empty hand.

I pour another handful for him.

"There a prize at the bottom?" he asks.

I peek inside the dark box and see a white envelope. I tip the box upside down and both crumbs and the prize fall into my palm. I carefully tear the envelope open, pull out a brightly colored card, and look it over.

"Is it the ink tattoo?" Dibs leans over my arm.

"No."

"Stickers?"

"No," I tell him, examining the card. "It's a Superhero Club Membership Card."

"Neat! Let's see it." He reaches for the prize and looks it over, then hands it back to me. "That's actually even cooler than the whistle."

"You think it's official?" I ask him.

"Maybe. But probably not as official as my Atomic Bomb Ring. That cost fifteen cents, plus one Kix cereal box top, and came with a satisfaction guarantee or your money back. That *has* to mean it's official. This was free in the box, probably doesn't mean as much. Still cooler than the whistle, though."

"Yeah," I agree, and slip the card into the bib pocket of my overalls.

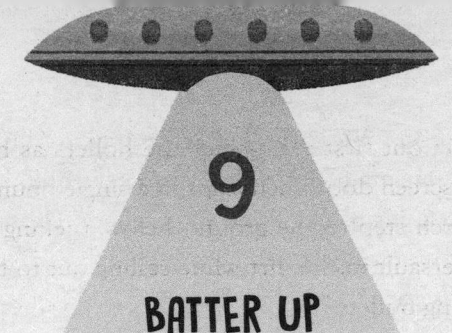

9

BATTER UP

July 6, 1947—7:05 p.m.

That evening after supper Dibs and I listen to our favorite program on the radio, *The Adventures of Superman*.

"*Remember, boys and girls,*" the radio announcer calls out. "*Don't miss the next installment of . . .*"

"Superman!" Dibs and I holler together with our fingers in the air as we fly around the living room, towels safety-pinned around our necks.

"*Up in the sky . . . Look! It's a giant bird! It's a plane!*"

"*It's Superman!*" we call out.

"*Superman is a copyrighted feature appearing in Action Comics Magazine. . . .*"

Daddy reaches over to the radio on the shelf from the davenport, where he's reading the paper, and turns the radio off while Momma points to the back door.

"You two Supermans," she calls from the rocking chair, her lap full of her knitting. "Out! No flying indoors!"

Dibs darts out first. *"Ka-pow!"* he hollers as he pushes through the screen door, then leaps in a single bound off the top back porch step to the ground below, tucking and rolling in a somersault in the dirt while calling out to the desert about speeding bullets.

With a hand on the door, I turn back and look at Daddy reading the paper on the davenport.

"Daddy," I say. "Want to throw out back with Dibs and me, maybe?"

Even though I already know the answer.

Daddy looks at Momma with Baby Kay on the floor as the baby stacks wooden blocks, and Momma gives him an encouraging nod. But it doesn't help any.

"Not tonight," he says, his eyes going back to his paper.

I sigh and let the screen door go behind me.

"Come on!" Dibs is hollering.

Clark Kent barks after Dibs and then scrambles up from the back porch to get into the mix of it.

"Vroom! Able to leap tall buildings in a single bound!" I shout, flying down the porch steps after him.

Dibs gives me one finger straight down.

Fastball.

I shake my head.

He gives me two fingers down.

Curveball.

I nod and wind up.

"Batta batta batta batta, *sawwwing*, batta!" Momma and Baby Kay sing from the back porch steps. Except Baby Kay's sounds more like *atta atta atta ing atta!*

Clark Kent is in ready position at shortstop to field missed balls. Except without a batter today, he's got nothing to field. Even so, he's the best shortstop around.

"It's a windup," Dibs announces. "And a pitch . . ."

The ball smacks Dibs's bare hands and bounces away behind him. "Strike one!" he shouts, shaking out his sore hands.

"Clark Kent! Heads up!" I holler out to him, and he darts toward home plate and off to chase after the ball.

Dibs spits on his red palms and wipes them on his overalls and I feel a small pain deep inside my bones. He never asks to use Obie's glove because he knows better. But I don't offer it, either.

It's his.

Momma gets up from the porch swing, holding Baby Kay in her arms, and disappears into the house. By the time Clark Kent finds the ball to give back to Dibs, Momma is walking down the back porch steps in dungarees, holding my Ted Williams Little League Louisville Slugger.

"Batter up!" Dibs hollers with a big beaver-tooth grin. "It's been a real long time since Mrs. Affinito's been up to bat. With a prior batting average of four hundred, she has had a hit every time she's been up to the plate. Let's see if Mylo Affinito can strike her out this time!"

Inside the house, I see the living room curtain move to the side and Daddy holding Baby Kay as she presses two sweaty baby palms against the windowsill, singing *atta atta atta ing atta!*

I bend at the waist, watching for Dibs's fingers.

One finger down.

I shake my head.

Dibs's lips tighten.

One finger down. This time more forcefully.

I shake my head again.

Then he just throws his hands up in the air at me, which in baseball-ese means nothing but in Dibs-ese means *Why won't you ever strike her out?*

"It's a windup . . . ," Dibs says again. "And a pitch!"

I send my best slow pitch in Momma's direction.

The bat makes a loud cracking sound when it finds the ball.

"And it's a hit!" Dibs hollers, standing straight up and shielding his eyes from the setting sun. "Clark Kent!" he hollers. "Heads up! Field it, boy! Go on!"

Clark Kent is darting toward left field after the ball, while Momma rounds the homemade bases that Daddy, Obie, and I built out of old milk crates, painted white, and nailed into the dirt.

"Get it, boy!" Dibs is running toward third to get Momma out. "Hurry up, boy!"

But Momma's too fast for all of us and makes it all the way home before Clark Kent can get the ball back to Dibs.

"And it's another home run for Mrs. Affinito!" Dibs calls between his hands. "With a batting average of four hundred, she's the first batter since Ted Williams to achieve this amazing feat since all the way back in 1941!"

"Woo-hoo!" I shout through cupped hands, my eyes searching for Daddy and Baby Kay in the window.

But they're gone.

Momma jumps up and down on home plate in her dungarees and throws her arms in the air. "Four hundred!" she shouts with a wide smile.

The widest smile I've seen on Momma in a real long time.

At least in one year, one month, and ten days.

10

TOMATO GUTS

July 6, 1947—10:55 p.m.

Dibs and I lie toes to nose again that night, while I tell you inside my head about the flying saucer sitting out in the field, and the pieces with the purple symbols, and the green eye, and about Gracie Delgado.

Wondering if you're still with me even though you're not in your bed where you should be. And wondering if you're mad about me not finishing that final comic book for you the way I promised you I would. I still haven't finished it. All the others ended with the Affinito Brothers' Superhero Duo saving the day.

Except the last one.

Which was the one that mattered most.

"I just don't get why we have to still lie like this all squished and sweating when there's a perfectly good bed right over there," Dibs complains at my feet. "It's just too doggone hot to sleep like this." He punches at the flat pillow.

"And this mattress is so lumpy, it feels like I'm lying on a big rock right in my back."

"What's the big deal? This is the way we've always done it."

"But that was . . . before. And I don't remember it being so lumpy back then."

"I don't know what you're complaining about, anyhow." I turn over. "I'm the one who has to smell your funky feet. These things should come with their own toxic warning sticker."

"My feet don't stink worse than yours do," he shoots back.

"Want to make a bet? Here's what the warning sticker should read. 'BEWARE: Breathing the noxious fumes off these funky feet can cause serious brain damage.'"

He grins big. "Well, your feet-stink is way more noxious than mine! Your sticker would say yours smell like a hot, noxious dog fart on a breezeless day."

That makes us both laugh.

"I'd rather my feet smell like hot dog farts than Baby Kay's diaper pail when Momma has to get on Daddy to empty it after three whole days. That's capital-N noxious."

We giggle even harder.

"Yeah, well, I'd rather smell like an old diaper pail than rotten fish after sitting in a bucket in the hot sun for three days with noxious vomit on it from a boy who just ate a bad batch of bean-and-cheese burritos with a side of gizzard covered in—"

"Boys!" Momma hollers up the stairs.

We suck air and stare wide-eyed at each other.

"Enough!"

"Yes, ma'am," I call back.

"Sorry, Mrs. Affinito!" Dibs hollers.

We look at each other and then shove our faces in our flat pillows and laugh our heads off.

I can't sleep.

The clock on the nightstand reads 1:00 a.m.

"Dibs," I whisper down at him. "You awake?"

"Yep," he whispers back.

"Where do you think they're from?" I ask him.

He doesn't hesitate. "Mars," he says. "Probably they were on some kind of mission to take over our planet . . . our minds . . . you know, that sort of thing."

I snort. "Where did you get *that*?" I ask him.

Dibs gives me a look like my brains really *were* sucked clean out of my head by the Martians out at the ship last night. "Where do you think? The Planet Comics series."

I scoff. "Oh, the Planet Comics series," I mock him. "The real-life guide to Martians."

"What we really need to worry about is the second shift that might come down angry and level us with their Martian weapons," Dibs says. "What do they want with us? And are they a hostile entity?"

I lean on my elbow. "What do you mean?"

"Like Martian mind control . . . or like what kinds of weapons do they have? Ray guns, phasers, stuff like that. What superpowers do they possess? Do they want to destroy mankind? Bring the human race to the very brink of extinction with a rampage of destruction and all that?"

I don't say anything.

"God made good and God made evil," he goes on. "Whether you're talking about Adam and Eve or Martians. The only difference is Martians are one million times smarter than us and they have powers far beyond what we can even imagine. If they want to take over Earth, believe me, they can do it."

"That's your comic books talking," I tell him. "You don't know it's true for real life."

"Yeah, well, that's what you said about the disk and you were wrong about that, too," he says. "You don't want to believe anything is true 'cause you're scared and that's a fact."

"And you're not?"

He doesn't answer me that time.

We lie there for a long while with no one saying anything until Dibs punches at the pillow again and turns over.

"There's something else I have to tell you," I say.

"Yeah?" He yawns.

"I hear something," I say. "Sometimes I think I do. I mean, not like with my ears. But it's something. Or it's . . . someone."

Silence.

"I don't hear anything," he says.

"No, I mean, not right now. I have been hearing someone calling for help and no one else seems to hear it."

Dibs's head pops off his pillow and I can feel his laser-beam gaze bore a hole straight through me.

"What do you mean? *Who?*" he finally asks.

"I think it might be . . . them," I say without looking at him. "It's someone or something . . . asking for help. My help."

"*Help?*"

"I think it could be *them*. . . . Th-the *Martians*." I whisper the last word. "I mean, I don't know who it is. 'Cause I don't see anything. Except sometimes I see these outlines on the backs of my eyelids. Does that sound weird?"

"Very weird," he says.

I sigh and flop back down on my pillow. "Forget it."

He stays sitting up, staring at me.

"Are you messing with me?" he finally says.

"No," I say.

"Swear?"

I sit up then, too, and look him straight in the eyes. "Swear."

Silence.

He's still staring.

"I'm telling you, I hear them. It's like . . . it's like it's my own voice but it's . . . it's their message, and they're asking for help . . . *my* help. I mean, I don't know . . . I haven't heard anything since we left yesterday . . . maybe they are talking to someone else by now. I hope they are, because I'm afraid that . . . you know . . . well . . . if they're not talking to someone else, then . . . then maybe they're not talking at all." I swallow the lump pushing its way up my throat from my gut. "You know what I mean by that?"

Silence.

I fold and unfold my fingers, waiting for him to say something else.

"You're not lying?"

I shake my head. "Nuh-uh," I say. "I'm telling you the truth. Cross my heart I am."

Dibs takes a deep breath in and then blows it out real slow, shaking his head from side to side. "Oh," he says then, slipping his legs out from under the sheet and swinging them over the side of the bed. "I knew it. This is exactly what I was afraid of."

"What?" I ask.

"The Martians have invaded your brain and taken over your mind." He points at me.

I push all of my breath out of my mouth and flop back down on my pillow again. "That isn't it," I tell him.

"How do you know?" he asks.

"First of all, I just know, and secondly, if it had happened, I would tell you so," I say.

"Oh, you would say, *Dibs, Martians have taken over my mind?*"

"Yeah, that's what I'd say."

"Of course a Martian who has taken over your mind is going to tell me they haven't. What am I, some kind of idiot?"

"Well, I don't know what to tell you, then."

"How can I really know that you're still Mylo and they didn't make the switch out there last night? Maybe that magnetic pull was some kind of Martian probe straight to your brain and they're controlling your every thought and movement from the mother ship. How do I know that their Earth mission isn't to spread the Purple Death—or worse—to all us Earthlings to destroy the population for total planetary domination?" He stands up now.

"What's the Purple Death?"

"Remember in that Flash Gordon movie we seen at the Roswell Theatre, *Flash Gordon Conquers the Universe?* Remember Ming the Merciless was sending down Death Dust to Earth, knocking people off, leaving only a purple spot on the foreheads of his victims?"

"Well, all I can tell you is that I don't have any immediate plans for a planetary takeover today or even tomorrow. But I can't promise anything after that."

"Let me think for a minute." He paces the floor beside the bed. "Tell me something that no one else but my best friend, Mylo Affinito, would know the answer to. Then we'll be absolutely sure they didn't take possession of your brain out there last night."

"Why would they take my brain anyway?" I lean up again on my elbow. "I'm not the one who's a genius, remember?"

"Come on," he says. "Say something only Mylo and me would know."

I take a deep breath and think hard about what to say. "Well . . . I want to be a pitcher when I grow up just like Spec Shea . . . ," I tell him while he examines me with his X-ray stare, his head to one side and his chin between his pointer finger and thumb. "And . . . if all the superheroes ran for president of the United States, Superman would win hands down."

"Everyone knows *that* one," he says. "Think harder."

"And . . . um . . . ," I go on. "And . . . I hate tomatoes but

I like the sauce. It's 'cause I can't even look at a cut-up tomato with its tomato guts oozing without wanting to puke. The innocent slaughter of it all. Tomato guts." I shudder. "Disgusting."

Dibs stands there staring and not saying a single word while he considers my answers.

"Well?" I say.

"How can you like the sauce but not the tomatoes? That's nuts," he tells me.

"I told you. 'Cause of the guts," I say.

He considers me again.

"So, are we good or what?" I ask.

He slips back under the sheet, gives his pillow a punch, and smiles at me.

"Yep," he says. "Only you would come up with something as stupid as tomato guts."

11

MARTIAN MIND-CONTROL CAPS

July 7, 1947—4:55 a.m.

"**I**'m going to have to bring back more than just pieces this time," Dibs tells me the next morning on the front porch steps. He finished his chores at his farm early, and then came back to wake me up for mine.

I yawn and pull on my boots. "Why's that?" I ask him.

"Mr. Funk didn't care two hoots about them pieces," Dibs tells me.

"Yeah?" I say. "So what's your plan?"

"I have to go bigger to help Daddy keep the farm," he says. "When Mr. Funk came out this last time, he was real mad. Yelled at Daddy until he was all red in the face. Then he got into his truck and said we had thirty days to get him the money or we'd be kicked off the farm. That was two days ago. And what if . . ."

"What if what?" I ask.

He swallows, his eyes watering at the bottom by the rim. "What if he leaves me, too?"

A pain hits me deep inside my bones. The very same pain I felt when I saw Obie sick in his bed.

"What's bigger than Martian ship pieces?"

"Proof."

"Proof of what?"

"Of a Martian," he says.

"I don't get it. How is having proof of a Martian spaceship landing going to fix your daddy's problems with the bank?"

"It just will, okay? I know it will," he insists. "It has to."

"What's that?" I point to his front bib pocket and hold my lantern closer to him. "Those the thin pieces from the craft?"

"Nope," Dibs says, pulling tinfoil squares from his overalls.

"That's just aluminum foil," I say. "What's that for?"

"Protection," he tells me.

"Protection from what?"

"Martian mind control, of course," he says. "I told you they'll probe your brain as soon as look at you, didn't I? Don't you pay attention? These will block the teleportation rays of their mind-control devices and keep our brains right where they belong, get it?"

The screen door opens and we jump.

"What in the world are you boys doing up at this hour?" Momma asks from the doorway as she ties her robe closed. "Your daddy isn't even up yet."

"We're, ah, we are, um . . . meeting the other kids to play this morning," I tell her. "Just trying to get chores done early, is all."

"Who?"

"Diego Ramos, Spuds, and Gracie Delgado," Dibs tells her with the foil pieces behind his back.

"Gracie Delgado?" Momma's eyebrows go up. "Maybe you could play out back here?" she suggests. "I can make summer sausage sandwiches and sweet tea for lunch."

"Ah." I look at Dibs. "We, ah—"

"We're playing out at Gracie's aunt and uncle's ranch today, Mrs. Affinito," Dibs tells her.

"Who's going to make lunch if Mr. and Mrs. Delgado are working the store?"

"We'll eat a big breakfast," I tell her.

"Yep." Dibs nods. "Are you making your churro hotcakes again?"

"How about I pack up some sandwiches for you to take with you?" Momma says.

I look at Dibs, and he looks at me.

"Sure, okay. Thanks, Momma," I tell her.

"Well then, finish up and come in for breakfast."

"Yes, ma'am," I say.

Momma opens the screen door and gives me one more long look before slipping back into the house. It's that look she has when I know she can see straight into me.

"You think she knew we were fibbing?" Dibs asks.

"You see that look she gave me?"

"Oh, yeah." Dibs nods.

"Momma has a way of knowing things."

"Like Superman's X-ray eyesight."

"Exactly like that."

12

HEAVENLY CHILI CHEESE DOGS

July 7, 1947—7:15 a.m.

Grown-ups say stupid things when someone you love dies.

I'm pretty sure they don't say them purposely to be rude, but what they say is still stupid.

Kids say what they mean. No candy coating.

Grown-ups candy-coat and cover up and sometimes even flat-out lie just so they don't have to say what they mean.

The top three dumbest things grown-ups say to you when someone dies:

1. He's in a better place.
2. Time heals all wounds.
3. I understand.

And there are even more I could add to that list if I wanted to.

Kids say it how it is. And even though sometimes it's hard to hear . . . it's better than what the grown-ups come up with because you know that kids really and truly mean it.

No candy coating.

The morning of Obie's funeral, Spuds's little brother, Bobby, came up to me and said, "Sorry your brother is dead."

And he really did mean it.

Gracie Delgado said, "Wish I could have known him better."

And she meant that, too. I could tell she did.

Even Diego Ramos, who doesn't have much nice to say about anything, said, "He was the best catcher I knew."

And he was.

The morning before our second Martian mission is set to begin, Dibs and I ride out to the cemetery to visit Obie first.

"You know what I was thinking about?" I ask Dibs on our way.

"What?"

"Something Joe DiMaggio said on the radio."

"What?" he asks.

"He said, *I want to thank the Good Lord for making me a Yankee.*"

"He said that?"

"Yep."

He nods. "Sounds good," he says.

"What's so good about it?" I want to know.

He shrugs. "What's wrong with it?"

"You think God's up there deciding what prayer He's going to grant and what one He's not? And then He picks the baseball prayer over all the others when people are suffering all over the world?"

"I don't know about all that, but I sure bet He likes baseball," Dibs says.

"Joe DiMaggio?" I ask.

"No," he says. "God."

"God?"

"Yeah," he says. "I bet you God likes it. You know, on His day off. I bet you He likes to watch over a Yankees game now and again . . . especially when they play the Dodgers. That's a good game. I wonder if He can order a hot dog with all the fixin's up in Heaven if He wants it. He's God and all—if He wants a hot dog with all the fixin's, He could make one, I suppose . . . I mean, He parted the Red Sea and created the world in seven days, He could probably make one with just a snap of His fingers. It's got to be a lot easier than the whole wide world. Might take a little longer if He wanted it with chili and cheese, though."

I put one hand on my hip. "What are you talking about?" I ask him.

"Ah . . . hot dogs?"

"We weren't talking about hot dogs," I inform him.

"No?"

"No."

"Oh, right, baseball," he says.

"Not that, either," I tell him.

"Weren't you the one that brought up Joe DiMaggio? Wasn't that you?"

"Yeah, but we were talking about God."

"We were?"

He doesn't say anything for a long while.

"*And* baseball?" he asks.

I sigh. "Never mind."

We continue to trot in the direction of the cemetery, me and Pitch out front and Dibs on True Belle lagging just behind.

After a long while Dibs is still on those stupid chili cheese dogs. "How hard do you think we would have to pray to have Him send us down a couple of those chili cheese dogs right now?" he asks. "My stomach sure could use one."

"We just had breakfast," I remind him.

"I can't help it. My stomach has a mind of its own."

"Good morning, boys," calls Mr. Haskell, the Corona Cemetery caretaker, who is busy hoeing the weeds sprouting out around Mr. Knudson.

HUBERT ALLEN KNUDSON
1801–1859

"Good morning, Mr. Haskell," I call back.

"Early-morning visit today, eh?"

"Yes, sir."

He nods and goes back to his weeding.

"You think they'll bury the Martians out here?" Dibs asks.

"Shhh," I hiss, looking over my shoulder to see if Mr. Haskell is listening. But he's too busy concentrating on his chores, his old crinkled fingers wrapped tightly around the wooden handle of the hoe that he's dragging through the dirt.

"You think they'll give them a proper burial?" Dibs wonders aloud, climbing down off True Belle.

"Why wouldn't they?" I tie Pitch's reins to the iron gate in the shade of a yucca tree.

"You think Father Kevin would do the eulogy?" he asks.

"I don't know," I say. "I don't remember Father Kevin saying anything about Martians in the Bible, do you?"

"No, but I think he only does funerals for Catholics. I don't suppose the Martians are Catholic," Dibs says.

"Why should it matter?" I say, hopping over Mrs. Hemmingson. "Father Kevin has a heart to love all people no matter what. Just like God wants us to."

"I have a heart like that, too," Dibs tells me, watching me hop over another plot. "With one exception . . . Diego meaner-than-a-snake Ramos."

"I thought his middle name was Paul," I say.

"Ha ha, very funny."

"Hey, don't step on Mrs. Hemmingson," I tell him.

He stops in his tracks. "Mrs. Hemmingson?" he says. "She don't care. She's dead."

"So? That means she likes getting one of your dirty-foot-in-the-face alarm clocks? And stop saying that word. I don't want to hear it again. Not one more time."

He stares down at the large stone marking Mrs. Hemmingson's place in our world. A reminder she was here and important to someone.

HERE LIES INGA OLENA HEMMINGSON
SEPTEMBER 30, 1834–JANUARY 12, 1904
WIFE AND MOTHER

"Fine." He takes a big step to the right, and then follows me as we hop over the others.

HERE LIES MAGNUS MCDOUGAL
JULY 11, 1808–JANUARY 3, 1901

A RANCHER AND HUSBAND,
FATHER AND GRANDFATHER
YOU WILL BE MISSED.

Sidestepping past:

JUAN SANTIAGO
FEBRUARY 2, 1902–APRIL 12, 1944
DEDICATED RANCHER, LOVING HUSBAND,
AND BROTHER
GONE TOO SOON.

Bypassing:

HERE LIES BRITA OLSEN
MARCH 29, 1850–DECEMBER 22, 1910
FRED'S WIFE AND THORA'S MOTHER
SIMPLY TREASURED.
REST IN PEACE.

Until we reach you. Next to Grammy and Pappy Hildago.
Dibs and I stand and stare down at your new home. I crouch
in front of the speckled headstone and stare at the script letters
scrawled across it, while Dibs cleans the dried leaves off it.

OBIE BROOKS AFFINITO
SEPTEMBER 6, 1934–MAY 27, 1946
BELOVED SON, BROTHER, FRIEND
WE WILL NEVER FORGET.

If it were up to me, I would have added:

NO ONE BRAVER.

"You missed a real good game on Wednesday," I tell you, letting my fingers trace the curly letters. "The Yankees took the Washington Senators eight to one."

Silence.

"Joe DiMaggio got on base twice," Dibs kicks in.

Nothing.

I lay my body flat on the ground, my bare back against the dirt and rocks, just the way you were lying in the coffin when they lowered you into the earth. I cross my arms over my chest and shut my eyes tight, holding my breath, wondering what it's like to be dead.

When my lungs ache and my eyeballs feel like they're going to burst, I gulp in air and cough. And I stare up at the world above me. The sun is already blazing hot up in the sky, shining through the fluffy white clouds swaying softly in the breeze above me. They are worlds away but look so close that I can almost touch them. So close that if I just lie here and search hard enough I might just spot you so I can pull you back down here where you belong.

"What are you doing?" Dibs asks, looking down at me.

"What do you think it feels like to be dead?" I ask him.

He sits down on the ground next to me, picking up tiny stones and tossing each one into the field past the fence.

"I think it feels cloudy . . . but the white fluffy kind, not the dark, angry monsoon kind. And not the lightning or thunder kind, either. More like peaceful and airy. Just like today's clouds are."

"Yeah?"

"Annnnd . . ." He searches the ground, looking for

another stone. "I bet they have every comic book ever written up there."

I laugh. "You wish," I tell him.

"Yeah." He laughs, too. "I do."

"Do you think people are really happy there?" I ask.

He shrugs. "That's what the Bible says."

"I don't see how Obie could be happy anywhere without us," I tell him. "It doesn't seem right. Not one bit of it does."

Dibs slides over and lies down next to me. And we stay that way, quiet, staring at the swirling cotton-ball clouds above us.

"That one looks like his catcher's mitt." Dibs points. "See it?"

"Yeah, I see it," I say.

Dibs sits up, holding his head in his hand, his elbow on the ground as he stares up at your stone. "We're going out to Mac Brazel's field," he tells you. "There's a flying saucer sitting out there, if you can believe that. Wish you were here now, going out there with us."

I pull myself up, too, and face Dibs.

"Hey," Dibs says. "You think they've got Martians up in Heaven? Maybe he already knows about 'em."

"Maybe," I say, reaching a hand out and touching the cool stone.

"Guess we'll see you later, then," I say, hoisting myself to my knees and wrapping my arms around the stone.

It feels cold in my arms and empty, too, like you're not here, either. Like you're lost somewhere out there and I can't find you.

"You know what?" Dibs asks me.

I let my arms drop. "What?" I ask, pulling myself up next to him.

"When it's my time to die . . ." His voice shakes on the last word. "The very first person I hope to see when I get to Heaven is Obie."

I turn to face him. There are giant drops hanging on the very tips of his bottom lashes, and I watch them fall on his cheeks in two straight lines down to his chin.

"That's the nicest thing anyone has ever said to me about my brother since he's been gone," I tell him.

"Nah," Dibs says.

"Yeah," I say. "It is."

"I didn't mean it to be nice," he says. "I meant it to be true."

"I know," I tell him. "That's the best part about it."

13

THE
PURPLE SPOT
OF DEATH

July 7, 1947—10:07 a.m.

"It's on the planet Mongo where Ming the Merciless has perfected the Death Dust that he has spread by rocket ship to humans on Earth. And if you get it on you, then you die instantly with a purple spot on your head." Dibs is going on to me on our way to meet the others out front of Richards's farm. "That's the Purple Spot of Death. Remember?"

"Yeah, I remember, but it doesn't make it real," I say. "It's a movie. Someone made it up."

"We are on our way out to see a Martian ship that crashed on Earth," he says. "Anything could be true now. Anything at all."

"Come on," I holler over to him, kicking my heels into Pitch's fat belly. "I can see them all up there waiting for us."

The plan was to meet at the debris field at ten o'clock. The others are already there, their horses in a line, sweating in the sun—Diego's Lupe, Spuds's Bazooka, and Gracie's Betsy Bobbin.

All three of them are leaned up over a piece of debris while Gracie jots something down on a bright red tablet. Except Diego seems more interested in trying to impress Gracie with his hairy lip than in exploring the Martian pieces.

"My dad says it's getting so thick that I'm going to have to start shaving soon," Diego is telling Spuds, but he's looking down at Gracie while he combs the fuzz.

Spuds squints. "They're so fine a razor couldn't cut 'em," he says.

"Are you blind?" Diego glares at him.

Spuds squints again. "The thing is, you have some hairs here." He points. "And some over in this spot, but there's nothing in the middle. You look more like a rabid dog with a bad case of mange," he says, laughing at his own joke.

Diego punches him. "Get out of here!"

"Oh! Oh! Here's one you'll appreciate," Spuds says then. "Why is the moon bald?"

Diego ignores him.

And Gracie doesn't seem to give two hoots about lip hair or shaving or why the moon is bald because she's too busy examining the pieces and writing in her tablet.

"Diego." Spuds tries again. "Come on, guess, why is the moon bald?"

"I don't care," Diego says, shielding his eyes from the sun.

"Hey, Mylo, Dibs," Spuds calls to us. "Why is the moon bald?"

"You get lost?" Diego asks us. "Thought you and Dibsey here must've chickened out."

"We were the ones out here first." Dibs puffs up his

chest. "If anything, you're the one with chicken parts in you, not us."

"Isn't anyone going to guess why the moon is bald?" Spuds asks again.

"H-h-hi, Gracie." I give her a quick wave.

"About how far does the debris field go?" Gracie calls out to me, getting right down to business. She's shielding her eyes from the sun with her pencil still in her hand.

"More than a mile in *every* direction," Dibs calls out dramatically, waving his hands slowly over the desert floor.

She scribbles in her tablet.

"He has no 'air!" Spuds tells us. "Get it? No *'air*. It's supposed to be *hair*." He laughs his stupid head off.

"Those same hieroglyphics on each piece?" Gracie asks.

"Except the thin pieces that look like the foil around candy bars," Dibs tells her.

She nods and scribbles more.

"What are you writing there?" Dibs asks, slipping down off True Belle.

She shrugs without looking up. "Just taking some notes," she says.

"Well, maybe write in your little book there that I was the first one to find these pieces." He points to her tablet.

She ignores him.

"H-hey there," I say, this time without the wave. "Glad you could, I mean, you know, it's good you can make it and all . . . so, ah, yeah."

She's still writing.

I can't help but wonder if there's anything in her tablet about me.

"She's not looking," Dibs mouths in my direction.

I give him a glare.

"Let's get going," Spuds says. "I didn't come out here to see pieces, I came out to see Martians. Come on."

"Wait," I say, slipping down off Pitch. "I just want to double-check that everyone is sure they want to go out there . . . knowing what we might see."

While we all circle around Gracie, she slips her tablet into a cloth purse lying diagonally across her.

"You mean dead Martians?" Diego smirks. "We all know there are dead Martians out there, Affinito. You think we're hard of smelling?"

"*That's* what that is?" Spuds asks. "Dead Martians?"

Dibs gives me a look, and then stamps a bare foot on the ground and points a stern finger in the direction of Diego and Spuds. "Mylo doesn't want to hear that word," he informs them. "Not one more time. You got it?"

I feel the hotness creeping up my neck and settling in my cheeks.

"Well, is everyone still in or what?" Diego takes a poll. "Anyone too chicken to go? . . . Anyone? . . . Butts?"

"Shut up, Diego!" Dibs shouts. "And stop calling me that!"

"All right, then," Diego says, reaching up for his saddle horn and slipping his boot into the stirrup.

"Wait," Dibs says. "Before we get on our way, we've got to take care of some official Martian business." He reaches up to True Belle, unzips a leather pouch attached to the saddle, and pulls out neatly folded blue and red bandannas. "It's for the smell, and also it catches the snot pretty good. You fold it in a triangle, like this." He shows them. "Then tie the ends around the back of your head."

The others just stare at him.

"It's only going to get worse," he says. "Believe me. This is nothing."

I grab my square first, and Gracie and then Spuds follow me. Diego just folds his arms across his chest. We make our triangles, cover our noses and mouths, and tie the corners together behind our heads.

"And," Dibs says, pulling the squares of aluminum foil from his bib pocket, "these are to prevent Martian mind control in all its forms. Probes, phasers, or the harvesting of brains out your ears. Martians will steal your brains as soon as look at you. You take the foil square like this"—he holds it over his head—"and mold it around your head, like so."

"Thanks anyway. I'm not a loaf of home-baked bread." Diego crumples his tinfoil square and tosses it back at Dibs. "I'm not wrapping my head in foil."

"I don't think you need to worry anyway," Dibs tells him. "Martians don't care to study any half-wits to further their cause."

"Hey." Diego sticks a finger in Dibs's chest. "Martians would love to have my brain."

Dibs laughs. "Nope," he says. "But it's funny that you think so."

Diego just scoffs and pulls himself up on his saddle while the rest of us secure our Martian mind-control-prevention caps on top of our heads.

Diego gives Lupe's belly a kick. "Let's get this show on the road!" he hollers.

"You need to let Dibs lead," I call after him. "He knows a shortcut so we can make it back by suppertime."

Dibs pulls himself on top of True Belle and trots past Diego, pulling his bandanna up to his forehead to show Diego a gleaming, big, bucktoothed smile. "You hear him," Dibs taunts. "I'm the boss, applesauce."

We clomp across dirt and gravel.

Stumble over rock and tumbleweed.

And push past the horrid stench that hangs thick in the air.

It's the same thing that happens when we lose a steer out in the field and find it days later. But there's a chemical smell, too. One that stings the hairs in your nose, makes your lips itch, and makes your throat feel scratchy, like you swallowed a wool sock.

The smell is even worse than it was the day before, making my mouth water and my throat gag behind my bandanna.

Up ahead I see Dibs lift his bandanna and spit into the dirt every few seconds.

Diego wipes at his nose with his forearm, probably wishing he had taken that bandanna when he had the chance.

Spuds keeps coughing.

And Gracie stays silent and stoic.

"Gracie?" I call up to her. "You okay?"

She turns to look at me over her shoulder. "Yes," she calls.

"I came prepared. I dabbed my uncle Joe's Aqua Velva under my nose this morning. I already heard about the fumes."

"That was good thinking," I tell her.

"Want some?" she asks.

"You brought it along?"

She nods and pulls back on the reins.

"Hold up!" I call out to Dibs.

"Here." Gracie stops. "This might help with the smell."

She digs through her purse. She pulls out the Aqua Velva bottle, opens it, and tips it over the top of her finger. "It's my uncle's aftershave. You can smear a little under your nose to block more of the smell."

We all circle around Gracie's horse for a fingertip of Aqua Velva.

"What if it's worse than all that and we're getting radiated?" Spuds asks, slowly smoothing the Aqua Velva under his nose. "No amount of aftershave is going to block Martian radiation rays."

"That smell ain't radiation," Diego says. "It's death."

No one says anything.

I turn to look at each and every one of them. "Anyone want to go back?" I ask.

Diego turns to me. "Do you?"

I can tell by the look on his face that he would like for me to say yes just so he doesn't have to be the one to do it.

But I can't.

Someone needs my help. Me. Mylo Affinito.

I don't know why and I don't know who . . . but I know I have to find out.

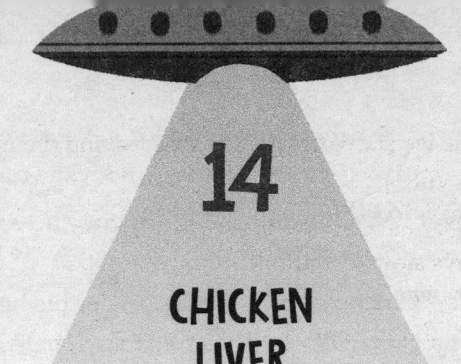

14

CHICKEN LIVER

July 7, 1947—11:45 a.m.

When I see the tall yucca up ahead and my guts start to wiggle inside me again, I know we're getting close.

"What's happening?" Diego pulls back on his reins. Lupe spits and huffs, coming to a sudden stop.

"Is that some kind of electrical current?" Spuds says.

"My insides feel weird." Gracie places a hand flat against her middle. "Like there's an invisible magnet trying to pull my inside parts to the outside."

"It's some kind of electrical force coming off the disk," I inform them.

"Or Martian mind control," Dibs says. "Make sure your anti-Martian-mind-control skullcaps are secured properly before we go any farther."

"It's there." I point. "Crunched up against that arroyo in the distance. Let's leave the horses in the shade and walk the rest of the way in."

One by one we slide off our saddles, leaving the horses to graze near the yucca.

Except Diego. "Maybe someone should stay here with the horses," he says slowly, without looking at us.

Dibs scoffs. "Chicken," he mumbles under his breath.

I give Dibs a glare. "No one has to go any farther," I say. "Don't come unless you want to."

"Gracie," Diego starts. "You should stay here with me and—"

"I'm going," she tells him. "I can take care of myself. I don't need any boy to do it for me. You can stay if you want."

I raise my eyebrows at Dibs.

Diego slips off his horse then and shoves his hands in his pockets.

"Are you sure?" I ask him.

He just nods, and we all start out in the direction of the broken ship.

Silent.

Even the desert is quieter than it should be, except for the hum of the electrical current, the scraping of our boots, and Dibs's bare feet against the gravel.

"Can you see the edge of it?" Dibs points, shielding his eyes. "See it? There!"

The pulling on my insides gets stronger with every step.

Diego stops. "The electricity is getting worse," he says.

"Yeah, but you get used to it," I tell him.

He doesn't say anything.

"You okay?" I ask.

"I think they're harvesting his brains," Dibs says with a

sly smile, adjusting his foil skullcap. "Should have listened to me when you had the chance."

"Diego," Gracie says. "You don't look so good. Maybe you should head back."

"Look at him!" Dibs exclaims. "I've never seen that color of green before. He looks like a Martian."

And that's when Diego burps real loud, and the burp turns into a gag, and then something brown and sloppy spurts straight out of his mouth.

"Holy cheese and jalapeños, Diego!" Dibs says, holding his own mouth and turning away. "What did you have for breakfast? A bad bowl of jambalaya with a side of gizzard—"

"Dibs," I say, stealing a glance at Gracie. "Leave him be."

Diego heaves again and a chunky mess forms a puddle at his feet. "We had leftover liver with our eggs." He wipes his mouth with the back of his hand.

"Yeah, chicken liver," Dibs mutters under his breath, smirking.

I give him a glare. "Don't crack wise," I hiss at him. "Just leave him be."

"Diego, there's nothing wrong with going back."

"You know, Diego," Dibs says, "they say the Martians' Purple Death starts to eat away at your brain little by little until you lose your mind entirely and go completely mad and then you just explode into tiny bits of blood and guts. I think upchucking is the first sign. You feel the squirts coming on yet? 'Cause that's the second."

Diego heaves again and more meaty chunks hit the ground. He straightens up and wipes his mouth again without saying anything.

"I'll take him back," Spuds offers. "You guys go on without us."

As Dibs and Gracie and I watch Diego and Spuds head back toward the tall yucca tree, Dibs calls out after them one more time. "Hey, Spuds!" he says. "What do you call a Martian who chucks up chicken liver in space?"

Dibs snorts, and I shoot him a look. "What?" he asks. "It's not like he doesn't ask for it. You hear what he calls me, don't you?"

"Just shush up."

"You taking his side now?" He scowls.

"It's not about sides," I tell him. "It's about taking the high road."

He folds his arms across his front. "The Bible says an eye for an eye," he says.

"Yeah, well, maybe that's not right," I tell him.

"You think God got it wrong?"

"God didn't actually *write* the Bible."

"Well, He *suggested* it."

"I'm just saying that I don't remember any stories in the Bible about an eye for an eye when someone chucks up liver on the way out to see a flying saucer for the very first time," I say.

Dibs slaps his palms flat against his thighs and sighs an exasperated sigh at me. "It doesn't have to be exact," he says. "You're supposed to read the stories of the Bible and apply them to real life."

"There isn't a story in the Bible that could possibly apply to this, is all I'm saying."

"You want to make a bet?" he challenges.

"I'm pretty sure there's no betting in there, either," I tell him.

"Neither one of you knows what the words in the Bible really mean," Gracie says.

Dibs turns to her. "Oh, and you do?"

She shrugs. "No one does."

"Then what's the point of even reading it at all?" Dibs asks, throwing his hands out.

"You know," she says. "To decide what kind of people we want to be. Like do you want to be the hero or the villain of the story?"

"Well, I know what kind of person I want to be in my story," Dibs tells her. "The kind that doesn't take nothing from no one." He bobs his head once, and then turns to me. "Especially from Diego Mean-as-a-Snake Ramos. What about you, Mylo? What would you be in your story?"

"M-me?" I stutter, shoving my hands in my pockets. "I— I'm not sure . . . brave, I guess."

They don't say anything.

"You want to know what L. Frank Baum wrote in the very first Oz book? It's what the Wizard told the Cowardly Lion," Gracie says.

"What?"

"He wrote, *The true courage is in facing danger when you are afraid.*"

"I don't remember that part," I tell her.

She smiles. "Maybe you need to read it again."

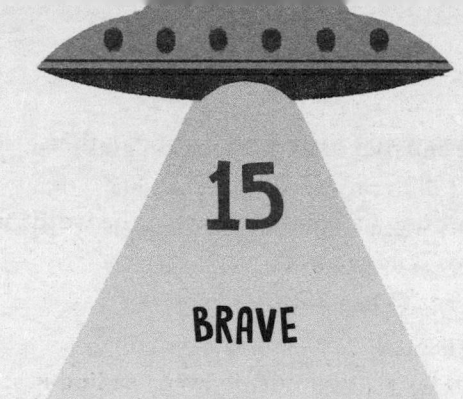

15

BRAVE

July 7, 1947—12:14 p.m.

"It's true," Gracie whispers through her fingers. "It's really true."

We stand in a line of three gazing at the slick oval disk, crunched and broken on one side against a desert arroyo.

"It doesn't look anything like Ming the Merciless's spaceship in *Flash Gordon Conquers the Universe*. That one looked more like a can of Ajax with a point stuck on top," Dibs whispers to me. "This one is flatter and smoother, more disklike with a bubble in the middle, don't you think?"

"Why do you think they crashed out here?" Gracie wonders aloud.

"The Earth's gravitational pull, probably," Dibs tells her. "Or maybe the Army Air Force radar interfered with their mechanics. Last night, that electrical force was even stronger, and it almost pulled all our guts right out of us and off to the mother ship for experimentation. But we held all our insides firm in place and told them they couldn't take 'em. We didn't have the tin foil to protect us . . . ," he blabs on.

And that's when something amazing truly happens.

Gracie slips her hand into mine.

Graciela Maria Delgado.

Her grip is tight.

It's sweaty and scared.

And something inside me flickers. Like a light switch or the blaze of a lit match, and I close my sweaty fingers tight around hers.

A silent, slippery promise that I will protect her.

No matter what.

I feel it in me.

And one other thing. I'm not ever scrubbing this hand to Z again.

"Dibs." I elbow him. "Don't scare her."

"I'm not scared," Gracie insists.

I turn to face her. "You're not?"

Her lips curl up at the edges, and her fingers tighten around mine. "Maybe a little," she says.

"I think you're brave," I tell her.

Her eyes meet mine again. Those Hershey's Kisses eyes with specks of Bit-O-Honey mixed in.

"You do?" she asks.

I nod.

"I don't see myself that way," she says. "Seems like no one does."

"What do you mean?"

"It's why I come to Corona for the summer," she tells me. "At home, all that's expected of me is to keep my dress clean.

But there's a lot more I want to do than keep clean. Out here I get to wear jeans and ride Betsy Bobbin and get dirt on my shoes. I think I'm meant to do something more in the world."

"Like what?"

I can see her cheeks flush as she focuses on her sneakers.

"I write stories," she tells me.

"I write comic books." I point to my front.

She smiles at me and I smile back.

That's when Dibs pokes his head in between us. "I think you're brave, too." He smiles with his big beaver teeth. "Way braver than those girls in the movies who are always screaming and carrying on. You aren't screaming or carrying on or nothing and those Martians could zap us with their ray pistols and probe our brains with their mind-control mechanisms at any minute. That says brave to me. No doubt about it."

"Ready?" I say.

Dibs nods and pulls his Atomic Disintegrator Pistol from his back pocket.

"Roger that!" he says.

We move forward, the three of us still in our tinfoil caps and Dibs with his stupid toy gun. We keep stepping forward until we're so close we can reach out and touch the cells on the underbelly of the ship.

"The energy field isn't as strong this time," I say. "You think?"

"Must be running out of gas." Dibs slips his pistol back into his pocket and wipes at sweat on his forehead.

"I doubt they fill up at the Sinclair," I suggest. "It's probably another energy source than gas."

Gracie reaches out toward the underbelly cells.

"Wait!" I say.

"What?"

"Don't touch it," Dibs says. "It might be radiating."

One thing I'm learning about Gracie Delgado is that she doesn't like boys telling her what to do, because she reaches out to touch it anyway. Which makes me think that Gracie is a lot like Obie.

Brave.

When her fingers first make contact she pulls away and then reaches out again, this time placing her palm flat against its smooth, shiny surface.

"It's warm," she calls out. "And . . . is it . . . it feels like it's moving. Almost like . . . it's breathing in and out. Real slow, though."

"You mean . . . like it's *alive?*" I ask.

She nods. "There's an opening, too." She points underneath. "Either it's a door or maybe it's just a hole where there shouldn't be one. See there?"

"They're probably watching us right now." Dibs adjusts his foil hat underneath his Yankees cap. "You aren't harvesting my brains today." He points up to the sky. "Not Dibson Tiberius Butte. No, sir!"

Closing my eyes, I take a deep breath, searching inside me for something. Anything that will give me the courage to do what I came here to do. To do what I know Obie would do.

And then I hear it again.

Help.

That same light switch flickers on inside me again. The lit match, blazing even brighter this time.

Hotter.

Stronger.

Rushing through my veins.

Burning up all the fear inside me as it goes.

I drop down to my hands and knees and crawl toward the opening underneath the disk. "I'm going in," I call over my shoulder.

"Hold your horses!" Dibs hollers after me. "Are you sure you should do that? What if they're in there waiting for you? What if they're in there ready to harvest all your Earthling guts for experimentation?"

"I don't think that's why they've come," I tell him, reaching out to the edge of the jagged opening and peeking inside.

Dibs and Gracie scramble on all fours behind me.

"How do you know what their purpose is here on Earth?" Dibs hisses behind me. "It's way too far to come all the way down here for a Sunday drive. They're here for a big reason."

"I can't say how I know. I just do."

Dibs puts his cheek right close to me and peers inside the disk, too. "I sure hope you're right about that," he whispers.

"What do you see in there?" Gracie asks.

"It's dark," I say. "It's hard to see anything. But it looks like a chamber up to another level."

Dibs coughs. "It stinks even worse inside than it does out here." He adjusts his bandanna higher up over his nose.

I look him square in the eye. "I'm going in," I say again.

"Are they telling you to? Is that what this is?" Dibs asks me. "Is that why you're doing it? On account of you think they're talking to you again? Because it could all be just a trick, you know. To nab your brains."

"What are you talking about?" Gracie asks.

"Don't—" I start.

"Didn't he tell you?" Dibs points a thumb in my direction. "This one hears 'em."

I sigh and drop my head.

"Hears . . . *who?*" she asks.

I look up at her as she stands there blinking at me. "It's not like with my ears," I tell her with a nervous laugh. "More like pictures behind my eyelids. Or a silent word bubble like in the Superman comic book that only I can see. I know that sounds kind of weird, right?"

She nods blankly.

"The thing is . . . ," Dibs starts. "There could be some live ones left in there. And then what? What if they pull you in for experimentation on your eyeballs or other circular-type, ah, body parts . . ." He clears his throat and raises his eyebrows at me.

"It's a chance I have to take," I tell him. "Someone needs help."

"You think that someone is in there?" Gracie asks. I turn back to the jagged hole, the fumes inside the ship making my eyes water. I wipe at them with my shoulder and readjust my bandanna high on my nose and my tinfoil hat secure against my skull.

"Yes," I tell her.

"Then you have to go," she says. "*The true courage is in facing danger when you are afraid.*"

I nod.

"You afraid, Mylo?" Dibs asks me.

I don't have to think long to answer that one.

"Yes," I say.

"That must mean you have a mess of true courage up in you already, then." He smiles.

I wrap my fingers around the edge of the opening and peer inside the disk again, and I think, *Maybe, just maybe he's right.*

16

SHORTSTOP

July 7, 1947—12:35 p.m.

Four years ago, when Obie was nine and I was only seven, Momma and Daddy took us to the Chaves County Fair. There were games to play and, if you were good enough to win, prizes, too. Daddy gave each of us five cents to choose whichever games we wanted to play. When Obie saw a brown bear hanging by a wire at the top of the baseball pitching booth, he spent all his pennies trying to pitch a ball through the small hole in the bull's-eye painted on a piece of wood.

The man at the counter was dirty, with one tooth missing in the front, a scraggly beard, and a cigarette barely hanging on between his lips. He would laugh each time Obie missed the hole, making the cigarette bob up and down and sprinkle ashes into the air.

"Got another penny, kid?" he would scoff at Obie each time.

When Obie had run out of pennies, he just shook his head.

"Too bad," the man sneered. "Step on up!" he shouted out to passersby. "Pitch the baseball through the hole and win a prize! Get three balls for a penny! Three balls for a penny! Step on up!"

Obie stared at the bear he had hoped to win.

I reached my hand way down into my pocket, grabbed my very last penny, and slid it over the counter toward the man. He handed me three baseballs.

I made it on my second throw.

And that afternoon as we were driving home in our rusty Ford pickup, my big brother had Shortstop in his arms.

The sharp jagged edges of the opening in the disk cut into the skin on my palms.

"We'll hold on to your feet out here," Dibs says. "That way you'll stay connected to this world no matter what."

I turn to face him. "Don't let go," I say.

"Never." He stands tall. "I promise you I won't. Not even if they harvest your brains and you turn into a Martian zombie."

I nod and turn back to the hole.

"Even if they suck every single one of your guts out," he goes on. "And your brains, too. I won't let go."

I nod again.

"Even if—"

"Okay," I tell him. "I trust you."

I yank my boots off and lay them in the dirt. I check my

Martian mind-control-prevention skullcap one more time, then wrap my fingers back around the sharp metal edges. I put my chin to my chest and feel the top of Shortstop's fur on my lips and then pull myself up into the tight chamber of the disk while Dibs and Gracie hold tight to my ankles.

It's dark and hazy inside the chamber, but up ahead I can see daylight streaming through the fumes, as if there are windows somewhere, even though we didn't see any on the outside. The smell is even stronger inside, and my eyes blur from the sting.

"Mylo!" Dibs calls up to me. "Tell us what you see."

I crawl slowly through the chamber, my sweaty hands slipping as I make my way deeper inside the first level of the disk. "I don't see anything yet!" I shout down at them. "But there's some kind of light up ahead. I have to go in farther."

I wipe sweat from my face.

My eyes ache and my lungs burn. Electricity pulls my guts to the very edges of my insides, demanding to come out. I choke and cough on the poisoned air filling my mouth and throat as I inch my way closer to the top of the chamber.

"There's light at the end," I tell them. "I'm going to keep on."

"Wait," Dibs calls back. "If you go much farther, we won't be able to hold on."

"Just a couple more inches," I call down to him.

"Gracie," I hear Dibs say below. "Whatever you do, don't let go."

"I won't," she says.

I slowly make my way to the light, the tips of my fingers

finding an edge and pulling myself even closer to the next level until I reach high enough to peek into the main area of the craft.

Light from the sun streams through the walls from every direction, and smoke and stink and fumes hang thick in the air.

With no metal fan to blow the hot haze in circles, it's even steamier inside than Momma's kitchen when she's baking her famous pecan pie on the hottest day in August. She won first prize at the Chaves County Fair two years running.

I wonder if Martians eat pecan pie.

"That's it, Mylo! You can't go any farther!" Dibs calls up to me. "We won't be able to hold on. Can you see anything yet?"

"The walls are windows!" I call down to them.

"What does that mean?" Dibs wants to know.

"You can see through the walls like they're glass. Top to bottom. I can see all the way back to the yucca tree where Diego and Spuds are waiting. I see Pitch and True Belle. Diego is still blowing chunks!"

"What else?"

"Gizmos!" I call back, choking and wiping more sweat with the back of my hand. "Like a bunch of small television screens, like they have at the Montgomery Ward's. Only without any speakers or volume knobs on 'em. There are a lot of bitty lights of every color on a console or desk of some kind. Some of the screens are black, and some have squiggly lines . . . and I can hear . . . static. Like what was coming out of Mordecai Lord's place that day. And I think . . . I think there might be some kind of radio transmission, too. Except it's not English. And they aren't regular words, either . . . just weird . . . noises. And small chairs, too. Like for little kids."

My head is pounding, and my eyes see dark spots hanging in the air. I squeeze my eyelids tight and then open them again. "Man alive, it's like that monsoon hit them on the outside *and* the inside," I tell them. "Everything's broken up all into pieces. Just like those same pieces with the purple symbols in Mac Brazel's field. Everything is busted up something awful."

"But do you see . . . *them?*" Dibs asks.

The sweat from my forehead drips into my eyes.

Help.

I suck air and choke on the fumes tickling and scratching their way down my throat, wiping a knuckle over one eye and then the other.

"I have to go in deeper," I tell them. "You can let me go. They're calling me again."

"No!" Dibs says. "I'm not doing it. I promised you I wouldn't."

"It's okay."

"It's a trap, Mylo," Dibs tells me. "Don't do it!"

I pull myself up farther into the main area, feeling their fingers around my ankles, yanking me back.

"What's he doing?" I hear Gracie ask. "I can't hold on much more."

"Mylo," Dibs calls. "We're pulling you out."

"No, don't!" I shout. "Not yet!"

"Is anyone here?" I call, squinting through the thick air.

I squeeze my eyes closed again, and this time when I open them, I see even more black spots and my head feels like it's spinning. Sweat keeps dripping, and my palms are stinging where jagged metal edges and pieces ripped through my skin.

"I can see another area toward the back of the ship," I call down. "You have to let go. It's okay."

I heave myself up higher, and they pull me back down.

"Mylo," Dibs calls from below me, inside the very bottom of the chamber now, too. "We are going to pull you out. You're too far in for us to hold on."

"Just a little bit farther—"

I freeze.

Something moves.

I hold my breath and stare through the haze.

"It can't be," I whisper.

Fingers.

Then a hand.

But not just any hand.

A skinny, bony, four-fingered hand.

Long fingers with pointy black fingernails and a tiny suction cup on each fingertip. The skin on its hand is like a cobra, slick and scaly.

And it's not green, either.

"I see one!" I shout.

"Gracie, on three!" Dibs yells. "We're pulling him out right now!"

Hands tighten around my ankles.

My palms slip against the metal chamber walls as my body is jerked downward.

"Wait!" I scream, feeling around for something to grab on to.

"Pull harder, Gracie," Dibs is saying. "Harder!"

"I am!" I can hear her shout.

I slip again.

"Wait!" I shout at them. "Stop pulling me!"

The four-fingered hand lifts from the floor of the ship. Reaching for me.

Me.

Mylo Affinito.

"He's alive!" I tell them, feeling another jagged edge slide under my palm as I grab on tight to hold steady.

The flying disk feels like a merry-go-round going way too fast now, spinning out of control as my head whirls and the dark spots fill in more spaces.

My stomach feels sick.

Dibs and Gracie pull harder.

I slip again.

"Wait!" I scream as my fingers cling to the final corner before I'm yanked back down the chamber.

I watch two gigantic, black, almond-shaped eyes peeking out from underneath a broken-up console. They stare, blinking just like the green light on that very first night of the crash.

Once, twice, three times.

Watching me.

While I watch them.

"I'm the one," I whisper to the desperate black eyes. "The one you've been talking to. I'm here to help you. I promise you I will. It's going to be okay."

"Pull harder, Gracie!" Dibs hollers. "They're not taking him up to their mother ship. Not if I have anything to say about it."

My fingers ache against the force.

My lungs beg for air.

My body feels like a limp, wet rag.

"I won't leave you," I tell the blinking black eyes. "I promise you I won't."

My fingers slip off the edge and I slide down the chamber, hitting the sides as I go. The last thing I remember are those black eyes.

And then . . . nothing.

17

TELEPATHIC SUPERPOWERS

July 7, 1947—1:55 p.m.

Someone is holding my head.

And I'm hearing voices.

But this time it isn't Martians showing me messages behind my eyelids.

It feels like my heart has taken up residence inside my skull and it's beating a fast and pounding bongo rhythm against my brain.

At least I know the Martians didn't harvest my brain. But maybe it would hurt less if they had.

Spuds: What if he's dead?

Diego: He's not dead, you dope.

Spuds: He ain't moving any.

Diego: He's still breathing, isn't he? . . . Look.

Dibs: Maybe they've infiltrated his brain, and his body is just a shell like on *The Whistler*.

Spuds: Is that a real thing?

Dibs: Sure it is.

Spuds: How can you tell if his brain is infiltrated or not?

Dibs: The eyes turn black as coal with no pupils.

Spuds: How are we supposed to know if his eyes are black as coal? They're closed.

Diego: Gracie, pull up his eyelid and check it.

Gracie: I'm not doing that to him!

Spuds: Do you think he really saw Martians in there?

Dibs: I think we should get him out of here. It isn't safe. And I don't know about you all, but I don't want to cross paths with any green and shifty Martians. They'll kill you soon as look at you. They'll spread their Death Dust and we'll be history. Just like that.

Spuds: Oh, hey, Dibs, what should you do if you see a green Martian?

Gracie: How can you tell jokes at a time like this?

Spuds: Come on! It's a funny one. What should you do if you see a green Martian?

Silence.

Spuds: Wait until it's ripe! Get it? Wait until it's *ripe*? Like bananas are green and then turn yellow when they're ripe. Get it? Wait until it's *ripe*.

Spuds laughs at his own joke.

"They're not green," I say then.

Silence.

I know it's my mouth that says the words, but it still

feels like I'm in the in-between and not quite back inside my body yet.

Diego: Did he say something?

Spuds: Mylo, did you say something?

Diego: Gracie, give him a poke and see if he'll open his eyes.

Gracie: I'm not poking him, either.

Dibs: Mylo? Mylo, can you hear me?

I feel a soft hand on my cheek. I know it's Gracie. It's got to be. Dibs would give me a dirty foot in the face before he'd ever give me soft touches on my cheek. And his hands are just as leathery as his feet are.

It takes every bit of strength in me to pry open my eyelids, and when I do, the sun is so bright I squint up at the shadowy faces leaned over me in a circle under the tall yucca. Gracie's shadow is the closest because she's holding my head in her lap, looking down at me, her foil hat still on the top of her head.

Pulling myself upright, I grasp at the gravel and rock, trying to steady the Earth as it spins around me. I squeeze my eyes shut and then I open them again.

"You okay, Mylo?" Dibs drops his knobby knees in the dirt next to me.

"What'd you say, Affinito?" Diego asks.

I cough at the dry dust coating my throat. "I said they're not green."

Gracie's mouth falls open and Spuds takes one giant step backward.

"Are you talking about the Martians?" Dibs asks.

"Yes," I say. I touch the back of my head where I can feel my heartbeat pounding and see blood on my fingertips.

"You lost your skullcap," Dibs says.

"You saw 'em?" Spuds asks.

"Yes," I say again. "And they're not green . . . they're gray."

I put my hand inside my bib pocket . . . it's empty.

I drop to my knees. "Oh, God," I whisper into my bloody palms.

"Don't worry." Spuds puts a hand on my shoulder. "There ain't nothing there a couple of Band-Aids won't fix."

"You don't understand," I say. "He's gone."

"Who is?" Dibs asks.

"What's he saying now?" Diego demands, pacing the outside of the circle.

"Shortstop," I whisper.

"Gone? You mean he's in *there?*" Dibs points in the direction of the disk.

I nod. "He must have fallen out." I get to my feet and dust the dirt from my knees. "I have to go back."

Everyone is shouting.

Diego is saying something about going back home.

Spuds is talking about being too young to die.

Dibs is hollering something about Martian mind control.

And Gracie is telling them all to hush up.

"What's wrong with you all?" she demands, her hands on her hips. "Can you just let Mylo talk?"

"Let me handle this." Dibs puts his hands up, pushes his way past the others to face me. "*Myyyylooo,*" he says real slow and loud with emphasis on each syllable. "*Has . . . your . . . brain . . . been . . . compromised?*"

"You're such an idiot, Butts. And take that stupid foil hat off your head." Diego grabs Dibs's Yankees cap and his tin-foil skullcap and flings them both to the ground. "You look like a moron!"

"Smart enough to keep my brain from being sucked out of my ears," Dibs tells him, picking the cap and foil out of the dirt. "The only reason they haven't tried to take yours is that they don't care to study humans as dumb as a stump."

"You better shut up, Butts!" Diego shouts at him.

Dibs holds up two skinny dukes. "Make me," he says, scowling.

"You're all morons," Gracie informs the boys. "Just shut up for a minute and let Mylo talk." She sits down next to me and pulls her tablet and a pencil out of her cloth purse. "Now, start from the beginning and tell us everything. Don't leave anything out," she says as she moves her pencil in graceful loops across the page.

"Did you really see 'em, Mylo?" Dibs asks. "Did you see real live Martian bodies?"

I wonder what else is in that tablet of hers and if she ever writes anything in there about me. If I had a tablet, I would write about the small mole right above her left eyebrow, which I've never noticed before. And that the skin on her hands feels as soft as the petals on Momma's bougainvilleas, which hang on the trellis that covers the front part of the house.

"No," I tell them. "I didn't see bodies."

"No?" Diego puts his hands on his hips.

Gracie's pencil stops moving and she looks up at me. "You didn't see them?" she asks.

"No," I say.

"I thought you said you did see 'em?" Dibs demands.

"You either seen 'em or you didn't, Mylo," Spuds calls out. "Which is it?"

"I did see one," I tell them. "But it wasn't a body."

"If it wasn't a body, then what was it?" Diego demands.

I turn to face Gracie again. "A Martian," I say, wondering if she'll write that in her book.

But her pencil stays still.

No one says anything.

"And he was alive, too."

Gracie starts scribbling furiously.

Spuds starts pacing in the dirt.

Diego starts to gag again.

Dibs just stares at me, still folded up on his knees in the dirt by my side.

No one says anything for a real long while, until Spuds finally stops pacing and turns to the group.

"I think we should all just go back home and leave it for the Army Air Force," he says. "That's it. We just . . . we just need to get out of here and . . . and. . . . and leave it be. We seen it, like we said we wanted to, right? We seen it. Now we just need to go before something real bad happens."

"Spuds is right," Dibs says. "We need to just go back and cross our hearts that we tell nothing to no one about it. Mr. Lord said we shouldn't come out here and he was right. We should have listened to him."

"Yep," Diego says. "I agree. We need to let the Army Air Force handle it. Come on, Gracie." He puts his hand out to help her up out of the dirt.

She's still writing.

"No," I say.

Diego drops his hand. "What do you mean, *no*?" He furrows his brow, ready for a fight.

"I mean I'm not going back," I tell him.

"Suit yourself, Affinito." Diego shrugs. "But we're leaving. Gracie?" He holds out his hand again.

She ignores him.

"What do you mean you're not going back, Mylo?" Dibs demands. "You have to."

I stand up then, take a long, deep breath, and brush the dirt from my overalls. My head feels heavy and dizzy, and the desert spins like another carnival ride until I find my feet under me.

"He needs my help," I tell them. "And I need yours if I'm going to help him out of there."

Spuds starts pacing again.

"What are you talking about?" Diego says.

I glance at Gracie, who's finally stopped writing and is staring up at me. "Dibs was right," I say. "I'm hearing something. Except it's not exactly words. It's like pictures . . . messages . . . on the backs of my eyelids."

"On the backs of your *what?*" Diego says.

"It doesn't matter. All I know is someone needs help. I don't know how or why it's me who knows about it, but it is . . . and . . . and so I'm helping whoever it is in that thing," I say. "But I can't do it alone. He thinks I can, but I know I can't. I need you, too."

"Well, I'm not going anywhere near there." Spuds shakes his head. "Not if there's some space monster inside that thing. Not on your life."

"This is life or death." I throw my hands up in the air. "They are living beings that need help. What does it matter if they don't look like we do? Someone needs help . . . . you help 'em. That's how it works."

"How many are there?" Gracie asks, chewing on her eraser.

I turn to look at her still sitting in the dirt. "I don't know."

She writes that in her book, too.

"Affinito, you're off your rocker, you know that?" Diego says. "*We* are going home. *You* can stay and do whatever you want. Best of luck." He turns toward Lupe.

"You don't understand," I say.

"I understand enough to know that you're starting to sound too much like crazy old Mordecai Lord. Next you'll be walking to the mailbox in nothing but a threadbare plaid bathrobe and eating attic bats, too," he calls over his shoulder.

"I've got it!" Dibs exclaims, his pointer finger in the air. "I know what this is! It isn't Martian mind control at all, and he ain't Mordecai Lord crazy, either." He stares wide-eyed at me. "It's . . . *telepathy.*"

Spuds stops pacing and slaps a hand over his mouth. "Is it catching?" he mumbles behind his palm.

"It isn't a sickness, it's a power. A *superpower.* In *Superman,* issue number forty-five, 'Lois Lane, Superwoman,' he has telepathic powers. He can read people's thoughts. Knows exactly what they're thinking without no one even telling him." Dibs gasps and puts a hand on my arm. "The card! It was real, Mylo! Like an actual sign that the universe has anointed you with superpowers . . . anyone could have gotten that Cracker Jack box. Absolutely anyone. But it wasn't just anyone . . . it was you. And now, just like Superman, you're *possessed of powers and abilities never before realized on Earth.*" He waves his arms.

Silence.

Dibs's hand shoots high in the air then with so much force it almost pulls his toes clear off the ground. "I call your Jimmy Olsen!" he hollers.

Diego blows air out of his mouth and shakes his head. "Butte, of all the dumb things you've come up with, this is by far the dumbest," he says. "Everyone knows Superman comes from a planet of supermen; he wasn't anointed by the universe. And for sure not through a Cracker Jack box."

Dibs ignores him. "Aquaman had it, too," he says. "He could talk to the marine animals and know exactly what they were thinking. Mostly just fish . . . but I bet if he got visited he could talk to Martians, too—"

"Butts, shut your pie hole already!" Diego commands.

Dibs doesn't hear that one, either. "That's it, all right! That's what he's got!" He looks at me with amazement. "*Cracker Jack telepathy.*"

"I don't get it," Spuds says. "He *caught* it from Cracker Jacks?"

"Wait!" Dibs shouts. "Mylo, tell me what I'm thinking right this minute." With his eyes closed, he massages his temples with his fingertips.

"Everyone just shut up for a minute!" Diego hollers with his arms straight out.

No one says anything.

"We're leaving!" Diego shouts. "That's it."

"Dr. Psycho was a telepathic supervillain in *Wonder Woman* number five, 'Battle for Womanhood,'" Dibs whispers to Gracie. "You might want to write that down in your little book there." He points.

"If you're going to write that, then make sure and put in there that Dibs doesn't know what he's talking about," Diego says.

Dibs scowls good and ugly back at Diego. "Then you should put in there that Diego's so bad up at bat, he couldn't hit water if he fell out of a boat."

Diego shows Dibs a fist.

Dibs pretends to shudder in fear.

And Gracie rolls her eyes at the whole thing.

"Do you think he needs a doctor?" she asks me.

Diego scoffs and kicks at the gravel with his boot.

"I don't know," I say. "But I have to find out."

"Dr. Psycho used his telepathic powers to enter Wonder

Woman's dreams, too . . . just like with this," Dibs says to no one in particular. "I'm just saying, same deal here."

"You read *Wonder Woman*, Butte?" Spuds says under his breath. "*Thaaaat's* pretty weird."

"I'm going back to help and that's all there is to it," I tell them all. "No one has to come if they don't want."

"Let's take a vote," Diego says. "All in favor of getting out of here, raise your hand." His hand shoots up first, followed by Spuds's.

Dibs gives me a sly smile and slowly raises his hand. "Sorry," he says.

"Okay, Gracie," Diego says. "Raise your hand."

Her eyes meet mine.

"*Gracie*," Diego says again.

She slowly tucks her tablet and pencil into her cloth purse. "No," she says flatly.

Diego's hand slips down slowly and his mouth falls open. "What do you mean, no?" he demands.

"I mean I'm not leaving," she says. "Not if someone's hurt and needs help."

I swallow hard. "Are you sure?" I ask her.

She gazes in the direction of the disk. "Yes." She bobs her head once, like she really means it.

"I don't believe this." Diego runs a hand through his hair.

"Hey." Spuds stretches his neck, pointing in the distance. "What's that?" he asks.

We all turn to see a tornado of dust billowing straight up to the sky off in the distance.

I shield my eyes with my hand.

"A dust devil?" Dibs says.

"It's a haboob coming this way, maybe," Spuds says.

"We better get out of here before that dust storm hits. I don't plan to be buried under a wall of sand with that Martian thing," Diego says.

Another gust billows through, clearing just enough of the dust and dirt and gravel and silt kicked up into the sky for us to see as plain as day.

"They're coming!" Dibs hollers.

18

A MARTIAN PRAYER AND A PROMISE

July 7, 1947—2:40 p.m.

A human chain of hands.

First me and then Gracie, Dibs, Spuds, and even Diego work together to climb up the side of a large arroyo way south of the crash site. I can't say for sure we weren't seen at all, but at least no one came after us when we saddled up and made our way out of there.

Once we all make it to the top of the rock, we army-crawl on our bellies across the flat surface to the very edge.

A covert parade of belly walkers.

One by one, we line up still against the rock and watch as the Army Air Force vehicles surround the crash site down below in one big roaring, red tornado of dust. I count fourteen vehicles altogether.

Seven jeeps.

Two flatbeds.

Five covered pickup trucks with tan-colored tarps over the beds.

"What do they need with two flatbeds?" Dibs whispers.

"Think they'll take the ship back with them?" I ask.

"It's round," Spuds says. "It's going to roll right off that thing."

We watch as men climb out of their vehicles in their 509th Bomb Group Army Air Force tan uniforms and scramble around in every direction, just like the cockroaches do in Dibs's kitchen sink when you turn the lights on.

The first group takes point all around the disk, their large guns drawn and ready for a hostile interstellar battle.

Another group works to set up camp, unloading trucks to the tune of harsh voices bellowing orders.

Tables are set up under a tent to the right.

Long black bags are laid out in the dirt on the left.

Another group of four soldiers pull bulky white suits with hoods over their uniforms.

Dibs pokes me and raises his eyebrows. "If they read the Planet Comics series, they'd know all they really need is the tinfoil squares on their heads."

A larger group forms a human chain, scouring the desert and picking up every single piece of debris. Even the ones still stuck in the high tree branches.

Another truck stops, and we watch four men exit the vehicle one by one, three of them wearing olive-green jackets over tan uniforms even though it's a million degrees out. Their medals and ribbons pierce their fronts and sparkle in the sun. And then we see one regular man who's not wearing a uniform. Instead he's in coveralls with dirt on the knees.

"Who's that?" Diego points. "That man there, out of uniform."

"Looks like a rancher," Spuds says.

"It's probably Mac Brazel," I say.

"Nah." Dibs squints. "Too skinny to be Mac Brazel. Maybe Mac Brazel called the Foster brothers in Texas about the crash and they came out to see it for their own selves. Maybe it's Jap or Henry."

We watch the men in the olive jackets as they huddle in their circle. But when they all fall into a line, looking straight out at the disk, we get a better look at them.

It's Dibs who gasps first.

"Do you see who it is?" He grabs my arm. "Do you?"

I stare, unable to speak.

And that's when we see the men in the white hoods lower a small body out of the bottom of the chamber.

"Look!" Gracie points.

A small gray body with coal-black eyes and limp gray arms hanging toward the ground.

"No," Dibs says under his breath.

My bones ache so deeply, I can feel the pain clear to my toes.

Dibs sits up and looks at me. "I think we need to pray for them," he says. "Right now, come on." He gets up and holds out his hands.

We all stand in a circle with clutched hands and bowed heads.

Even me.

"I'll start," Dibs says. "Lord God, please help these Martians. I know there's one still alive in there, God. Please watch over him and make sure he gets home." He clears his throat. "Where he belongs."

Then Gracie. "They're probably real scared to be here on a planet where they don't know anyone and don't know the language," she says. "Give them peace in their hearts to know there are people here who want to help them."

Diego clears his throat and shifts his feet. "I don't know what to say," he tells his boots.

"Just say what you feel," Gracie tells him.

He nods. "They have family," he starts, his voice low and gravelly. "And friends who want them home. Please see to it that someone helps them get there."

Then I see him glance at me.

I look away.

"Spuds," Dibs says. "Your turn."

"Oh, um, God? I don't know if this is your territory, but there are some creatures over that way that don't look like they're doing so good. I think even if it isn't your job to watch over them, you'd do it, you know, 'cause you're God and all."

And then it's my turn.

The others stay silent, eyes closed, waiting on me.

But I don't know what to say to Him.

"Mylo?" Gracie finally says. "Do you want to add anything?"

I nod.

"I made a promise," I whisper. "Please let me keep it this time."

"Amen." Dibs says it first.

Everyone follows.

Even me.

We stay in our circle, hands still clasped, gazing back and forth at each other.

Unsure what to do next.

"We need to make a pact," Diego finally says. "No one says anything about us being out here today." He points to each one of us, his eyes stopping on me.

I nod.

"Everyone put a hand in," he says, holding a flat palm out in the center of our Martian prayer circle.

Spuds puts his hand over Diego's, then Dibs, then Gracie, and then me.

We stand in our circle of secrecy. Sweaty palms stuck together tight in a slippery hand-sandwich pact. Our eyes locking on each other in a silent understanding of the importance of what we've seen.

What it means for them.

What it means for us.

And for the entire universe, too.

"Gracie," Dibs whispers in her direction. "Did you put that part in your book about Diego not being able to get a hit?"

But Diego isn't even listening.

His eyes are glued to mine.

"Affinito," he says. "What in the Sam Hill is your daddy doing out there with the Army Air Force?"

19

THE WRONG BOY

July 7, 1947—4:15 p.m.

At the black mailbox, Dibs and I sit quietly for a long while, him on True Belle and me on Pitch, thinking about it all.

"You don't hear him no more, do you?" Dibs finally says.

I shake my head.

"Was that the one?" he asks. "The one they pulled out of the ship? Was he the one you seen in there?"

I don't say anything.

"He wasn't moving . . . do you think it was . . . he was—" he starts, and then stops.

He doesn't ask me the question that he doesn't want an answer to.

A question I don't want to answer.

I swallow back the rush of tears in my throat and wipe at the ones pushing their way to the rims of my eyes.

"Mylo?" Dibs whispers, studying me, his Martian mind-control-prevention tinfoil square still molded tight against his head underneath his Yankees cap. "You crying?"

I shake my head, but the tears squeezing out between my lashes make me a liar.

I swat them away with an angry hand.

"I promised him," I say, my voice squeaking and cracking on each word. "I promised him."

Dibs stands there staring at me without saying anything.

I push more tears off my face, but they're coming down like hard rain. And with that kind of mess going on, there is just no putting on a brave face. So I just stand there crying like a big baby right in front of him.

"And you want to know what else?" I wipe my nose again.

He nods.

"The most important thing I have of Obie's is gone now, too. The one that means everything."

"You have a lot of things of his still," Dibs says.

"Nothing that smells like him anymore. Shortstop smells just like him. He was the only connection I had left."

I scoff and snot shoots from my nose. "Some kind of superhero, huh?" I say.

Dibs doesn't answer at first. Then he says, "I think it'd be okay if Superman cried. Shows he's part human, too. Super-heroes have to have a human heart or they wouldn't care enough to help those who need it."

"He isn't part human," I say. "He's from Krypton, a planet of supermen and superwomen."

"Maybe by birth he is," Dibs says, pondering, "but that doesn't mean he doesn't have the heart part. They all had it. Remember when Jor-El and Lara put him on the space vessel as Krypton was exploding? They sacrificed themselves for him to live here on Earth. That's heart."

"I guess."

"Maybe the Army Air Force will help the Martian," Dibs says. "Bring him to the base hospital and help get him back to his family. You think the Army Air Force has a heart for Martians?"

"What if they don't?" I ask. "What if they keep him prisoner and he never gets back home ever again? What if his family has to wonder where he is, too? Wonder why he isn't back home with them?"

"So maybe we do something more."

"We?" I say. "I thought you raised your hand back there, along with the others."

"Yeah, well, maybe I changed my mind," he says. "I may not be a Cracker Jack superhero like you, but I have enough stuffing in me to declare myself your Jimmy Olsen."

"Don't you get it yet? There's nothing special about me," I tell him. "Not one single thing. I don't know why you can't see that."

"I see what I see, and what I see," he says, "is that you're the closest thing to a superhero I've known here on Earth."

I wipe my eyes with my forearm. "Just 'cause a box of Cracker Jacks says so?"

"No. On account of the courage I see . . . even before Cracker Jacks knew about you. What you did today," he says, shaking his head. "Going inside the disk and then deciding to go back when the rest of us chickened out . . . that was something, all right."

"Yeah, well, I sure don't feel very brave."

"You want to know why else I think you got a whole lot of courage stuffed up in you?"

I nod.

He turns his head toward the house. "You keep on going," he says, real quiet this time. "You keep on, even after Obie died. Especially on the days you might not want to. And I know there are those days, even though you don't say it out loud. Because I know you."

I look up the drive now, too.

"He's home," Dibs says, jutting a chin at his daddy's rusty Ford pickup parked in front of the house. "Probably wondering where I've been."

"Just come home with me," I tell him. "Momma's making your favorite for dinner tonight. Fried chicken with mashed potatoes and her famous lumpy gravy."

He shakes his head. "Can't," he says.

"Why not?" I ask him. "Why can't you?"

"'Cause I haven't been here all day. I have to see what's happening."

"What do you mean?"

"I mean what if this is the day Momma comes back for me?" He rubs at the saddle horn in his hand. "What if Daddy's drank so much that he doesn't pen up the pigs right and they get out? We already don't have the money for Mr. Funk and, well, if we lost the pigs, too . . . it'd be real bad. What if Mr. Funk comes back early and no one is here and he decides to take what we have?"

I don't know what to say to all that.

"Guess I'll see you tomorrow," he says.

I nod. "So long."

"So long." He shakes the reins and kicks True Belle's fat belly.

I watch after him as he goes.

I watch while he makes it up the drive, then slides off True Belle and finally trudges up the front porch steps.

Awaiting his doom.

I watch long after he lets the screen door slam behind him and the yelling starts.

It hurts my heart to listen and not be able to do anything, so I kick Pitch's belly and get on my way home. The silence of the stifling desert air all around me stings my ears and aches me to my bones with every step.

No more whispers.

No more screams.

Nothing.

I pull the Superhero Club Membership Card out of my pocket as I ride, running a finger over the words. Words that aren't mine.

Words that will never be.

I rip it in half first, and then I rip it again and again and again until all that's left is tiny pieces, and I throw them up over my head and into the wind. Then I kick my heels into Pitch's belly even harder.

"Yah!" I scream.

She starts into a trot and moves into a full-on gallop, breaking away from it all.

I shake the reins again.

Faster.

But no matter how long her strides, the gray is always just one arm's reach away.

It's dark and it's deep and you can never find your way out. The air inside it hurts your lungs and your skin, worse than any scrape or sore. It's an ache that pains every part of you and takes your strength and your breath.

It takes everything.

It's an agony that reaches so deep inside and holds on so tight you don't think you'll ever breathe again.

And you're not sure you even want to.

"Please let me be!" I holler back over my shoulder.

But the gray never listens.

I pass the ranch and Corona General, too.

I ride without stopping as Pitch takes long, sleek strides down Highway 54 and through the iron gates, running until I reach the one and only place where I know you are.

Even though I can't feel you there, either.

OBIE BROOKS AFFINITO
SEPTEMBER 6, 1934–MAY 27, 1946
BELOVED SON, BROTHER, FRIEND
WE WILL NEVER FORGET.
NO ONE BRAVER.

I slip down off Pitch and drop to the ground in a pile of bones, throwing my arms around the cool stone marking his place in this world.

And I cry.

I cry like I'll never ever stop.

Never ever catch my breath.

Never ever breathe again.

"I miss you," I choke out through the tears filling my throat, my warm cheek against the cool, slick stone.

Silence.

"Can't you hear me, Obie?" I scream at the sky. "It's Mylo. Your brother. I can't find you!"

Low thunder grumbles in the west.

"I've gone and done it again . . . promised something I had no business promising. And I messed that up, too. I can't fix it and God isn't listening. I know you're here somewhere. I know you can hear me. Please just answer me!" I beg the sky. "Tell me what it takes to be as brave as you!"

Bucket-sized tears stream down from my lashes and drip off my chin and out my nose and I let them.

"Maybe you're mad at me?" I ask, squeezing his stone even tighter. "Because I couldn't keep my promise to you? And that one was on a spit shake, which makes it a million times worse. But you made one to me, too. You said you wouldn't leave me. You promised you wouldn't. No matter what, you promised. But I can't find you. Not even here. You're just gone and you shouldn't be. This wasn't supposed to be the end of your story."

Silence.

"And you want to know what else?" My voice catches. "I knew it was a lie when I said it," I tell him. "I knew it but I said it anyway because I wanted it to be true. But maybe you lied, too."

Nothing.

"I tried, though," I tell him, dropping my chin to my chest and wrapping my arms around my knees. "I prayed with all I had in me. And I hoped. Back when I had hope in me, I did."

A gust whips up, blowing gravel, and one tumbleweed gets stuck against Gracie's great-great-grandmother.

VALENTINA GRACIELA DELGADO

JULY 4, 1862–DECEMBER 2, 1933

BEAUTIFUL, STRONG, KIND.

A SPIRIT TO BE RECKONED WITH.

I wipe my nose on my forearm again. "Nothing I did worked," I say. "And now you're gone. Gone from this place, gone from the house . . . and gone from me. Shortstop is even gone now, too."

I lie down on my back against the sharp pebbles, staring up at the darkening storm clouds above me, letting the tears run straight into my ears.

"I need you to come home," I tell the sky. "It's the only way your ending can be right."

Help.

I jump to my feet when I hear it, peeking around Obie's headstone and scanning around the other stones that mark very important places in this world.

I look over at Mr. Beckman, wondering if he heard it, too.

IN LOVING MEMORY OF
PIERMONT BECKMAN
APRIL 1, 1842–JANUARY 4, 1899

"Did you hear that, Mr. Beckman?" I ask him.

But he doesn't answer me, either.

"Hello?" I call out. "Is someone out there? Mrs. Delgado? You hear something?"

Silence.

I squeeze my eyes shut and listen hard.

"Hello?" I say again.

This time I hear something that almost knocks me right off the heels of my boots.

Mylo.

"Y-you . . ." I swallow. "You . . . know me?"

Nothing.

"I want to help you," I tell him. "I really want to. But you picked the wrong boy. I'm missing my courage part."

No one answers.

"It's just gone!" I shout out to the sky.

Silence.

"And God left out the muscles, too."

Still nothing.

"Hello? D-do you hear me?" I call. "Did you hear me about picking someone else?" I plop my bag of bones back down on the ground, my brain feeling too worn out to do anything more.

An owl hoots at me from somewhere in the distance.

And something scuffles in the dirt.

I shoot straight up again, scanning between headstones and past trees. It's getting dark now, with another summer monsoon rolling in.

Wind whooshes.

Gravel rustles.

Thunder rumbles.

And then a footstep.

My neck stretches left, then right. "Are you there?"

And another footstep.

"Dibs?" I call, squinting into the darkness. "If that's you trying to scare me, you'll be sorry."

Silence.

I know it's Dibs.

It's got to be. He'll jump out with a bloodcurdling *Boo!* and get a couple of big yuks about it, too. He'll yuk it up for weeks, reminding me of it. Like that time he hid in the chicken coop and *Boo!*ed me something awful two winters ago. It took him nine whole months to forget about it.

Of course it's Dibs.

Thunder rolls and I feel a drop of rain hit my shoulder, and then another one.

The thick air sticking against me.

"I know it's you, Dibs," I call out, putting my hands on my hips. "You're not funny."

The thunder answers me first and then the wind.

I watch the tumbleweed let loose from Mrs. Delgado and move on toward the black iron fence.

"Dibs?" I call, louder this time. "If it's you, I'm going to give you a knuckle sandwich so hard that—"

Another footstep and then a scuffle and then . . .

An eye.

One big black eye peering out at me from behind Mrs. Vandebrink.

HERE LIES LILLIAN VANDEBRINK
AUGUST 14, 1802–MAY 22, 1888
FRED'S WIFE AND ELMER'S MOTHER
R.I.P.

An extra-large gray hairless head is watching me.

Four long, skinny fingers wrapped around the stone.

Fingers with pointy black fingernails and suction cups where the fingerprints are supposed to go.

I suck air and freeze in fear, my eyeballs stuck on the large black eyes watching me.

Me.

Mylo Affinito.

Then the hand is reaching toward me.

Closer.

Closer.

There's something clasped between the gray fingers.

He takes a step out from behind the stone. And then another one, until he's standing close to me, in a silky tan flight suit that's as tight as his skin. At least two heads shorter than me and one shorter than Dibs. He's skinny, too. Even skinnier than Dibs is, if that's even possible. Like six-year-old-boy skinny, with a watermelon-sized head. Purple hieroglyphics are printed up and down one arm, just like on the shattered pieces out in the desert.

I stand frozen.

My feet cemented to the ground as he reaches one hand slowly toward me. It's just as Dibs said it would be. Interstellar Martians here to suck our brain out our ears as soon as look at us.

Something is inside his hand as he reaches closer.

Ming the Merciless's Purple Death.

Martian mind-control at its best.

A teleportation device from the future powered on and ready to beam me up to the waiting mother ship.

Why didn't I listen to Dibs when I had the chance?

The visitor drops whatever's in his hand at my feet.

Dibs would warn me about a clever Martian distraction to catch me off guard so that when I take my eyes off him . . . Ka-pow! My brains are sucked out of me in a single second.

I slowly peel my eyes from his, glancing down at the dirt in front of me. Then back at him and then back at the dirt again.

I drop to my knees and scoop the small brown bear from the ground.

Shortstop.

I carefully dust the red dirt off him, and then bring him slowly up in front of my nose.

I close my eyes tight.

And I breathe him in.

Right between his ears where the fur is loved almost clean off.

I fill my lungs as full as they will go and hold all of our memories inside me until I have to breathe them back out again.

Obie.

He's there.

The oil from his leather catcher's mitt and the dirt from the pitcher's mound we built out back.

And his courage.

20

LEAVE IT BE

July 7, 1947—6:05 p.m.

It's a million degrees in the hayloft, and a wicked wind is starting up outside.

I can't say exactly how we got from the cemetery to the hayloft except that he took my hands in his and made some weird sounds and then there was this strange pulling inside me and then a haze of clouds and dreams. Like I was sleeping but wide awake at the same time.

And then I was home.

With a tiny gray man from outer space.

I scurried him up to the hayloft before Daddy finished in the field and went to wash up with the Ivory for supper.

The smells of Momma's fried chicken and mashed potatoes and her famous bourbon pecan pie weave in and out of the open door of the hayloft, reminding me I haven't eaten since breakfast. Momma's uneaten summer sausage sandwiches spoiling in the heat, still in my saddlebag.

We sit staring at each other.

Me and him.

Me, melting in the summer heat. Him, dry as a bone.

Drips run down my temples. Buds bead up over my top lip. Streams slide down between my shoulder blades.

I wipe my forearm over my forehead and through my wet hair.

"You don't get hot, huh?" I ask him.

If I had my tablet now, I would make a list of questions to ask a man from Mars that would take up every page.

Front and back.

And I bet there wouldn't be one single line with a question as dumb as what I just asked.

Not even at the very bottom of the list when I was running out of questions. My tongue tastes the salt from the sweaty beads on my lips. I can't take my eyes off him. Wondering what's the best thing to ask.

"You speak English?" I ask him.

He blinks at me with his gargantuan, glassy black eyes. Considering me, as his hairless eyebrow bones go up and down, wrinkling and unwrinkling his sweatless forehead.

I wonder what he sees when he looks at me through those eyes.

An Earth Martian.

Five strange, suction cup–less fingers on each hand.

Fine hair everywhere but the upper lip, where it's supposed to be.

Rivers of sweat.

His bony bald brow wrinkles up and then down. Up and

then down. He's examining me. I wonder what's on his list of questions. He probably wouldn't ask anything about the sweat. I wipe my face again with the back of my hand.

That one goes without saying.

"Mylo!" Momma calls from the front porch. "Supper is ready!"

If only Momma could know. But she can't. No one can. We all made a pact at the arroyo. And if I were to ever break that pact, Momma would be the very last person I would tell, even though she's one of the first people I *want* to tell. She'd have me scrubbing to Z with the sloppy bar of Ivory until the end of time.

"Coming!" I holler.

"There is so much I want to ask you," I whisper to him. "I figure you know a whole lot of things on account of your head being so big and all. No offense or anything. It's not a bad thing to be bigheaded. Lots of people have big heads. I mean, not as big as yours, of course, but . . . well, Dibs says it's 'cause of you being so big-brained. So it's a good thing and it suits you. You're probably real smart, is all I'm trying to say."

His big black eyes blink at me.

"On the other hand, your ears are nothing but holes," I tell him. "Makes me wonder if you can hear me at all."

He tilts his head.

"I keep asking you questions that aren't on my list . . . if I had a list, that is. If I had made a list of things I'd want to ask a real live Martian," I tell him. "But who makes a list like that? Who expects they're going to have a face-to-face meeting with a man from Mars? Sorry . . . I don't know why I keep rambling on . . . just nervous, I s'pose."

I watch as the Martian adjusts his fine-threaded tan flight suit, which looks more like a second skin than fabric.

"If Dibs were here, he'd know exactly what to ask you," I say. "Or . . . Obie. He'd know, too."

He's still adjusting things.

"That's my brother."

The screen door slams. "Mylo!" Momma calls again. "Where are you?"

I lean out over the sill of the open door of the loft and wave down to her.

"Up here, Momma!" I holler. "I'm coming!"

The Martian scuttles over to the door, trying to get a bug-eyed, fat-headed peek, leaning this way and that, while I try to block him from view.

"Hurry up now," Momma tells me, catching wild wisps of hair dancing across her face from the monsoon blowing in. "Daddy's all washed up already and the fried chicken is getting cold. What are you doing up there?"

"N-nothing," I say, sliding from one side of the window to the other. "Be right there!" I grab the Martian by the arm and dive down into the mounds of loose hay.

He tumbles on top of me.

"You can't let them see you," I whisper. "It's not safe for you. Get it? We have to keep you hidden. *Hiiiddden*," I say slowly.

He blinks at me again and then sits up, raises one eyebrow, pulls a gold band out of a pocket, and places it over his head.

I point a shaky finger at it. "What in the Sam Hill is that thing?"

He leans one knee down in the hay, pulling more things from invisible pockets in his skintight flight suit.

"What are you doing?"

He sets something on the hay in front of me.

I need to squint to make it out.

It's a small card.

A square piece of cardboard.

I bend at the waist to get a closer look. And then reach for it, my fingers shaking. His skin feels smooth when I touch his palm. I quickly grab the card and examine it closely, turning it over and running my finger across the front and back where it was ripped. "It's my Superhero Club Membership Card?" I whisper.

The same Superhero Club Membership Card that I ripped into tiny pieces at Dibs's place. The Cracker Jack pieces I threw into the wind.

"You can't even see the scars where I ripped it."

I jump and shove the card in my pocket.

"Mylo!" Daddy barks. "Your momma told you it's suppertime. What are you doing messing around in here?"

I scramble to the edge of the hayloft and peer over the rail.

"Ah, yeah, Daddy," I call down to him, wiping more dripping sweat. "Sorry."

"Don't you hear your momma calling you?" His voice is stern and his jaw rigid. "It's way too hot to be spending time in here. Come on now."

"I'll be right in," I say.

"I said now."

"Yes, sir."

I don't know what to tell the Martian as his brow bone moves up and down, so I just leave him there and climb down the ladder while Daddy waits and watches.

He opens the barn door for me and follows me out.

"Daddy?" I say before we reach the porch steps.

He doesn't answer me.

It seems that Daddy's got a whole lot on his mind since Obie died. So much that he doesn't ever seem to hear or see anything that's happening right in front of his face. And now there's even more on his mind, I suppose, on account of him being out at the crash site. And right this minute, his being an ostrich with his head in the sand when I need him most makes my brain feel like exploding.

Daddy never said a whole lot. Even before now. But if he did have something to say, you made sure to listen up real good because it was bound to be important. No good-for-nothing chitchat ever came out of him. And he played baseball out back with us and taught us about ranching. And after supper some evenings and on Sundays, too, he'd strum the guitar on the porch and we'd sing songs like "Clementine," "This Little Light of Mine," and "You Are My Sunshine."

But he's different now.

He hardly talks at all anymore and when he does he's usually barking. And the guitar hasn't been picked up for a long while.

And now there he was out in the desert around Corona,

New Mexico, with the Army Air Force, examining a Martian crash. Daddy in his coveralls and the men in their uniforms.

When I look up at him right this minute, I wonder if I even know him at all anymore.

"Daddy?" I try again. "Do you believe in flying saucers?"

He stops short and looks down at me. "Your momma told you to stay away from Mac Brazel's field, didn't she?" he barks at me.

I stare at him.

"Yeah, but—" I start.

He leans down so he is face to face with me, his nose almost touching mine, a heavy palm set on top of each shoulder.

"I know things that you don't know," he tells me, then glances toward the house.

"Like what?"

"Doesn't matter," he says. "What matters is that you do what you're told. You need to leave it be." He stands up straight again and starts walking.

I watch him for a minute and then scramble after him, taking three steps for every one of his.

"But what if someone needed help?" I call. "What then?"

He doesn't even look at me this time. "Leave it be," he says with a swipe of his hand like it's the end of the discussion.

I stop and stare after him as he makes his way up the porch steps.

My cheeks catch fire and my fingers curl into tight fists as I watch him and his stupid, stuck ostrich head buried so deep in the red New Mexico dirt that he can't even see what's important.

My mouth wants to scream at him.

My fists want to punch him in his high, heavy chest until he wakes up from his cloud of gray.

My feet want to stomp hard up each one of those porch steps so that everyone in our house knows just how much mad I have stuffed up inside me, because I don't have the words.

Mad that comes quicker than it used to and stays longer than it should.

Mad that scares me because it didn't used to be there and I don't want it to stay.

Most of all, I want to tell him with the swipe of my own hand that this isn't the end of anything.

He doesn't even understand . . . this is only the beginning.

21

IN THE
SHADOW OF
THE MOON

July 8, 1947—12:45 a.m.

I finish an entire tablet full of questions that night after supper. Every single page filled.

Front and back.

I know I can't possibly ask the Martian every single solitary thing I'm wondering about because that would take a lifetime.

Multiple lifetimes, maybe.

The thing is that every time I get an answer to one of my questions, I come up with another whole slew of new things to ask. So last night I decided to narrow it down to the top three things that I really need to know. Which I wrote on the very first page.

These are the most important questions I could think of. Ones that are so important, so momentous, that they might just save the human race from the brink of extinction, and the Earth, too.

All of it resting on *my* shoulders.

Me.

Mylo Affinito.

The top three questions to ask a Martian when he crash-lands on the planet:

1. Do you really probe brains?
2. Are you here to spread the Purple Death?
3. Do you know Superman?

I never knew how hard it is to climb down a trellis with bare feet.

Mostly 'cause of the thorns.

They poke into your skin like tiny needles and you can't holler out in pain or even stop to sop up the blood when you're sneaking down after midnight to check on a Martian hiding in your hayloft.

But it's also hard to climb down a trellis in the dark while it's still wet from the monsoon that blew in and blew back out again, with a tablet full of Martian questions, while making good and sure not to break off any of Momma's bright pink bougainvilleas, all at the same time.

But I keep on until one foot touches the ground and then the other.

There's one faint light glowing from the porch that stays on each and every night. Momma turns it on after supper, at dusk, so that anyone who might need something, even in the middle of the night, knows this is the place to come to. But I know this is something Momma wouldn't understand. She'd just tell me to wash with the Ivory, mind my business, and let the men who handle it do what they need to do.

I scramble across the mud puddles in the drive and push open the barn door.

"Are you here?" I whisper into the darkness.

Silence.

One muddy foot at a time, I step up the hayloft ladder until I make it all the way to the top. In the light of the full moon shining through the hayloft door, all I see is hay.

He's gone.

And I can't help but wonder again if any of it happened at all. Maybe I dreamed it up. Maybe I am *crazy*.

"Hey, ah . . . you, you . . . Mr. Martian," I whisper. "You in here?" I stretch my neck to scan each stall below. "I have my list of questions ready for you."

Pitch neighs at me.

Daddy's horse, Throgs Neck, doesn't even bother with me. He just keeps on chomping from a damp hay bale.

Nothing.

I sigh and climb down the ladder. When I pull the barn door open again, I see something I'll never forget. Not in all my days left on Earth.

Him.

The Martian.

Standing straight and tall in the shadow of the moon with his eyes squeezed tight and balancing his tiny feet on the top of a square fence post. His four-fingered hands stuck flat against each other like he's saying a Martian prayer, arms straight out and pointed up at the moon. A thin gold band secured tight around his gigantic head.

Then I think of a question I forgot to add to my tablet.

4. Do you know God?

I figure he might. I mean, he lives closer to God than I do. Maybe he's even seen Him up there, giving each other a neighborly howdy when they pass on by.

I stand in the doorway of the barn, watching him.

"Are your people coming to get you?" I whisper into the darkness.

He turns to look at me and then back up at the sky as I make my way over to him. When I reach him, he motions for me to stand on the next post over from his.

I pull myself up and stand straight just like him. Then he takes his headband off and reaches out to hand it to me. I look at it hanging from his four-fingered hand.

I can just hear Dibs now.

Don't you do it, Mylo. That's a brain probe if I've ever seen one. And Martians will harvest your brains as soon as look at you.

I swallow down the fear clutching my throat and reach my hand in his direction.

The headband is thin.

As thin as the silver foil Hershey bar wrapper pieces we saw out in Mac Brazel's field. But the headband is strong, too. And flexible, like a rubber band with a sleek gold surface that shines like diamonds. On the inside are millions of the tiniest suction cups I've ever seen.

I slip the thing over my head first, and then stretch it back up so it sits flat across my forehead. I can feel the same energy that was coming off the ship pushing its way into my brain. Silent energy. The Martian places his palms together again and lifts them high, pointing toward the trillions of brilliant stars in the sky, and I do the same.

Then I wait.

But all I feel is the wind picking up, forcing the rusted windmill's blades around and rustling up loose gravel from the drive. Tiny rocks and dirt prick my skin. I can feel the dirt sticking to the sweat in some places.

I open one eye and turn to look at him. "What am I supposed to do?"

He breathes slow and deep.

I close my one eye and do the same.

And that's when the pictures come. One by one, flooding the backs of my eyelids. Answering every question I've ever had in my entire life. Answering the questions I haven't even thought to ask. Not with words . . . with pictures and with thoughts wired directly to my brain. Moving pictures, like a movie or something. And not in black-and-white, either. In Technicolor, just like at the Roswell Theatre. It reminds me of the scene in *The Wizard of Oz* when Dorothy's house lands in Munchkinland and she opens the door to a world of color she never knew could exist.

A land full of answers.

The pictures rush at me fast. Too fast. I can't even think quick enough to keep up with the flood.

Martians come in peace, they don't probe brains, they're a million times smarter than human beings—just like Dibs said—they don't know the Purple Death or Superman, but they know . . . *Him*.

And they pray, too.

There are even answers about you, Obie. Ones that I wanted to know, and some I didn't realize I needed to know.

I get answers to questions that I hadn't even thought to add to my tablet. Answers nobody would ever guess in a million years.

But the biggest one of all: the Martian isn't from Mars at all.

And he's not even a *he*.

She's a *she*.

"Mylo!"

My eyes pop open and I suck air.

Daddy's scrambling down the porch steps in a pair of pajama bottoms and no shirt, while Momma's in her billowing flowered nightgown, her arms wrapped around one of the pillars that hold the porch in place.

"Mylo!" Momma hollers again, catching the wild wisps as they fly in her face.

"What are you doing?" Daddy demands, rushing at me and stomping fast, heavy feet through the puddles in the drive toward me. "Get away from that thing!"

22

MARTIANS DON'T EAT ICE CREAM

July 8, 1947—1:15 a.m.

Momma's pacing the kitchen floor while Daddy keeps running his fingers through his hair and blowing heaving breaths out of his mouth like he's blowing up a balloon.

"Make sure you scrub all the way to Z," Momma tells me, her arms wrapped tight around her while I push Ivory suds between my fingers at the kitchen sink.

"I'm already on T," I say.

"Well . . . start again."

I peer over my shoulder at her. "All the way back to A?"

"That's right," she says.

I turn back to the sink, roll my eyes, and start the alphabet all over again, shifting Ivory suds between each finger while Momma and Daddy try and figure out what to do.

"I don't want that thing in this house, Bud," Momma is saying. "I won't have it."

"I thought you always said everyone is welcome here," I remind her.

"Yes, well, with one exception," she informs me, staring out the glass at a real live Martian girl still standing straight and tall on the fence post out front. "And mind your business—I'm talking to Daddy."

"But it isn't a thing at all, Momma, and she ain't from Mars, either," I tell her. "I made it to Z again. Can I rinse now?"

She stops pacing and stares at me.

"Can I?" I ask her.

She nods.

"What are you talking about, Mylo?" Daddy asks.

"Well, first off . . . she's a girl." I wipe my hands dry on the embroidered rooster.

Momma's mouth falls open and for a second I'm afraid she's going to tell me to scrub all the way to Z again, but instead it just closes again without a single thing coming out of it.

"And it turns out, she isn't from Mars at all," I say. "She's from a place called Europa." I smile real wide and look back and forth between them.

First at Momma and then at Daddy and then back at Momma again.

But they don't say anything.

"It's the smallest of the Galilean moons floating out there around the planet Jupiter," I say, and then wait.

Still nothing.

"And get this," I say. "The moon was named after the King of Tyre's daughter in Greek mythology. And on their planet, *girls* are more the boss of things than the boys are. They even have a girl president on their planet, if you can believe that one. I mean, I could believe that Momma could be president or even Gracie Delgado one day. Except I wonder where a girl would go to the bathroom 'cause I bet all they have in Washington, D.C., are men's rooms. Right? Is that right, Daddy? They'd probably have to make a ladies' room special. Otherwise she'd have to hold it all day long and Momma says it's never good to hold it."

I look at Momma and then Daddy.

Silence.

"Anyway, not only is she a girl, she's not even a grown-up yet. She's eleven like me, in Earth years, which only makes her almost one in Jupiter years. But she explained it like this . . . like how it is with dogs, you know like for every one dog year it's like seven in people years. Get it? So for almost every twelve people years, it's like one in their years."

"What was a Martian child doing on a flying disk?" Momma says real slow like she's trying to wrap her brain around everything.

"It was a special field trip," I say. "Along with the grown-ups, she and her brother got to go along. That's the one who's at the base . . . her brother. She says he's okay for now, but she needs to get to him so they can go back home. And you're not listening, Momma. I told you, they aren't from Mars. I figure if they aren't from Mars, then they aren't Martian. So I'm gonna call them Moontians." I beam at my own genius.

"Moontians?" Daddy says.

"Good, right?" I push Momma's flowered curtains to the side and steal another glance out at her still standing straight and tall on the fence post.

Daddy doesn't answer me.

I turn to Momma.

"Right?" I ask her. "Moontians, get it? But I don't know her name yet. We didn't get to that one. I guess I forgot to ask."

"Mylo," Momma says. "H-how do you, how do you know all of this? These . . . these details?"

"'Cause," I tell her. "The Moontian let me wear her little gold headbandy thing and it showed me all these answers to all these questions I had. First with these sort of pictures on the backs of my eyelids, and then the facts just stayed stuck up into my brain for permanent. Pretty neat, huh? I feel a whole lot smarter than I did before. Like . . . like . . . *seventh-grade* smart instead of just going-into-sixth-grade smart."

Momma looks at Daddy and then back at me and then I watch her eyeballs go straight up while she crosses her front with the Father, Son, and Holy Ghost.

"Lord have mercy," she tells the ceiling.

Momma always says that when she crosses herself.

"You don't have to worry, Momma," I tell her. "No matter what Dibs says about them, they come in peace. She told me so. They didn't come for an interstellar invasion to take over our planet or even to probe our brains for experimentation. They're here to *help* us, Momma . . . not to hurt us. They didn't come for none of the stuff that Dibs said they did. Although I s'pose it's going to take some fast talking to convince Dibs of that. He thinks of the Planet Comics series as the bona fide Martian Bible. Wait till he hears they aren't from Mars at all. He's going to flip his lid."

"Mylo," Daddy says. "You said they're here to help us? Help us with what?"

"Daddy . . . we are destroying our planet," I tell him. "And everyone who's anyone knows it, too. Out there they do, anyway." I point out the window toward the night sky. "The only ones who don't seem to know it is us here on Earth. The nuclear bombs in Japan and the practice ones that went off in the desert here, they're causing damage all the way to Europa and beyond. We aren't just hurting each other on this planet; we're hurting others out there, too. They don't have war in Europa—she doesn't understand why we have it here. Even with that big noggin of hers, she can't figure out one good reason for it. And come to think of it, I can't, either. Dibs says their brains are a million times smarter than ours are. Maybe that's why they don't have war there. No hate, either. She told me so. Can you imagine a world like that?"

I wait.

For something.

Anything.

Just so I know they heard me. I mean, really heard me. And that they believe me, too.

But Daddy doesn't even open his mouth. He just slips down into his chair at the kitchen table like a bag of bones and Momma starts up with the pacing again.

"And they picked me, Momma," I tell her. "Me." I push the curtain to the side again and peer out at her. "And I'm going to be the one to get her home, too."

My chest is bursting and it's the first time I've ever felt so much strength inside me. That there really might be courage somewhere inside that was just hiding all along. I feel like a real live Superman who's going to save the world from chemical annihilation. *Tune in next time, boys and girls, and learn how Superhero Mylo Affinito saves mankind from extinction! Brought to you by Kellogg's Pep, the buildup wheat cereal.*

I stand there, staring at them with my hands on my hips. "Well?" I demand. "Aren't you going to say anything?"

"Mylo," Momma starts.

Here it comes.

Momma will know exactly what to do. Momma always knows. Now that she's had her Mississippis to take it all in, she'll have the exact words to make everything right.

That's the way Momma is. No matter what.

"Yes, Momma?"

"Mylo . . ."

I glance over at Daddy and then back at her. "Y-yes, ma'am?"

She stops pacing and meets my eyes.

"Wash your hands."

"*Again?*"

"That's right, and don't leave out any of the letters."

I sigh and grab the sloppy bar of Ivory. I guess Momma doesn't have the words when it comes to Moontians.

When the Moontian is finally done talking to the sky or baying to the moon or whatever it is she's doing out there, I convince Momma to let her actually come inside the house.

Which is a big deal, since Clark Kent isn't even allowed in the house and he's family. But I think Momma agrees to it more because she can keep a watchful eye on her than anything else.

Momma's not quite convinced yet that the Moontian is here on friendly business.

I even let the Europa visitor sit in Obie's spot.

It's only the polite thing to do.

Momma dishes up two big bowls of Chocolate Swirl ice cream. I can't say I've ever been allowed to have a bowl of ice cream after midnight before, but I think it has something to do with Momma trying to keep things as normal as possible.

As normal as things can be when a Moontian comes visiting.

"You go ahead there and have your ice cream." She points from the sitting room doorway. "Me and Daddy are going to talk in the next room. We'll be right here."

"Okay, Momma." I scoop up a spoonful to show the Moontian how it's done. "See? Like this."

"Don't, ah ... don't ... just don't *touch* anything." Momma peeks once more around the doorway, wrinkling up her nose.

"See?" I hold out the spoon. "You scoop first, and then you eat it."

She stares down at her Chocolate Swirl and then sticks a long, skinny gray finger in it and pulls it out again.

I scoop up another big mouthful and focus in on Momma and Daddy's hushed voices in the next room. Although I can't make out the words so well, there is no mistaking the way they're spoken.

Harsh tones hurl back and forth.

Sharp and biting.

Rigid and angry.

It makes the Chocolate Swirl churn inside my belly.

Once in a while some words sneak out of the whispers and reach my ears. Words like *Army Air Force* and *Mac Brazel* and *even the Battle of Los Angeles*.

"Stay here," I tell the Moontian. "I'm going to go and listen. I know that seems like the wrong thing to do here, but if I didn't listen when I wasn't supposed to, I'd never know a single thing that goes on around here."

She blinks her glassy black eyes at me and then stares back down at her bowl of ice cream, sticking in another finger to touch the chocolate part of the Chocolate Swirl.

"It's cold," I tell her. "But it tastes good. I mean, it's no Peppermint Bonbon, but it's still ice cream. Momma got Chocolate Swirl 'cause it was on sale this week even though Peppermint Bonbon is way better. But you can't taste it unless you put it in your mouth . . . unless your tasters are in your suction cups. Which I guess they could be, huh?"

She doesn't even wrinkle up her forehead this time 'cause she's so focused on the bowl in front of her.

"Wait here," I say again. "I'll be back."

I slip out of my seat and creep over to the doorway to listen.

Momma is crying.

I know it on account of the sniffling.

"I thought we were done with all this," she's saying. "You promised me you were done with all this."

"I didn't bring that thing here, Luce," Daddy tells her. "It's here because of Mylo."

"And you don't think that has anything to do with you? They called you out to the desert today, didn't they?"

"They needed my help," he says.

"Well, you could have said no," she tells him. "Now look what's happened. I want you to get that thing out of here. Who knows what kind of interstellar germs it's carrying into this house?"

I hear Daddy blow air out of his mouth in a blast and after he does, his words come out softer and slower. "You know I can't call the base and tell them she's here," he says. "They will do the very same thing they did the last time. That's exactly why I left the service. I didn't agree with how they were treating these . . . these beings. You said you agreed with that decision, remember? What makes you think they won't do the same thing to these little people again? Right now the Army Air Force believes all the creatures are dead except the one they brought to the base hospital. They don't know about this one. And if I'm the one to tell them . . . can you imagine what will happen to us? I'm sorry, I won't do that. She stays . . . at least until I can figure out what to do. I don't understand you, Luce." Daddy's voice softens even more. "You're the first person to give someone a hand when they need it. How is this any different? They need our help."

"It's Mylo," she says. "What if . . . I just can't . . . lose him, too—"

"You won't," Daddy tells her. "I promise you."

Silence.

A floorboard creaks underneath my foot.

Momma's voice snaps sharp. "*Mylo!*"

I scramble on my tiptoes back to my seat at the table, almost sliding clear off my chair and onto the floor.

The Moontian is still staring at her ice cream, but now she has it all over all her fingers as she mushes it between them. Just like Baby Kay likes to do.

"You don't play with it," I tell her. "You eat it. Like this." I shovel in a big, cold spoonful. "In your mouth, see?" I open up my mouth to show her.

"Mylo?" Momma peeks her head around the corner.

I snap my mouth closed, swallow down my Chocolate Swirl, and wide-eye her.

"I—I wasn't listening."

"*Mylo?*" Momma's voice is stern.

I lower my chin in my chest

"I was listening."

She just sighs and shakes her head.

23

A FLYING
DISK CAPTURED

July 8, 1947—1:30 p.m.

Maybe Jor-El McRoostershire the Third doesn't know it yet. Or even Pitch or any of the other animals in the field. But the world will never be the same. Not just because a real live Moontian from outer space is living in our house, but also because it's the first time in history that the Army Air Force tells the world we aren't alone.

> July 8, 1947 Roswell Daily Record
>
> RAAF CAPTURES FLYING SAUCER ON RANCH IN
> ROSWELL REGION
>
> The intelligence office of the 509th
> Bombardment group at Roswell Army Air Field
> announced at noon today that the field has
> come into possession of a flying saucer.

But it's hearing the morning news on KGFL Radio out of Roswell that changes absolutely everything.

"Headline Edition July eighth, nineteen forty-seven. The Army Air Forces has announced a flying disk has been found and is now in the possession of the Army. Army officers say the missile found sometime last week has been inspected in Roswell, New Mexico, and sent to Wright Field, Ohio, for further inspection. . . ."

I place my hand on Daddy's arm. He's come in early from the field for lunch and stays longer than normal, reading and rereading the newspaper article about the captured disk while he mumbles to himself and shakes his head.

"Daddy," I say. "They took him? They took him to Wright Field?"

He shakes his head again. "Not yet—the transfer is set for Friday."

"They can't take him there. They just can't."

Dibs was a no-show for breakfast, and he's not here for lunch, either. The Moontian is picking up the pieces of fried chicken that Baby Kay flings off the side of her high chair and setting them back on top for her. Then Baby Kay screeches a high-pitched giggle, claps her tiny hands, and throws another piece over the side.

Baby Kay didn't need hardly any time to figure out that the Moontian is okay by her. Baby Kay hasn't learned yet that if you look different you aren't okay. Babies are that way. Full of love no matter who you are.

"I'm not sure there's much we can do about that," Daddy tells me.

"Momma says that about Dibs, too, but I don't understand why we can't do more," I say.

Daddy pulls his ostrich head from the red New Mexico dirt for a moment and meets my eyes.

The telephone rings on the side table in the hall.

"Hello?" Momma says into the receiver.

Baby Kay screeches again and claps her hands. "Oonton! Oonton! Mo! Mo!"

"Yes, Mrs. Manuela," Momma says. "Of course, yes . . . yes, we will be there. Pardon me? The Battle of Los Angeles?" Momma shoots Daddy a couple of eye daggers left over from their private talk in the sitting room last night. "No, I don't think I've heard of that."

Momma listens some more while Daddy goes back to his paper.

"A weather balloon?" Momma asks. "You don't say. Well, the Army Air Force isn't saying anything about a weather balloon this time, are they? A capture of a real flying disk is in black-and-white now for all the world to see. Yes . . . yes. We will see you then. Thank you for calling." Momma places the receiver back in its cradle.

"What was that all about?" Daddy asks without looking up.

"She says she's been trying to get through for hours. The phone wires are jammed and Mary Anne Kane, the telephone operator in town, says there are calls coming in from all over the world to the base and the newspaper and the radio station, wanting more information about that flying disk." Momma sighs. "But she phoned to say that Father Kevin has called a special church meeting later today to talk about what's being reported in the papers. Mrs. Manuela said there are a lot of people feeling uneasy about this being a sign it's the end of the world."

Daddy's eyes meet mine again and I watch him roll them to the ceiling and back down.

And then . . . *he smiles.*

Not just any smile.

That bright white one.

The one where I can see that his one front tooth laps just a smidge over the other front one. It's the smile he used to smile while he strummed the guitar on the porch or was fielding balls on the field we built together out back. He's an even better fielder than Clark Kent because he can actually catch them before they hit the ground.

It's been a long while since I've seen that smile. I've seen the straight-lipped one for folks at church, but not this one. This smile gives you the feeling that everything will be okay. No matter what.

I smile, too.

He leans in close to me. "If they met her"—he motions toward the Moontian—"they wouldn't be carrying on about all that nonsense, now, would they?"

"Yaaaay!" Baby Kay cheers.

I watch the Moontian hiding behind Baby Kay's high chair, every few seconds peeking her watermelon-sized head around one side and then the other to surprise the baby.

Baby Kay screeches and claps her hands each time. "Oonton! Oonton! Mo! Mo!"

I turn back to Daddy. "No," I tell him. "They sure wouldn't."

24

SUPERHERO
SIDEKICK

July 8, 1947–3:00 p.m.

After lunch, Momma, Daddy, Baby Kay, and I all pile into Daddy's truck and head over to pick up Dibs. I leave the Moontian up in my bedroom with a stack of comic books. On the way to Butte Rise and Shine Pig and Poultry, Daddy tells me I'd better keep quiet about the Moontian for now.

"Even to Dibs?" I ask.

He looks over at Momma, who's trying to sway Baby Kay's curls in one particular direction. Baby Kay isn't sitting still for it. "No! No! No!" The baby shakes her head.

"He's family," Momma says. "There's no way to keep it from him."

"For now, let's keep it between us," he says.

What Daddy means to say is on account of Dibs's big mouth, he could get us all in some big trouble. I heard Momma and Daddy through the floor last night after we all went to bed and the Moontian went back out to her fence post to talk to the moon. Daddy said this was top-level security clearance kind of information and none of us should have it.

The thing is . . . Dibs isn't just anyone. He's my best friend in the whole entire universe.

Even if he has the biggest mouth in all the land.

I want to tell Daddy I can't make any promises, but I stay quiet instead.

I pull a comb through my Brylcreemed hair in front of Daddy's rearview mirror, checking to make sure the side part and the comb marks are straight while Daddy bounces the truck up the dirt road toward Butte Rise and Shine Pig and Poultry to pick Dibs up for a special Tuesday church meeting called by Father Kevin. Momma rang him earlier to let him know we'd be coming for him.

We smell pig stink when we hit the halfway mark.

Daddy pulls up the drive, sets the brake, and climbs out to fetch Dibs while I pull at the collar of a fresh Sunday shirt wind-dried out on the line.

I'm already melting in the sun.

"Stop messing with it," Momma warns.

"It itches me," I complain.

But she's still too busy trying to find a direction to comb Baby Kay's flyaway curls while the baby wrestles for her freedom.

"No omb! No omb!" Baby Kay demands, shaking her head from side to side.

While Daddy stands at the front door of Dibs's house, a loud engine roars up the drive behind us, and through the back window of our truck, I see Mr. Butte pulling up in his rusty Ford pickup.

"Uh-oh," I mutter under my breath. "He's home."

"Mrs. Manuela had plenty to say about him this morning, too," Momma whispers to me. "She said they finally had to just throw him out of Jake's bar last night and he ended up sleeping on a bench out front."

"He left Dibs home alone all night?" I ask.

Momma stays quiet.

Mr. Butte pulls up next to us with a real ugly scowl stuck to his face.

The *ugliest*.

"Uh-oh," I say again. "He looks mad."

We watch as he pulls himself out of the driver's seat and stumbles off the running board and onto the ground. Momma nods to him through the open window, but he doesn't say *hey* or anything. He doesn't even remove his stained fedora from his head.

"Momma?" I say.

"Quiet now," she warns, her eyes stuck on Mr. Butte's back as he makes his way up to the front porch. He misses the bottom step and lands on one knee, quickly grabbing at the rail to hoist himself straight again. When he reaches the top, Daddy gives him a nod and Mr. Butte hurls words at Daddy in a way that doesn't look neighborly at all. Even though I can't hear them.

Dibs comes out of the house in his Sunday shirt. The same wrinkled button-down shirt as always, which is ten sizes too big and probably tucked down to his knees underneath his overalls, with a grease-spotted blue tie cinched at his neck to keep the whole mess in place. On Sundays, instead of wearing his backward Yankees cap, he pulls a crooked part down the center of his head and slicks each side back with way too big a dab of Brylcreem, much bigger than he needs to tame his buzz cut. Dibs stands still behind Daddy, watching the men hurl their words.

"Momma?" I say again.

"Yes?"

"Why can't we help him?"

She sighs. "We do what we can."

"Can't we do more?"

Momma stops, letting out a long sigh, and for a moment Baby Kay wins her battle for freedom. "I've offered many times, Mylo." She sighs again. "I just don't know what else to do. So . . . we do what we can."

I watch Daddy take ahold of Dibs's hand, and together they come down off the porch as Mr. Butte throws more angry words against Daddy's back. And this time, since he's shouting so loud, I hear some of them. I'm not going to say what those words are, but they're definitely not the kind of words that neighbors are supposed to use. If Momma caught me or Obie using those words, she would have made us put a whole nickel in the penny swear jar.

"Come along, Dibs," Daddy says, low and firm, keeping a strong hold on Dibs's trembling fist.

Daddy opens the driver's-side door on our old Ford while me and Momma scooch over to make room.

Dibs smiles big at us while he climbs up into the truck.

"Morning, Mrs. Affinito," he says, showing her his big beaver teeth.

Just like he does every Sunday when we pick him up for church. Except this isn't Sunday and today there's a dark purplish mark just above his left eye.

My insides ache when I see it.

He punches me in the arm. "Big-Bellied Betty had a litter of ten piglets early this morning," he gushes. "I named every single one after Yankee players. There's Yogi . . ." He starts counting on his fingers. "DiMaggio, Bobo Newsom, that's the runt of the litter, and—"

"She didn't have any girls?"

"Yeah, but I named them after Yankee players, too," he tells me. "I figure they don't know any different."

"So you did that all by yourself?" I ask.

He shrugs. "Well, Big-Bellied Betty did most of the work. Hey, Mrs. Affinito." He leans over me. "Is that your fried chicken I'm smelling?"

Momma pulls a brown paper bag with grease spots on it from her purse and passes it to me, and I pass it to Dibs.

"Thank you, ma'am!" Dibs says, pulling open the bag.

"Not at all," Momma says.

And when I look up and see the way she's looking at Dibs, I just know her insides are aching, too.

Daddy turns the key and puts the truck in reverse while Mr. Butte stares after us through bloodshot eyes, simmering with his own mad on the stoop.

I turn to watch him through the back window of the truck as Daddy bounces down the drive, with a whole bunch of mad filling my belly. I see him trip one more time on the porch steps, give up, and crumble.

Broken.

Alone.

And even though my brain would never tell my bones to do it, they ache for him, too. I guess my bones have a mind of their own.

When we finally get to church I'm about to burst from having to wait all the way to Roswell to tell Dibs about the Moontian.

I pull him over to a quiet corner of the lobby while Momma, Daddy, and Baby Kay greet neighbors and pretend there isn't a visitor from the moons of Jupiter in the bedroom reading my collection of Superman comic books.

"Come on," I whisper to Dibs, pulling on his sleeve. "I have something I have to tell you."

"Hey, what's the big idea? You're mussing me up," Dibs complains, tightening the giant knot on his dirty tie. "I want to look my best for the Lord."

"You think God gives two hoots about what Dibson Tiberius Butte is wearing today?"

"God sees everything." He stands straight. "And you got to score points where you can."

"Points for what?"

"Heaven, you dope," he says. "What do you care, anyway? I thought you weren't speaking to Him."

"Who says I'm not?"

"You don't think I noticed your fake Father, Son, and Holy Ghost crossings for the past year? There ain't nothing about you that I don't know, Mylo Affinito. Not one single, solitary thing."

"You want to make a bet?" I wrap my fingers around his skinny arm and pull him farther into the corner.

"Where are we going?" he demands.

"I have something big to tell you," I whisper. "So big you aren't going to believe it in one million years. Not a billion years. That's how big it is."

His eyes open wide. "You got a doozy?"

"This is so much bigger than a doozy," I say. "I don't even know what to call it." I stretch my neck to make sure no one is listening and then put my hands on his shoulders.

"A double double doozy?" He wide-eyes me.

"Bigger," I tell him.

"Bigger than a *double double*?"

"She followed me," I say.

He blinks.

And then blinks again.

"Who?"

"Who do you think?" I say.

"Good morning, boys." Mrs. Delgado waves another lace hanky at us as she makes her way toward the ladies' room door.

"Oh, ah, good morning, Mrs. Delgado," I say. "Is Gracie here?"

Mrs. Delgado dabs at the sweat on her neck with the hanky. "She's already inside," she says, pushing the ladies' room door open. "Which is where you boys should be."

"Yes, ma'am," I tell her. "We're on our way."

Dibs and I wait until the door swings closed again.

"Wait a minute," Dibs says. "Is this a Gracie Delgado doozy? Because I don't want to hear no more about how you want to kiss her on her lips."

"I didn't say I wanted to kiss her anywhere."

"You did too say it," he insists. "And it was disgusting then, so if that's what you're trying to tell me, you can keep that doozy to yourself. I don't need to hear any more of that mushy business."

"Will you shush up already so I can tell you?" I say. "She followed me all the way to the cemetery."

"*Who?*"

I take a deep breath.

"*The Martian,*" I mouth.

He stands there blinking at me.

"Nuh-uh." He shakes his head.

I nod. "Sure did."

He blinks at me some more. "No fooling?"

I shake my head. "Nope."

"Where is he now?"

"She's a she, not a he, and she's reading comic books in my room, if you can believe that one," I tell him. "I assigned Clark Kent to stand guard."

Dibs stares at me for at least ten Mississippis this time. But I gave him even more than a double double to consider, so I figure he can have his ten Mississippis to wrap his brain around it all. I suppose I needed way more than ten when I first laid eyes on a real live Martian peeking out behind Mrs. Vandebrink.

"He can't be a girl," Dibs says.

"Well, she is," I say. "And she's not from Mars, either."

"Hold it." He stretches out both palms in my direction. "There is nothing in the Planet Comics series about any girl Martians. And I've never heard of any spacemen from anywhere but Mars. How do I know they didn't suck your brain right out your ears for Martian mind control?" He eyes me suspiciously.

"Dibs," I tell him, putting my hands on his shoulders again. "They aren't like that at all. They come in peace. They're here to help us."

"Mmm-hmm," he says, still eyeing me good.

"After church I'm going back out to Mr. Lord's place," I tell him. "I think there's something he might be able to help us with. Are you with me?"

"I mean, there isn't anything about any girl Martians in *Superman* or *Aquaman* or nothing."

"What about Wonder Woman?" I ask him.

"Yeah, but she's not a Martian," he says. "She's made out of clay and comes from Greek God mythology. Her powers aren't extraterrestrial. Totally different."

"Well, I don't know what to tell you. She's a girl and that's all there is to it. And there's more, too."

"Don't tell me you let her sleep in Obie's bed," he warns me. "After all those nights with your noxious feet in my face and that lump under your mattress."

"She doesn't need it. They don't sleep," I say. "Not like we do, anyway. Not in a bed with a pillow and covers. She gets energy in the shadow of the moon. That's how she recharges herself, kind of like how we do when we go to bed. Get it?"

He blinks at me again.

"Like the moon is the Shell station and she's a Ford pickup?"

"Not exactly," I tell him.

Mrs. Meadows, the church secretary, begins playing the organ near the altar to let us know God is ready for us.

"I'll tell you more later," I say. "So are you still in? Do you really want to be my Jimmy Olsen? Because I really need you to be."

Mrs. Manuela begins to sing "How Great Thou Art" from the nave of the church and I know Momma well enough to know her neck is stretched as far as it will reach as she's looking for us and wondering why we don't have our rears in the pew where they should be.

Dibs is still thinking about my question.

"Well?" I finally ask. "What do you say?"

He puffs up his chest, puts his hands on his hips, and gives me his very best superhero sidekick pose. "Your trusty assistant is ready for duty, Superhero Affinito!" he says, with a crisp salute to his forehead. "*And together we will save the whole wide world from certain Martian annihilation!*"

"I told you they come in peace, didn't I?"

He sighs and drops his shoulders. "Yeah. But that doesn't sound as good."

Turns out that it's not the end of the world.

Even though *we* already knew that.

But Father Kevin had to do some dancing at the pulpit

to convince some of the townspeople that they didn't need to hide in their cellars, and to reassure the rest of the town that everything was just fine and there was no threat from a Martian invasion.

After the church meeting, the adults stand in small groups sipping warm lemonade from a pitcher that's been sitting in the sun and gossiping about what they've heard around town. Young children run on the grassy yard playing tag, swing on the swings, or hang upside down from the monkey bars.

Dibs and I line up at the homemade baked goods table. I grab one sugar cookie and two lemon squares, while Dibs slips a sugar cookie into each pocket of his overalls and then piles four lemon squares on a paper napkin. Mrs. Meadows glares at Dibs over her gold cat-eyed glasses but doesn't say a single word.

Diego and Spuds find us sitting under the big elm tree eating our cookies and squares.

"We have something to tell you all. Where's Gracie?" I ask them.

"You going to eat all those?" Diego grabs the top bar from Dibs's napkin.

"Hey," Dibs protests with his mouth full. "Get your own."

"I did." Diego smiles. "Then I ate 'em. Cookie Warden, Mrs. Meadows over there, won't let me have any more."

"Yeah, well, I ain't your lemon bar getter," Dibs informs him.

"I told you she won't let me, didn't I? Pass me over another one."

"No." Dibs rounds his shoulders and folds his arms over his stash.

When I see Gracie coming toward us in a pale blue dress with a small lace collar, I feel the tops of my ears catch fire.

"Holy buckets, Affinito." Diego laughs at me, almost choking on his lemon bar. "That's quite a shade of red you're sporting there. You could lead a sleigh with those ears."

Spuds laughs so hard that bits of lemon square fly out of his mouth.

"Like a beacon," he chimes in. "Look, now it's spreading up his neck, too."

"Are you going to listen up or what?" I ask.

"Venetian Red in the box of Crayolas." Diego slugs Spuds on the shoulder.

They laugh their stupid heads off again.

"Like the color of the blood when my daddy cuts the heads off the chickens." Spuds slaps his knee.

"Good one," Diego says, and then they elbow each other in the sides. "Hey, ketchup. Red as ketchup!"

They bust another gut.

"Are you guys going to listen up or not?" Dibs hisses. "Mylo has something to tell you all about last night."

Diego pops the last of Dibs's lemon square into his mouth, and it leaves powdered sugar on the tips of his upper-lip hair.

"I thought we all made a promise we weren't going to say anything about what we saw out there," Diego says. "And not one day later, here you are running your mouth. Can't you ever keep that thing shut?"

"Yeah," Spuds agrees, checking over his shoulder. "Shut up about it! I don't want to get in trouble."

"I know that's what we said," I say. "But something's happened."

"Yeah, something's happened," Dibs repeats.

"What?" Gracie asks, kneeling down next to me.

"You're playing with fire, Affinito," Diego warns me. "I heard this is all top secret stuff and the Army Air Force was out there for hours making sure nothing was left at that crash site. You need to leave them to it."

"I can't," I tell him.

"Yeah, we can't," Dibs says.

"Anyone who's still in, meet me at our barn tomorrow night after supper. I have something very important to show you."

Diego scoffs at me.

"Even more important than a double double doozy," Dibs adds.

"We already took a vote and all decided we're done." Diego stands up.

"Yeah, well, that was before," I say.

"Yeah," Dibs repeats. "That was before."

"Before what?" Diego demands.

"Red as Dorothy's ruby slippers!" Spuds hollers out with his finger in the air.

Diego laughs, and they poke their stupid elbows at each other again.

"*Before* one of them followed me home last night," I blurt out.

They all stare at me with eyes like saucers and mouths wide open.

"Who did?" Spuds asks.

"One of them," I say.

"Th-the . . . *gray* people?" Gracie whispers.

Diego snorts.

"You're such a liar, Affinito," he says to me, and turns to Gracie. "He's lying. There's no way. I don't believe a word he's saying. We saw them drag that body out of there. We saw them. That thing was dead."

"He's not dead," I tell them. "But there's another one and I'm going to help get them home. But we have to hurry because they're shipping the one at the base hospital out to Wright Field by Friday. Anyone who wants to help them, meet me tomorrow night after supper in our barn and you can see for your own selves."

"Yeah, you can see for your own selves," Dibs echoes.

"You're lying." Diego waves his hand at me.

That's when Dibs jumps into the center of our circle with a flourish, waving his arms and ending in his superhero assistant pose, his fingers clasped to his hips and his chin high in the air.

"*Laugh, all of you,*" he tells them in his Superman radio announcer voice with his gigantic tie and wrinkled shirt tucked to his knees. "*But a time will come, my friends, when you will wish you heeded the words of Mylo Eugene Affinito! Superhero extraordinaire!*"

25

ZUCCHINI
SQUASH

July 8, 1947—6:45 p.m.

"That is one *big* head," Dibs says, staring down at the Moontian sitting on my bed.

I nod. "Sure is," I say.

"I mean, gigantic," he says.

"Yep," I say.

"That's got to be the biggest noggin I've ever seen in all my life. Like a watermelon before they ball the innards into a fruit salad. No wonder their brains are so big—they've got all that space to fill."

"She's real smart, for sure," I say.

"Like As in arithmetic smart?" he wonders aloud.

I look at him. "A-*pluses*."

After church, I took Dibs up to my room to see her. Gracie couldn't wait until our after-supper call to arms in the barn with the others, so she rode Betsy Bobbin to our ranch to meet her, too. The Moontian had already made it all the way through *Superman* issue number one, "Champion of the

Oppressed," to issue number 110, "Mother Goose Crimes," while we were at our special Tuesday meeting at church.

"I can't believe it," Gracie says, sitting down on my bed next to the Moontian. "And she's really a girl?"

The Moontian blinks at Gracie.

"I'm a girl, too," Gracie tells her, reaching her hand out to touch the Moontian on the sleeve of her tan flight suit like she's making sure that what she's seeing with her own eyes is true.

"Yep," I say. "And she's our age in Earth years, but only one in Jupiter years. Weird, huh?"

"She's not even a grown-up," Gracie says.

"Nope," I say.

"Can she speak English?" Dibs asks.

"She didn't," I say. "I mean, at first she was silent and then she started making noises, you know . . . beeps and clicks . . . like in the disk, but now it seems like she's trying to say words. Kind of like Baby Kay does when she's learning how to talk. Sounding words out, mimicking us, that kind of thing."

"Like a parrot," Dibs says.

I look at him. "Not at all like that."

"Can you speak?" Gracie asks her.

We wait.

Silence.

"What's with that nose?" Dibs blurts out. "It's like just two holes and nothing else." He tilts his head left and then right. "You think he can smell with that thing? I mean, you think it works?"

"How should I know?" I say. "And he's a she, remember?"

"Well, doesn't she talk to you?"

"Not about stupid stuff like nose holes."

"What, then?" he asks. "What do you two talk about?"

"Important things," I say.

"More important than the things *we* talk about?"

"Yeah, we talk about humans destroying the planets and the universe, other civilizations out in other galaxies, peace between worlds. Important things."

"Well, what about . . . ?" Dibs raises his eyebrows.

I turn to him. "What?"

"You know, does she . . . *go to the bathroom?*" He mouths the last word real big.

I click my tongue and roll my eyes. "You're disgusting."

"Why is that disgusting? Aren't you even curious?"

"No," I say.

"Curious about what?" Gracie asks.

"Nothing," I say before Dibs has the chance to open his mouth.

"But you said ask her important things, didn't you? Don't you think *that's* important?"

"Do *you?*" I ask.

He thinks about it, and then crosses one leg over the other. "Right now, I do."

I roll my eyes again. "Momma brought her into the bathroom once, but she didn't seem to need it. Plus, she never eats anything. They must get all their energy from the moon like we get ours from food."

Dibs thinks about it. "I'd rather get mine from the moon if it meant I never had to eat Brussels sprouts again."

"Or broccoli," I agree.

We stand quietly, watching while Gracie tries to teach the Moontian a rhythmic clapping game.

"Then you clap twice . . . like this, see?" she says, clapping her hands.

"What about Superman?" Dibs asks me. "Did you ask if they know him?"

"That question is even stupider than the nose hole question," I tell him. "You think I would ask her something so dumb when I could ask her anything in the whole entire world? The whole entire universe?"

He raises his eyebrows. "You asked, though, right?" He shows me his big beaver teeth.

I shrug. "Yeah, I asked."

"And what'd she say?"

"They don't know him."

He smiles. "I knew you asked," he says.

"Are those the comic books you write?" Gracie points at the stack of homemade comics in the open drawer of the nightstand between the two beds.

"Yeah," I say, feeling the Venetian Red filling in the tops of my ears again.

"Any girls in them?"

I look at Dibs. "Ah . . . well, ah, I guess—"

"That's a no." Gracie looks at the Moontian again and shakes her head. "Probably should add some, huh?"

"Yes," I say.

"That sure is a jim-dandy of a headband on her head," Dibs says. "Think it's a *human* mind-control-prevention skullcap?"

I smack him in the chest with the back of my hand. "That's

exactly what *I* asked her," I say. "Actually, it's for communication transmission and translation. That's how she knows what I'm saying and how she's learning our language. It also gives me information. She put it on me."

Dibs blinks at me. "It's a *what?*"

"It's how she knows what we're saying, and when she puts it on me, it answers questions that I didn't even know were swimming around in my brain. It's also how they operate the disk. There isn't any ignition in that thing, or pedals, buttons, or rearview mirrors or anything. They put their hands on this screen and then think about flying and it flies. Their minds do all the work. And it's also what's going to get them home. She just has to get to her brother at the base. She's not leaving here without him."

"No phasers?"

"No phasers."

"No mind-control devices?"

"Not any of those, either," I inform him. "But there's this one other thing she's got. It's like a magic wand and it glows green on the end of it. And it puts broken things back together again. Like new. I ripped up my Superhero Club Membership Card, and she just zapped it whole in a single blink." I pull it out of my pocket to show him. "Can't even see where the rips were."

He examines it front and back. "Well, why didn't she just point that thing at the disk and fix that?" he asks.

"I don't know the answer to that one," I say. "I guess she left some answers out."

"You asked her about Superman but you left that one out? It's a pretty important one, don't you think?"

"You're absolutely, positively sure they come in peace?" Gracie asks me.

"Yep, they came because of the atom bomb," I say. "They saw that thing going off from space. Each one of them."

She nods.

"The bombs reverberated throughout the entire galaxy. They thought we went and blew up our planet for good after all the mess we made down here and up there. They were surprised to see us even still alive at all."

We don't say anything else for a long while.

"What about her name? Did she tell you her name?" Gracie asks, giving the Moontian a green plastic bracelet from her cloth purse and slipping it over her wrist.

"I guess I forgot to ask that, too," I say.

"What do you think she wants to be called?" Dibs wonders aloud.

I shrug. "Didn't say. Should we give her a nickname, you know, like with Spuds . . . at least until we figure it out?"

Dibs rubs his chin between his thumb and forefinger, considering. "You mean like Zucchini Squash?" he suggests.

I turn to him. "What? No, you dope, I don't mean another vegetable. I mean a nickname that fits her like Spuds fits Spuds. Know what I mean? Like Spuds is round and dimpled like a potato. Get it?"

We stare at the Moontian again.

"What about No Hair?" Dibs says.

"That's just stupid."

"Suction Cup?"

I roll my eyes. "No way."

"Crash?"

I put my hands on my hips and give him a good glare. "That's the worst of all of them. And why remind her of that? You're just going to hurt her feelings."

"You think she has feelings?"

"Of course she does."

"How can you be so sure?"

We all stare at her again.

The Moontian pulls the headband off her head and hands it to Gracie.

Gracie hesitates, looking at me again.

"I did it," I tell her. "It doesn't hurt. It just feels like the energy we felt at the ship. She just wants to talk to you. It's okay."

Gracie carefully slips the headband over her dark brown braids and then closes her eyes.

"What's she saying?" Dibs asks her.

Gracie is quiet for a long while as we watch her eyeballs underneath her lids moving quickly left and then right over and over.

"Looks like she's sleeping," Dibs says.

"It feels kind of like that," I tell him. "And then it feels like you've just woken up from a dream. But a real clear one with bright colors, like when Dorothy opens the door to Munchkinland."

We watch Gracie slowly open her eyes.

Dibs's hand shoots up in the air. "I call seconds," he demands.

"Wow!" Gracie says, searching through her bag and pulling out a red tablet and pencil. "Girls can be anything in

Europa. Anything at all," she gushes. "Her mother is a scientist on her planet and her aunt is the mayor of one of the towns. An actual mayor, of all things!"

"A woman mayor?" Dibs says. "That doesn't sound right."

"Oh, it's right, all right." Gracie beams.

"Well, did she tell you her name?" Dibs asks.

"The best translation to our language," Gracie tells us, staring wide-eyed at the Moontian, "is Moon Shadow. And she does have feelings. Lots of them. She feels them all the way down to her space girl toes."

We all stare at her.

Moon Shadow.

A being from another world.

Someone who has changed everything we thought was true.

"Hold on," Gracie says, touching her fingers to the band still wrapped around her head. "I think she's got something real important to tell us. Yes, Moon Shadow? You can tell us anything. Anything at all."

We all lean in close and wait.

The tiny Moontian opens her mouth and then closes it again. Then she opens it and closes it again. When she opens it a third time, we hear a beep at first and then a click and then she's trying to use her tongue to say something.

Her very first human word.

We all stare wide-eyed at her.

"K-k-k," she starts.

"You can do it, Moon Shadow," Gracie tells her.

And then she does it. She says her very first word.

A real important word, too.

"*KA-POW!*"

We all bust a gut laughing and realize for the very first time that this tiny being from a moon across our solar system has become something even more important than we could ever have dreamed of.

Our friend.

26

A MOONTIAN COVER-UP

July 9, 1947—9:05 a.m.

"**I**s that Gracie?" I shield my eyes from the sun and gaze at the road out front of the house.

Dibs is helping me finish up chores the next morning when we see her turning Betsy Bobbin up our long dirt drive.

He shields his eyes, too. "What's she got?" he asks, setting down a pail of chicken feed.

"I think it's a newspaper."

"What's she hollering about?"

"They did it again!" she calls out to us, waving the newspaper high over her head.

"Did what?" I call back.

She pulls hard on the reins, bringing Betsy Bobbin to a halt in front of us.

"Here." She tosses the paper down to me. "They took it back. All of it. They just went and took it all back."

"Who?" I ask.

"The Army Air Force."

"They took what back?" Dibs asks.

"The disk," she says. "They said it wasn't any disk at all. They just plain went and took it all back."

"What'd they say it was?" Dibs wants to know.

"I'll give you one guess," she says.

"No, they didn't," he says.

"They sure did." She nods.

"Not a stupid weather balloon," I say, unrolling the paper.

"That's exactly what they're saying. Even after telling the whole world what it really was yesterday."

"What are we, a bunch of idiots?" Dibs leans a chin on my shoulder to get a look, while Gracie slips off Betsy Bobbin and stands behind my other shoulder.

Together we read the front page.

> July 9, 1947 Roswell Daily Record
>
> GEN. RAMEY EMPTIES ROSWELL SAUCER
>
> RAMEY SAYS EXCITEMENT IS NOT JUSTIFIED
>
> GEN. RAMEY SAYS DISK IS WEATHER BALLOON
>
> An examination by the army revealed last night that mysterious objects found on a lonely New Mexico ranch was a harmless high-altitude weather balloon—not a grounded flying disk. . . .

"How . . . what . . . It's unbelievable. How can they even say these things? They're just flat-out lies. Stinkin', lousy lies." Dibs stomps around in the dirt, kicking up loose gravel with his bare feet.

"A *weather balloon*," Gracie says. "Just like Mrs. Manuela said happened in the Battle of Los Angeles. Fourteen hundred rounds fired at it and all they can come up with is a *weather balloon?*"

"They took it back," Dibs mutters again, shaking his head, kicking more gravel. "Like just because they say it's true we have to believe it? Believe it like we don't have our own eyes? Our own brains?"

"And that's not even the worst of it," Gracie goes on.

Dibs stops kicking and stares at her.

"They took Mac Brazel into custody this morning."

"Into custody?" Dibs says. "What is that supposed to mean? He ain't no criminal."

"They arrested him for telling the truth?" I ask.

"Mrs. Manuela said Mac Brazel gave an interview to the Roswell radio station last night on tape about the whole thing and it was supposed to air on the radio today. But now that the Army Air Force has changed their mind about what they want people to know, they went in and threatened the radio station about playing that taped interview on the air. Said they'd shut them down if they played it. A matter of national security, they said. Now they're escorting Mac Brazel around Roswell to give new and improved interviews at the radio and the newspaper both, to say the exact opposite of what's true. But Mac Brazel won't straight-out lie, so who knows what they'll do to him now."

"Can they do that?" I ask.

She shrugs. "They're doing it."

"What about your daddy?" Dibs asks her. "Isn't he a general at the 509th Bomb Group? Isn't he in charge there?"

She shrugs. "Kind of, but Washington, D.C., is really in charge. Daddy doesn't normally talk about stuff that goes on at the base, and I'm in Corona this summer so I'm not spending time out there like I do sometimes."

"*The base?*" I ask her. "You spend time on the Roswell Army Air Force base?"

"Sometimes I go with Daddy on weekends when he has work to do or when Momma is busy with the younger kids and wants me out of her hair. Except I'm not allowed everywhere," Gracie explains. "There are some locked doors and even one wing that I'm never allowed to be in. Mostly, I read in Daddy's office. But it's quiet on the weekends and sometimes I explore, and once I made it to this one hallway and I got in some big trouble. *Big* trouble."

"What's in that hallway?" Dibs asks her.

She lifts her shoulders up again. "All I know is it's *need-to-know.*"

"What does that mean?"

"It means if you don't need to know it for your specific job in the military, you don't get to know it. Need-to-know, get it?"

"So once Mac Brazel gives his new interviews to the radio and the newspaper, what then?" Dibs asks her. "Will they let him go?"

"I don't know that, either," she says. "If you don't do what the government says, they can do whatever they want to you. Even imprison you for treason."

Dibs swallows. "*Treason?*" he says. "What's that?"

"When you commit crimes against your country," she explains.

"Since when is telling the truth crimes against his country?"

"That's the whole point," she says. "If you don't do what they say and go along with what they want, they can accuse you of that. Remember what I said about national security? If they want something to be a secret, you keep that secret, or else. So I guess Mac Brazel is doing what they say so they'll leave him be. See that other article there?" She points to the paper.

July 9, 1947 Roswell Daily Record

HARASSED RANCHER WHO LOCATED "SAUCER" SORRY
HE TOLD ABOUT IT

. . . Brazel said that he had previously
found two weather observation balloons on
the ranch, but that what he found this time
did not in any way resemble either of these.
"I'm sure what I found was not any weather
observation balloon," he said. "But if I
find anything else besides a bomb they are
going to have a hard time getting me to say
anything about it."

"But that's not even the worst of it," Gracie says again.

"Wait." Dibs sighs hard. "You already said that. You got more bad news?"

She nods. "The worst. The Army Air Force is going door to door in Corona making sure no one is hiding any of the pieces. And making sure everyone knows to keep their mouths shut about it."

My heart stops beating and fear washes over every single bit of me. "What do you mean door to door?" I ask her. "Every single house?"

"That's what Mrs. Manuela said at the store this morning."

"Holy cheese and jalapeños," Dibs mutters, and starts pacing in the dirt.

"They know there were others out there," she goes on. "More than just Mac Brazel."

Dibs stops. "You mean like . . . *us?*"

"I don't know about that," she says. "But Mrs. Manuela said they've been to the Martins' place, to the Beasleys', and out on the Rivera ranch, too." She counts on her fingers. "So far they haven't collected a single thing, but they're not going to stop until they find what they're looking for."

"Gracie," I say. "A-are they looking for anything else?"

She bites on her lower lip. "That's the question," she says softly.

"Mylo," Dibs says. "What now?"

"Moon Shadow . . . *KA-POW!*"

We all shield our eyes and look up at Moon Shadow leaning on the sill of my bedroom window and waving a comic book between two of her long, skinny gray fingers. Today she's wearing a stiff, clean pair of brand-new overalls that Momma picked up at the Montgomery Ward's in Roswell so that she could wash the Chocolate Swirl out of Moon Shadow's flight suit and hang it on the line with the rest of the laundry.

Clark Kent lifts a drowsy head from the top porch step, still minding his post after I assigned him the duty to protect Moon Shadow at all costs.

"She may not know Superman, but she sure likes him." Dibs smiles up at her.

"We have to protect her," Gracie tells me.

I nod.

"And we have to get her home," Gracie says.

I nod again. "No matter what the Army Air Force says or does, they can't erase everything," I tell them. "No matter how hard they try to."

Dibs's and Gracie's eyes meet mine in silent agreement.

"If all they're doing is looking for pieces, that means they still don't know about her. And if they do know about her . . . well, either way, we have to have a plan to hide her."

"Where?" Gracie says. "Is there any safe place in Corona where no one will go looking for her?"

"KA-BLAM!" Moon Shadow calls from the window.

"I brought some things with me today," Gracie says. "Books and homemade flash cards, and I'm going to help her learn more words."

My running list of the greatness that is Gracie Delgado:

1. Her heart.

I put my hand in the middle of our three-person circle, Gracie puts hers on top of mine, and Dibs puts his on top of hers.

A promise. A very important one, too. A promise that means life or . . . *death*.

And it's all up to us.

Dibs turns to Gracie again. "Gracie?"

"Yes?"

"Can you field a baseball?"

Gracie's eyebrows scrunch together. "What does baseball have to do with anything?"

Dibs smiles, showing me his big beaver teeth. "Actually, a lot more than you'd think."

27

FRIED
ATTIC BATS WITH
A SIDE OF HAM

July 9, 1947—10:35 a.m.

After chores Dibs and I head on over to Mr. Lord's place with a loaf of Momma's bread under my arm while Gracie stays back with Moon Shadow.

"Mr. Lord?" I call through the ripped screen. "You here?"

"Of course he's here. Where else would he be?" Dibs whispers.

I give him an elbow to the ribs.

"It's me, Mr. Lord . . . Mylo Affinito, and Dibs Butte, too."

Heavy footsteps pound the floorboards, making their way to the screen door.

Today he stares silently at us through the ripped screen like a rabid dog who's lost his bark. His white hair is still in need of a dab of Brylcreem and his dingy plaid bathrobe is pulled tight around his skinny middle.

I hold out Momma's bread. "Zucchini," I tell him.

I hear Dibs croak a swallow.

Mr. Lord pushes open the screen door. "Tell your momma I said thank you kindly," he says, taking the bread.

I reach inside my bib pocket and pull out my Superhero Club Membership Card for him to see.

He takes it and examines it, flipping it over and then over again. He stares down at me from under the heavy wrinkles. "What do you want me to do with this?" he asks me.

"She fixed it," I say.

"Who did?"

This time it's me who croaks a swallow. "I think you know who," I tell him.

His brow lowers over his bloodshot eyes just like the shady awnings over the Corona General Store's front windows.

He *does* know. I can see it in his eyes.

"I told you to leave it be, didn't I?" he says. "Let me guess, you're one of the ones that were out there, aren't you?" He shakes his head. "The ones they're looking for."

I can feel Dibs's eyes on me.

"I told you it's too dangerous, didn't I? They'll figure it out and come looking for you. This is a level of clearance that is so top secret only a handful of people know about it. And you kids aren't in that group. Don't you understand what could happen to you? Someone messed up and released this story to the press and a bomb exploded. People from all over the world calling and wondering if we are under attack. So now they're covering it all up. Saying it was all a mistake. And they are going to great lengths to fix this mess. You don't even have a clue as to what you're up against."

"*T-treason?*" Dibs squeaks out.

"Go home," Mr. Lord says. "Roller-skate. Play your games. Be kids. Leave it alone."

I straighten my shoulders and stand as tall as I can, like a dutiful soldier ready to face a battle. "I can't, Mr. Lord," I say.

He shakes his head again.

"What are all those ones and zeroes in your tablet?" I ask him. "It has to do with . . . *them*, doesn't it?"

"Leave those Martians be!" he barks. "You hear me?"

"Ah, excuse me, Mr. Lord." Dibs points a finger in the air. "But, um, technically . . . they're Moontians, not Martians."

Mr. Lord stares hard at Dibs.

"'Cause they ain't from Mars. They're from one of the moons orbiting Jupiter. Get it? Europa, to be exact."

Mr. Lord doesn't say anything.

"And also, when someone needs help, you help 'em," Dibs goes on. "That's what it says in the Bible, anyway. I mean, not those exact words or anything, but something like that, because no one really knows what the Bible means, they just do the best they can." He leans close to me. "Did I get what Gracie said right?" he whispers.

I nod.

Mr. Lord explodes. "You don't think I know what the Bible says, boy?"

"Well, that's sort of hard to say, really, 'cause, you know, because, ah . . . well, you're never in church on Sundays," Dibs mutters. "No offense, but you're the only one who's not, so I figure maybe you don't."

"How do you boys know those men are from a moon or-biting Jupiter?" Mr. Lord asks him.

Dibs points a thumb in my direction. "On account of his eyelids," he says.

Mordecai Lord eyes me.

"I know because she told me," I say.

"*She?*"

"The Moontian," I tell him. "A boy and a girl. Two of them survived, Mr. Lord. One is at the base hospital and one . . . well, one is . . ."

Dibs shakes his head at me. "Don't tell—"

"One . . . is in our house," I tell Mr. Lord. "Moon Shadow. She's at home with us."

The scowl on Mr. Lord's face falls off him in slow motion and his lips form a stern, straight line.

But he has no words.

I guess even Mordecai Lord, with all his military history, needs his Mississippis to get used to the idea of Moontians visiting us.

"Mr. Lord, we need your help," I tell him. "*They* need your help. We're going to get them back home. With or without you. But I figure with you, we have a better chance at it."

He hesitates.

"Nope," he says then. "Nope. It's just too dangerous. Especially for children. I said you need to leave it be and that's it."

"Are they really sending you messages, Mr. Lord?" I keep on.

He scratches at his chin whiskers and chews at the hairs that hang too long over his upper lip.

"They are," I say. "And they have been for a while, too."

"On your eyelids?" Dibs asks him.

"Please, Mr. Lord," I say.

He fills his cheeks and then blows a gush of air out of his mouth.

"Come on," he says, stepping aside in the doorway. "I can show you, but you can't tell anyone."

Dibs and I look at each other.

"You mean . . . *inside?*" Dibs squeaks again, pointing a finger at the doorway.

We both stretch our necks and peer through the screen door.

It's dark in there even though the sun is shining on the outside, with ratty drapes and tattered, yellowing shades pulled down over the front windows. There's a small wooden table with all the chairs pushed in and dirty dishes piled high in the sink and an open cupboard filled with jars of Skippy Creamy. And one large boiling pot on the stove.

Dibs wide-eyes me. "That some kind of stew you got cooking up there?" he asks.

"That's right," Mr. Lord says. "Are you coming or what?"

I straighten up again and take a long, deep breath. "Yes," I say, taking a step across the threshold. Behind me, my tried-and-true assistant.

My Jimmy Olsen.

The screen door bangs behind us and we blink to help our eyes adjust to the darkness.

"You want something to eat?" Mr. Lord asks.

"Y-you mean from the pot on the stove?" Dibs stutters.

"No," Mr. Lord says. "That's rabbit stew . . . won't be ready for hours yet. I got peanut butter, though. And I have spoons. And zucchini bread, of course."

"N-no, no, thank you, sir," I say, pressing my lips together.

"Come on back this way." Mr. Lord waves his hand at us as he trudges through a maze of stacked boxes and large books to the back sitting room behind the kitchen.

We follow him to a place that should have a davenport, a reclining chair, and a radio like anyone else's sitting room, except Mordecai Lord has a big wooden desk with a rusted lamp and tall bookshelves filled with large grown-up books that look like the science section at the Roswell library.

Newspaper articles litter the walls. Some tacked up and some stuck up with yellowing tape. All of them with headlines about flying disks that people have been seeing in the skies all over the United States and beyond.

On the corner of the desk stands a large wooden picture frame. A woman, her arms wrapped around a boy about my age.

Mordecai Lord Jr.

I know him by name only on account of when you live in a town as small as Corona, you usually know everyone's business.

Whether you want to or not.

Some details true and others not.

I pick up the frame and stare down at the smiling faces. The same kind of smiles as the ones on me and Obie in the picture on the night table between our beds. The kind your mouth smiles when you think endings happen the way they should every time.

Even when they don't.

"Is this your family?" I ask Mr. Lord.

He nods without saying anything, sits down in a cracking leather chair, and rolls himself closer to his desk.

"Sorry," I tell him, setting the frame down again.

He's focused on the radios. "Sorry for you, too," he says. "It isn't right."

"No," I agree.

He clears his throat. "This is what I wanted to show you," he tells us, turning the knobs on the dusty radios lined up in front of him.

Stacks of tablets are piled by dates and years. The 1947 tablets in this pile and the 1946 tablets in that one. In front of him sits a large black microphone.

"What is all this?" I ask as Dibs leans in to read the articles tacked to the walls.

"It's my ham radio setup," Mr. Lord says.

"Do you get *The Adventures of Superman* on that thing?" Dibs asks.

Mr. Lord snuffs a chuckle out his nose. "Not exactly," he says. "Not that kind of radio."

Dibs loses interest then and goes back to the articles.

"Have a seat." Mr. Lord motions to some stacked boxes on the floor next to his chair. "This is a communication device. I can pick up certain signals—let me show you what I've been doing."

I slip one hip down on top of a box marked CLOTHES in messy handwriting.

"Hey," Dibs calls out. "This one on the Battle of Los Angeles?" He squints and leans in closer. "An actual picture?"

he asks. "This is the disk they tried to shoot up? This is an actual picture of it?"

"Weather balloon," Mr. Lord scoffs.

"Mrs. Manuela told us all about it. Fourteen hundred rounds and they couldn't take down a weather balloon. Who would have thought they would come up with the same stupid excuse? *Again*. Like we don't have eyes."

"It's all need-to-know," Mr. Lord says, still focusing on the radio dials.

"Yeah, but who decides who needs to know and when they can know it?" Dibs asks. "Because we need to know a bunch of stuff and no one seems to want to tell us any of it."

Mordecai Lord is busy turning dials and flipping switches. "The government believes that people cannot accept the possibility that there might be life on other planets. They think all religious and financial institutions would fail and people would go nuts."

Dibs raises his eyebrow at me. "*Nuts*, you say?"

"Do you think that would happen?" I ask Mr. Lord.

"I think the public deserves to know the truth," he tells me. "That's why I left the military when I did. I was involved with this at a very high level and I wanted to tell the public and they wanted to keep it a secret."

"That's why you left?" Dibs asks.

"Didn't really have a choice," Mr. Lord tells us, still turning dials. "They made that decision for me. But they call me back every time they receive new signals from outer space. And again now after the crash, to read the binary messages coming through."

He continues to turn dials left and then right.

Right and then left.

Fuzzy static and then a click. Static and then a beep.

Then snippets of voices in between bouts of fuzz.

"You think that was another flying disk, Mr. Lord? Like the one in Los Angeles?" Dibs pulls up a chair right next to Mr. Lord now that he's his longtime friend and not the fried-bat-eating man feared by all the kids in all the land.

"It was absolutely an interplanetary vehicle of some kind," Mr. Lord tells him. "And they know it, too."

"No ifs, ands, or buts about it?" Dibs asks.

"Not a one." Mr. Lord nods once like he really means it.

More static.

Dibs picks up a plaque from the desk and examines it closely. "What was your rank?" he asks.

"What? No, never made it all the way to a four-star. I was a two-star. A major general."

Dibs seems satisfied with that answer and sets the plaque down again. "When were you in?" he asks.

"A long time ago," Mr. Lord replies.

"So you weren't a spy, then?" Dibs asks.

Another snuffed chuckle escapes Mr. Lord's nose. "Well, if I was, I wouldn't be able to tell you that, would I?"

Dibs snuffs his own chuckle. "S'pose not," he says.

"It's here somewhere," Mr. Lord says. "I know it's here somewhere. I just had it this morning."

"Are you saying there were flying disks visiting Earth way back when you were in the military, too?" I ask Mr. Lord.

"That's right."

"I thought you said they came because of the bombs." Dibs leans over Mr. Lord to look at me.

Mr. Lord stops adjusting his dials and stares at me, too.

"I said that's why they came this time. She didn't say anything about other visits."

"The atom bomb?" Mr. Lord asks me.

"Yes, sir," I say. "They said the nuclear radiation is damaging our planet and everyone else's, too, and they come here to see what we're doing."

"And you know this how?"

"His eyelids," Dibs says. "Remember?"

Mr. Lord doesn't say anything.

"She's starting to learn our language, but before that she was communicating directly to my mind—"

"*Telepathically,*" Dibs announces proudly with his chin up and his big beaver teeth showing.

"And she has this headbandy thing," I go on. "For communication and translation."

"I know exactly what you're thinking, Mr. Lord, but you don't need to worry none," Dibs reassures him. "They didn't harvest brains. I made good and sure of it." He gives me an elbow in my side. "Go ahead and tell him about the whole tomato guts thing."

I watch the corners of Mr. Lord's mouth turn up until he's full-on smiling, showing all his crooked, coffee-stained teeth.

It's the very first time I've ever seen him smile. In my whole life.

For a second, the gray lets him go. Like he's slipped from its grasp when no one is looking and he can finally breathe again.

Can finally be free.

Just then the static stops and out of the speakers of the ham radio come beeps and ticks and tocks and clicks.

Just like inside the disk.

"This is it!" Mordecai Lord exclaims. "You hear that? I made contact with this frequency . . . and I'm translating the binary. It's almost like Morse code, but not quite." He grabs a tablet and turns to a fresh sheet. "Binary is a mathematical code of communication using just zeroes and ones. This is where I'm tracking the number sequences in these tablets."

"Mr. Lord," I say. "Do you have anything translated yet?"

"Only bits and pieces," he says, scribbling down more numbers. "That came over yesterday." He points to a loose sheet.

I pick it up and stare down at it.

"I wasn't exactly sure what it meant . . . until now," he says.

01000111 01110010 01100001 01110110 01100101
01101100 01111001 00100000 01101001 01101100
01101100

Gravely ill.

01010011 01110111 01101001 01100110 01110100 01101110
01100101 01110011 01110011 00100000 01101101 01101111
01110011 01110100 00100000 01101001 01101101
01110000 01100101 01110010 01100001 01110100
01101001 01110110 01100101 00100000 01110100

01101111 00100000 01101101 01100001 01101011
01100101 00100000 01101001 01110100 00100000
01101000 01101111 01101101 01100101 00100000
01100001 01101100 01101001 01110110 01100101
00101110 00001010

Swiftness most imperative to make it home alive.

Dibs and I read it and then suck air and stare wide-eyed at each other across Mr. Lord.

"Mr. Lord," I say. "We really and truly need your help. Please."

He looks up from his paper.

I watch the edges of his mouth curl up again, showing that same coffee-toothed smile.

Then he nods just once, like he really means it.

28

A
REAL-LIFE
LEX LUTHOR

July 9, 1947—6:15 p.m.

They arrive in the middle of a massive red dust devil right after suppertime.

Three large Army Air Force trucks with big white stars painted on the doors barreling down the road.

But we're ready for them.

We first see them coming in the distance, kicking up loose dirt and gravel, while we eat Chocolate Swirl ice cream from big bowls out on the front porch.

Momma and Daddy with Baby Kay on the porch swing, and Dibs and me on the front steps.

"Here they come," I say, looking over my shoulder at Daddy.

Baby Kay is too busy focusing on the tiny bites Momma is spooning out for her to notice. "Mo," she demands. "Mo ocklit swull!"

Daddy gives a nod to Dibs and me to let us know it's all going to be okay. And I know it will be. Because he says so. Even if he says so with his eyes and not his words.

They've already been to Dibs's house.

The trucks and the men in their uniforms.

Some in fatigues and others in their tan button-downs with the tie tucked tight inside their shirt just under the third button. Dibs says there was only one wearing a dark olive jacket with stars on the epaulets. Dibs can't remember how many stars, but he did say the officer was bald as a cue ball.

Just like Lex Luthor.

They searched the house top to bottom, finding every single piece Dibs had collected out there. And they left with a warning.

He'd better not go and spout off about what he'd seen out in the desert to anyone or there'd be consequences to pay.

Big round tires turn up our dirt drive, kicking up even more dust.

Roaring engines whirl and sputter.

Daddy stands tall and strong, filled with his courage, his jaw rigid and his eyes locked on the parade of military vehicles making their way up our drive.

It reminds me of Obie.

Same jaw.

Same stance.

Same courage.

"All right, everyone," Daddy tells us. "Let's head inside."

Angry boots pound the dirt outside, then up each step of the porch.

Boom . . . Boom . . . Boom . . .

Low voices grumble.

Clark Kent is whining, his nails scraping the porch as he paces it, staying true to his duty. Even he is filled with his very own doggy courage.

An angry fist slams hard against the screen door.

Bang . . . Bang . . . Bang . . .

"Army Air Force." A deep voice cuts through the steamy kitchen. "Official business."

Bang . . . Bang . . . Bang . . .

There was never a reason to be scared of the Army Air Force before. They fight the bad guys. They preserve life and freedom. They protect us and keep us safe from the evil in the world. Daddy was even one of them, and same with Mr. Lord. Mr. Lord had two stars, and stars are a real big deal in the military.

They're the good guys.

Dibs and I sit like statues at the kitchen table and Momma takes Baby Kay into the back while Daddy lets the soldiers in.

One man in an olive jacket with three stars on his shoulders steps forward, removes his hat, and tucks it under his arm.

Bald as a cue ball.

Dibs wide-eyes me and mouths two words. "Lex Luthor."

"I'm Lieutenant General Nesbit Jones," the man tells Daddy. "Lieutenant Colonel Affinito, I presume?"

"That's right," Daddy says. "Can I help you with something, sir?"

"We are here to talk to you about the activity that has taken place out in a field past the Foster Ranch."

"I guess you haven't seen the papers," Daddy says. "Looks like that was nothing but a weather balloon, fellas. Sorry you made the trip out for nothing."

The man turns to look at me and then at Dibs and then back at Daddy.

"You been out that way?" he asks.

"No, sir." Daddy stands tall with his arms crossed.

There's a minute of silence while the three-star general decides whether to believe Daddy.

"Anyone else in this household been out that way that you know of?" He side-eyes us again.

Dibs croaks a swallow.

"No, sir," Daddy tells the man.

There's another moment of silence while the man considers Daddy's answer.

"I understand you have two children. Is that right?"

"Three," Daddy corrects him.

The man pulls a small tablet from his pocket and flips to the page he's looking for "Right." He nods. "I need to speak to . . ." He squints down at the page. "Obie . . . Obie Affinito," he says, looking back up at Daddy.

Daddy doesn't say anything for a bunch of Mississippis, and with each one, my heart beats even faster.

"Our son Obie passed last year."

The man nods again, pulls out a pen from the same pocket where he got the tablet, and makes a mark across the name written on the page with one quick, heavy motion.

Daddy's eyes meet mine.

My cheeks burn.

My teeth clench.

My eyes narrow.

The mad comes quick this time, first down in my belly and then all the way up to my brain. It's strong and fierce and makes me clutch my fingers into fists and think of the kinds of words that Momma wouldn't like one bit.

Dibs must have his own storm brewing inside him, because he stands up then, shoving the kitchen chair back and letting it scrape against the floorboards. "You don't need to cross him out of your pad like that!" he shouts. "Like he doesn't matter. He may not matter to you, but he matters to us."

The man stares wide-eyed at him. "Didn't we talk to you out at the Butte place?"

Dibs puffs up his bony chest in the lieutenant general's direction. "That's right," he says.

"I think you're in enough trouble, son. Best to keep your mouth closed."

Daddy puts a hand on Dibs's shoulder. "Dibs, why don't you go in with Mrs. Affinito and the baby."

Dibs nods and gives Lex Luthor one more good glare, and then he makes his way out of the kitchen. "It's down-and-out rude is what it is," he keeps muttering as he heads to the back.

The man looks down at his tablet again, and then at me. "Are you . . . Mylo?" he asks. "Mylo Eugene Affinito?"

I don't say anything.

"Mind if I talk to the boy?" he asks Daddy.

"I've already told you," Daddy says. "No one's been out that way."

"I imagine you've already heard we collected pieces out at the Butte farm," the lieutenant general says.

"So?"

The man smiles. "Do you mind?" He motions to the table. Daddy nods. The man sits.

"Lieutenant General Jones, sir," one of the soldiers says. "Would you like us to search the property outside?"

Lex Luthor nods and places his hat on the table without ever once taking his eyes off me.

I watch the men through the kitchen window as they scatter across the ranch, and that's when I see something out of the corner of my eye.

Moon Shadow's fine-threaded tan flight suit.

After Momma washed the Chocolate Swirl stains from it, she hung it out to dry on the line right between Dad's Fruit of the Looms and her cotton dresses.

We forgot the clothesline.

Lex Luthor reaches inside his front jacket pocket and tosses a crumpled-up tinfoil Martian mind-control-prevention skullcap across the table in my direction.

I stare down at it.

"Want to tell me something?" His words float above him in a bubble like any other supervillain in any Superman comic book.

I fill my lungs all the way to the top and bring my eyes up to meet his. "About what?" I ask him.

He smiles again. A straight-lipped smile without any teeth to it.

Sweat beads pop out on my chin.

The rooster clock ticks over the sink.

The fan blows on high.

And a single drip of sweat slides down the side of my temple.

But I won't blink.

The longer he stares, the more sweat beads pop out. They're everywhere now as he stares me down. Waiting for me to break.

My heart is pounding.

Inside I'm hoping with all that's in me that the men don't notice the flight suit of the Moontian from Europa that we are harboring in a very special hiding spot.

"Don't sit there presuming I'm stupid, boy!" the lieutenant general shouts, scaring Baby Kay in the back bedroom.

She howls good and loud, just like with the lightning. Probably thinking in her tiny brain that if she howls the loudest he might just go away.

She howls again.

He leans in close. "I'm a lot smarter than you think I am."

I don't say a word.

"I know you were out there."

I don't blink.

"You want to know how I know?"

I won't give him the satisfaction.

"Your friend Mordecai Lord," he tells me.

I blink and look over at Daddy.

He's pacing now, back and forth in front of the stove, his arms still crossed.

Chin on his chest.

His jaw rigid.

Eyes locked.

I shake my head at the lieutenant general. "No, he didn't," I tell him. "He wouldn't say any such thing."

"My boy just delivers bread to Mordecai Lord's place once a week," Daddy says.

"If you don't mind, I'd like to hear it from the boy," Lex Luthor barks at him over his shoulder, never once taking his eyes off me.

Another sweat bead drips down the side of my temple.

The long hand on the clock hits the twelve, and a mini rooster pops out of a small wooden door and crows seven times. When it's done, it goes back to ticking.

Tick . . . Tick . . . Tick . . .

"Answer me!" the booming voice shouts.

I jump.

Baby Kay howls her loudest howl yet.

"I—I—" I start. "I forgot the question."

He shoves the kitchen chair back with his tree-trunk legs and it crashes to the floor.

I don't know what Momma would charge in the swear jar for something like that but I bet it's a whole lot more than a nickel. No one has ever done anything like that to Momma's house before.

"Let's go. Right now!" he shouts, his palms flat on the table and the tip of his nose close to mine.

So close that a speck of angry spit lands right on me.

Baby Kay howls again from the back bedroom.

He leans even closer. "You better start talking," he demands with a cloud of coffee breath.

"I told you, he wasn't out there," Daddy answers for me again, louder this time. "He doesn't know what you're talking about. I won't stand here and have you bully him into saying something he doesn't know anything about."

"Tell him he was here with us and that's the end of it!" Momma hollers from the back bedroom.

Lex Luthor doesn't move. "I am not going to tell you again," he says sternly. "I'm going to need to hear it from the boy."

I croak a swallow and look him straight in the eye. "I don't know nothing about anything, sir," I tell him. "Mordecai Lord is a crazy old man. All I do is bring him bread once a week. Bread Momma makes him so he doesn't starve in that old rickety house of his."

"Tell him about the bats!" Dibs calls.

The man's eyes narrow into buttonhole slits. "So that's it. You're telling me you weren't out there?"

"All I know is what's in the papers." I look back at Daddy and he nods. "Just another weather balloon." The edges of my mouth curl up. "Right?"

"Let's lay our cards on the table, shall we?" Lieutenant General Jones whispers. "You have something I want. No one else may know you have it, but I do."

Moon Shadow.

He can't know.

It's impossible.

The others wouldn't have said anything—we made a promise on a spit shake. No one goes back on a spit shake. It just isn't done.

Mr. Lord wouldn't tell them about her.

It wasn't on a spit shake, but he meant it just the same. I know he did.

I cross my arms and lean tall and straight against the back of my chair and stare hard at Lieutenant General Jones. There's nothing he can say to make me blink. Nothing. He can yell all he wants, but he's getting nothing from me. I won't break, and he can't make me. When Dibs and I play the staring game, I always win. Dibs can't keep a straight face for more than three Mississippis. Four, tops.

I'm the reigning champ.

And he can't change that. Just like he can't change what's true, no matter what the papers say.

Do your worst, I want to say to him. I'm not afraid of you.

A soldier stomps up the front steps and pushes the screen door open enough to slip his head inside. "Sir," he calls. "You might want to take a look at this."

The corners of Lex Luthor's mouth begin to curl until it's a full-fledged smile. But not a bright smile like Daddy's smile is, or even Mr. Lord's. This smile is a smile that doesn't like to lose.

And will do anything to win.

Lex Luthor puts his hat on his head and follows the soldier out the door.

"Good job, Mylo," Daddy tells me, striding to the window and motioning for me to join him.

He places a heavy arm across my shoulders.

It feels warm and strong. Like Daddy's finally coming back to us. The way he used to be.

It makes things feel true.

Safe.

And right again.

Together we stand and watch the soldiers huddling in a circle, examining something.

"We forgot the flight suit," I tell him, pointing to the laundry on the line.

"That's not it." Daddy squints. "They've got something else."

"It's a piece from the crash site," Dibs says, running up from behind us. "I planted it as a decoy, you know, just in case." He smiles with his big beaver teeth at us.

"Good job, son," Daddy says, and lays his other arm across Dibs's shoulders. "This is a hard thing . . . and, well, you boys handled it just fine. I'm proud of you both."

Although he tries to hide it, I see Dibs's eyes water for just a second before he wipes at them with the back of his arm. It makes me think he probably doesn't hear words like that much from anyone.

29

FARAWAY STARS

July 9, 1947—7:45 p.m.

The sun is setting behind arroyos as the sky grows dark. A nighttime stage for the stars as they pop out in the sky, one by one. No monsoon blows in from the west tonight, just a welcome cool breeze that gives you a shiver and makes chicken skin pop out on your arms.

I lie still underneath it all, my head in my hands against your stone, wondering which star is yours.

More faraway stars then pop as the sky grows darker by the minute.

Must be a million of them now.

A million and one.

A million and two.

The whole thing makes me feel very small. And it seems as though the more answers I get, the more questions I have. I have more now than could ever be confined to one notebook.

The biggest question . . .

Who am I, and why am I here?

Looking above me at all that I still have yet to learn makes me think there is a real important answer to that question.

Maybe it's an answer that Moon Shadow can't give me. Or Momma or Daddy, either. Maybe it's an answer I have to figure out all by myself.

Moon Shadow is perched on top of Mrs. Vandebrink's stone, gassing up on the Moon's rays in her new overalls and undershirt. And truth be told, she's even wearing a pair of my Fruit of the Looms under there. Momma says there's never an excuse for not having clean underwear on. I guess Momma-logic applies to Moontians, too. Momma even taught her how to scrub space germs off her four-fingered hands with the bar of Ivory. She showed her how to suds up in the crevices between the suction cups. And since Gracie's lessons yesterday, Moon Shadow not only knows how to scrub to Z, she's saying more words all the time.

The stars wink at me from above, sparkling and blinking in the darkening sky. I feel so small under all that space tonight. So many glowing stars mixed in the vastness. I think of all the distant places and worlds I will never ever see.

And somewhere up there . . . is you.

My brother.

Where are you up in all that mess, Obie? I ask. So much has happened. So much I need to tell you about.

I knew this was the place.

Here she would be safe. Between Mrs. Vandebrink and Mr. Beckman. Watched over by Gracie's great-great-grandmother Valentina Delgado, *a spirit to be reckoned with,* and Magnus McDougal and Juan Santiago.

And here with you, too, Obie. I knew you would watch over her.

I knew you would protect her.

I hear voices in the distance.

Clomping horseshoes.

They're coming.

Gracie leading the way for Spuds and Diego and Dibs for our call-to-arms meeting to save the Moontians.

I stand up and wave to her.

"Over here!" I call.

"I thought we were having our meeting in the barn," I hear Spuds complaining.

"This is where we hid her from the Army Air Force," Gracie is saying.

"You should know I'm not crazy about cemeteries," Spuds informs her. "And there's only one thing I hate worse than cemeteries and that's cemeteries in the *dark*. The sun is going down, you know. It's almost all gone. How long is this going to take? Is it dusk or night right now? Because I'm not supposed to be riding out in cemeteries at night."

"What's the big deal?" Gracie asks. "We know everyone here. And if we don't know them personally, we know their families. These are our people. Our community. Our town's history. There isn't any place safer."

"What about ghosts?" he mumbles. "Ghosts live here, too . . . *especially at night.*"

"And Obie," I hear Gracie say. "Our friend Obie is here."

"Gracie, did you know that kid could catch a mean baseball?" Diego asks. "Didn't matter what you threw him, either. A fastball, a slider, a curveball, a split finger, even an illegal spitball, it didn't matter. The kid never missed. You couldn't trip him up no matter what type you threw him." He laughs. "Couldn't throw a ball to save his life, though. Even just in the infield. Remember that, Spuds?"

"Yeah," Spuds says. "And I also know that if he were still alive, he wouldn't want to be creeping around the cemetery at night, either."

"Will you quit being such a baby?" Diego says.

"*You're* a baby," Spuds snaps back.

They're getting close now.

"Hey, Gracie," Spuds says. "What kind of pants do ghosts wear?"

She sighs. "I have no idea," she says.

"Come on, guess. Diego, guess."

"I don't care," Diego says.

"Boo jeans," Spuds tells them. "Get it? Boo jeans. It's supposed to be *blue,* but I said *boo* instead because they're ghosts. Get it? *Boo jeans?*" He laughs his stupid head off.

Diego sees her first. "Wh-what . . . wh-what . . . Spuds, do you see what I see?" His voice is shaking and squeaks on the last word.

"Oh, boy . . . oh, man . . ." Spuds starts to mumble the Our Father under his breath. "*Our father, who art in Heaven . . .*"

"That's her," Gracie tells them. "Moon Shadow. It's okay. I'll protect you."

"*Thy kingdom come,*" Spuds goes on. "*Thy will be done . . .*"

"What are you boys so scared of?" When they reach Obie's stone, Gracie climbs down off Betsy Bobbin.

"On Earth as it is in Heaven," Spuds goes on. "Give us this day our daily bread."

Moon Shadow opens her eyes and lowers her hands and stares back at the boys. "Tune in next time, boys and girls, as we see Moon Shadow plummet toward Europa on her way back home through the stars. Brought to you by Kellogg's Pep," she says.

I look up at Gracie, and we laugh.

"She really likes Superman," I tell them.

"Oh my good God," Diego mumbles.

We sit in a circle next to Obie's stone, my lantern glowing bright in the middle. It feels nice to be all together again. Us boys used to play baseball out back all the time, but it's been a long while since that's happened.

Tonight, only Dibs is a no-show.

Maybe he changed his mind about the whole Jimmy Olsen thing after all.

Or maybe he got consequences because he's not a need-to-know and he knows way too much.

"There was one big guy with a head as bald as a cue ball that told me he would bury my bones in this desert if I didn't tell him everything I knew about what we saw out there," Diego says.

It's taken Diego and Spuds more Mississippis than I can even count to get used to the idea of Moon Shadow. Spuds wouldn't even come down off Bazooka for a good long while. He went through the Our Father, the Hail Mary, and the

Glory Be before we could convince him that she was okay. He missed the Tuesday church meeting when Father Kevin told us the world wasn't ending.

"So, did you?" I ask. "Did you tell them?"

"Nope," Diego snaps. "I told them I didn't know anything. They didn't find my pieces, either. Did *you?*"

"I didn't say a thing," I say. "But he knew."

"He knew what?" Gracie asks.

"He knew about her."

"Did he say that?"

"He didn't say it exactly, but he said I have something . . . and he wants that something and he plans on getting it. Those weren't his exact words, but that was the gist."

"He could have been talking about the pieces," Gracie says.

I think about that. "Yeah," I say. "But you had to be there. It seemed like he was talking about something else, too."

"Who would have told?" Diego asks, and then turns to Spuds. "Spuds, was it you?"

"Don't look at me," Spuds says. "They haven't even come out to our place yet. But I did hear Mrs. Manuela talking at Corona General and she said the Army Air Force called up Mr. Owens at the Ballard Funeral Home in Roswell asking about coffins."

"She *said* that?" I ask.

"Sure did. I heard her tell Mr. Delgado right at the counter."

"*Coffins?*" Diego mutters.

"That's right," Spuds says. "And who do you think those coffins are for?"

"Them?" I say.

"Either them or . . . *us*," Diego mutters.

Gracie rolls her eyes. "They aren't for us," she says.

"Easy for the general's daughter to say," Diego mutters.

"Oh . . . go comb your lip," she says.

Spuds bursts out laughing so hard he falls on his back, while I chuckle behind my hand.

Diego just seems happy that Gracie has finally acknowledged his hairs. He feels them with the tips of his fingers.

I'm sorry Dibs missed that one because he would have loved it. He might have asked Gracie to be the manager of our baseball team, whether she can field a ball or not, after that crack.

"If none of us were the ones who told, it had to be Mr. Lord," Gracie says.

"No way he did that. Never. Not in a million years." I shake my head.

"Then who?" Spuds says.

"Hold it," Diego says. "Someone's coming."

I stand up and hold my lantern out. "It's Dibs," I say.

Dibs ties up True Belle and dashes in our direction, hopping over Robert Goodman and Mrs. Delgado and bypassing Brita Olsen and Mrs. Vandebrink.

"Where have you been?" I ask him.

He stops next to our circle, his skinny chest pumping up and down as he tries to find his breath. He bends at the waist and puts his hands on his knees and then hocks a good loogie into the wild desert grasses.

"You'll never guess what happened," he huffs.

"What?" Diego asks.

"They got him, too." Dibs spits again.

"Who?" Gracie says.

"Mordecai Lord," he tells us. "They came and took him away still in his dirty plaid bathrobe. He's gone. And we're next, I just know it."

30

NABBED

July 9, 1947—9:45 p.m.

I bang on the door for the third time.

"Mr. Lord!" I holler, peeking between cupped hands through the screen door.

Silence.

No sounds coming from inside.

No gruff voice or stomping footsteps or smell of man sweat or rabbit stew boiling on the stove.

No wild hair that needs more than a dab of Brylcreem to tame it or faded plaid robe, either.

Daddy's headlights light the porch, but inside it's dark.

"Mordecai!" Daddy hollers, pounding a heavy fist against the door.

"They nabbed him all right," Dibs mutters. "Mac Brazel, and now Mr. Lord. We're next. I just know it. They'll take us and throw away the key."

"Tell me again what you talked about with Mordecai," Daddy says to me.

"He has this radio," I say. "But it isn't a regular radio. It's—it's—"

"It's a roast beef radio," Dibs pipes up. "But it doesn't broadcast *The Adventures of Superman*."

"No, it wasn't roast beef," I say.

"Meat loaf?"

"No . . . Ham!" I point at him. "It was ham."

"Right, ham."

"And there are these noises that come through it, and he writes numbers in his tablet, but only the ones and the zeroes, none of the other numbers."

"Binary," Daddy says.

"Yes, that's it. That's what he said. Binary code," I say.

"Do you know who he was communicating with?"

"Them, for one." I point to the sky.

"You think Mr. Lord is really crazy, Mr. Affinito?" Dibs asks, cupping his hand around his eyes, trying to get a look inside.

"No, Dibs," Daddy says. "Not even close. He's a very, very smart man who has done amazing things for his country. My guess is that he found out some things he wasn't supposed to."

"I actually kind of like him, now that we got to know him," Dibs says. "You think he chopped up his family?"

"What?" Daddy says. "Who would say such a thing?"

"See?" I tell Dibs. "People *do* make that stuff up."

He shrugs. "You think the attic bat thing is made up, too?"

I roll my eyes.

"You think we're next, Mr. Affinito? I mean, you think since we aren't need-to-know, they'll come for us, too?"

"Need-to-know?" Daddy asks.

"You know, you can't know it unless you need to know it and we don't need to know it so, you know . . . we shouldn't."

Daddy gives Dibs a few blinks before he says, "Let's take things one at a time. I'm sure everything will be fine."

Daddy pulls open the screen and hollers one more time. "Mordecai!"

Nothing.

"Think we should go inside?" I ask Daddy.

Daddy nods and steps over the threshold, turning the kitchen light on.

Same dirty dishes in the sink.

Same kitchen table with all four chairs pushed neatly underneath.

I follow Daddy and Dibs follows me.

"You think they're surveilling this place?" Dibs whispers.

"Who?"

"What do you mean, *who*? The military," he says. "Who else?"

"There isn't anyone around for miles."

"Doesn't need to be," he tells me. "You can't *see* anyone now, but they could be watching his house through a camera from a craft flying high above the clouds that can film an ant on the ground, it's so high-powered."

"That's absurd." I roll my eyes. "That could never happen in a million years."

"You're so stuck in your own little world," Dibs tells me.

I turn to face him. "What in the Sam Hill does that mean?" I ask him.

"It means you don't have any imagination about what's

possible just because it isn't happening in your neck of the woods. That's what it means."

"Where would you get that?"

"Gracie." He smiles.

"*She* said that about *me?*" I ask.

"No," he says. "She didn't say it about you. She said it about the Army Air Force. She said other things about you."

"Like what?"

"She didn't say anything as disgusting as wondering what it would be like to kiss you, if that's what you're wondering."

"I'm not wondering anything about that," I snap. "Just tell me what she said."

"Believe me," he says. "You don't want to know."

"Yes, I do," I say. "I do want to know."

He smiles even bigger. "She said she thinks you're smart."

I feel the burn on the tops of my ears first and then in my cheeks. "She did?" I ask. "Did she really say that?"

"Hey, I did my best to set her straight," he tells me. "I told her your whole deal about the tomato guts and your tendency to choke when Miss Hanratty calls you up to the blackboard to do arithmetic problems and the time Eunice Snodgrass punched you and stole your Bit-O-Honey."

"It wasn't Bit-O-Honey," I say. "It was a box of Cracker Jacks."

"Still," Dibs says.

"Did you really tell her all that about me?"

He laughs. "Nah, but I did tell her about your noxious feet."

I turn and punch him in the arm.

"Boys," Daddy calls from the back room.

We snake our way through the stacked boxes to the back, and when we get there we find Mr. Lord's desk completely torn apart.

"Holy cheese and jalapeños," Dibs says under his breath. "They sure enough did come in here and arrest him. It wasn't like this yesterday."

"Look at this." I rush toward Mr. Lord's desk. "The radios are smashed on the floor. And where are all the stacks of tablets?"

"Look at what they did," Dibs says, bending down and picking something off the floor.

I take the broken picture frame from his hands.

Shards of glass are littered over the faces of Mrs. Lord and Mordecai Jr. I brush the broken glass off the frame and onto the floor, careful not to scratch up their special smiles. The ones that think endings always happen the way they should. Then I set the frame upright and leave it on top of the desk where it's supposed to be.

"Lex Luthor warned me that something real bad could happen to me and they were going to find Momma and do something bad to her, too, if I didn't keep quiet about all this. Then they took Mac Brazel and now this. This isn't going to end good. I can just feel it."

"Dibs," Daddy says. "Help me pick these books up and get them set back upright in the bookshelf."

"Should I check things out upstairs?" I ask, peering up the darkened staircase.

"I'm sure not going up there," Dibs informs me.

"You can look for clues down here with Daddy," I tell him.

"What kind of clues?"

"I don't know, just look for something out of place." I wrap my fingers around the banister and slide my boot onto the first step.

He stretches his arms out on both sides. "*Everything* is out of place," he tells me.

"I'll be right up," Daddy says. "Just give me a minute here. Mr. Lord doesn't need to come back to a mess like this." He begins sliding books back into the case and picking up the busted radio parts.

I take the stairs two at a time until I hit the landing and find the light switch on the wall.

The first door is open, and when I peek inside I can see it's a bedroom with one messed-up double bed, the sheets in a tangled ball, a night table on either side, and raggedy flowered curtains hanging at the window.

"Mr. Lord?" I call again.

Nothing.

The next door is the bathroom, and that's empty, too.

I stop in front of the very last door.

It's closed.

I take a deep breath, put my hand on the glass knob, and turn it.

The door creaks a loud, long groan as I push it open and peek inside.

"Mr. Lord?" I whisper this time, not sure if I want an answer.

Nothing.

My fingers feel the wall next to the door for a light switch and when I find it, I flip it up.

It's a boy's room.

A stifling, stuffy boy's room perfectly preserved in dust, like there hasn't been a door or window open to it in years.

It smells of musk and cedar wood and age. On the dresser are perfectly lined-up picture frames. One of a boy on a horse, one of Mr. Lord as a young man holding a baby, and one of the Lord family all together, the three of them at a church picnic in Roswell. I can even see a young Mrs. Meadows in the background monitoring the baked goods table in her cat-eyed glasses.

On the bed is a crocheted bedspread pulled tight.

Without a wrinkle in it.

And one small brown bear sitting up against the pillow. I pick up the bear and breathe him in at the top of his head.

But all I smell is dust.

I wonder if this bear once smelled of his boy, too.

There's another frame next to the bed on the side table. Mr. Lord with the boy, both of them wearing baseball gloves. I barely recognize Mr. Lord because of his smile. The same one Daddy used to have that's big and white with a light in his eyes. A smile he had when there was joy inside him.

And hope, too.

Long before the gray swallowed him whole.

"You find anything up there?" Dibs calls from the bottom of the stairs.

I wipe the dusty glass against the leg of my overalls and set the frame back down.

"No," I call to Dibs, and head back to the landing. "Did you find anything down there?"

"Just one big mess is all," he calls back.

When I flip the light switch off and start to pull the bedroom door closed behind me, something catches my eye.

Something shiny between the mattress and the box spring.

I reach down and touch it. It's metal and sharp on the edge. I pull on it and the piece slips out from under the mattress. An I beam from the wreckage. A thin strip of metal with the same purple symbols on it as Moon Shadow has down her sleeve.

I pull up the mattress.

"Hey!" I yell down to Daddy and Dibs. "I found something."

"Attic bats?"

"No."

"Pickax?"

"Just get up here already," I holler.

I hear Dibs's bare feet slapping against the wood steps behind me and then Daddy's boots, and soon Dibs's hot breath is over my shoulder.

"What is it?" he asks.

"Look." I point under the bed.

"The Boogieman?" He belly-flops to the floor and gazes under the bed.

"No, just look." I hold up the mattress for Dibs to see.

The mattress has been hollowed out and filled with pieces from the crash site. All the broken-up parts are held in by long crusty strips of masking tape across the bottom of the mattress.

He whistles. "Mr. Lord struck the mother lode!" he says, grabbing a piece from the stash.

"That's why he's a two-star," Dibs tells me. "Two-stars know how to hide pieces of a Martian ship when they need to." He examines the strip of metal in his hand. "Guess he was out there, too," he says. "You think he saw the Moontians? Bet he wasn't brave enough to go inside, though. He may be a two-star, but he isn't a universe-appointed superhero like you. He probably doesn't eat Cracker Jacks."

"I don't know, but look at that." I point. "There are all his tablets, too." I army-crawl through the dust, scooching farther to reach the tablets. I drag out a pile of the 1943 ones and a pile of the 1942 ones, too. All with the ones and the zeroes in them.

"What did you find?" Daddy is kneeling behind us now.

I hand the tablets to him and he takes them, piling them all together on the night table. Then he stops. He picks up the picture of Mr. Lord and his boy and stares down at it.

"Here's the last of them, Daddy," I tell him, handing him the final piles of tablets.

He sets the frame down and starts to thumb through the filled pages.

"Are any of them decoded, Mr. Affinito?" Dibs asks.

"Some," Daddy says. "I'll take these back with me and decode the rest."

I stare at him. "How do you know how to do that?" I ask.

His eyes meet mine but he doesn't say anything. And I wonder just how much there is to know about Daddy that I never knew before.

"Geez, Mr. Affinito," Dibs says. "You're just like the Clock. He's this highfalutin crime-stopper who looks like a regular guy in a three-piece suit, but he wears a mask to hide his identity when he's solving mysteries and fighting injustice. All the other highfalutins don't have a clue it's him. You don't have a calling card with a clock on it by chance, do you?" Dibs gives me an elbow.

Daddy gathers all the tablets in his arms and turns to Dibs. "Not with me." He smiles big, making his way out the door.

31

THE
MOONTIAN
RESCUE

July 10, 1947—10:05 a.m.

All us kids meet up at Corona General Thursday morning.

Everyone is in.

Even Diego, and especially Spuds, whose biggest goal now is to teach Moon Shadow how to tell a joke right.

Dibs and I make it to the store first. Mrs. Manuela is already at the counter, sharing her daily news updates.

"Mrs. Manuela," Mrs. Delgado is saying, "they already said it was all just one big mistake. It was a weather balloon. Didn't you see the paper?"

"Oh, I saw it, all right." Mrs. Manuela smiles smugly.

Gracie is on her stool in rolled-up blue jeans and a pink T-shirt, winding her hair and still reading from the same book she had with her before, *Comet in Moominland*.

I make a mental note to ask Mrs. Bishop about that one on my next trip to the Roswell Library.

"Hi, Gracie." I wave.

Her eyes meet mine, and she smiles.

"You boys hear that Mac Brazel is back home?" Mrs. Manuela asks.

"He *is*?" Dibs says. "They let him go?"

"That's right, with a shiny brand-new pickup, too."

Dibs and I look at each other.

"Before the crash in the desert," Mrs. Manuela goes on, "the Army Air Force had a reward for anyone finding evidence of a real live flying saucer. Three thousand dollars."

"*Three . . . thousand . . . dollars?*" Dibs repeats each word real slow.

"I'm not saying it's true." Mrs. Manuela fans herself with an embroidered hanky. "But sure seems to me Mac Brazel got that money to keep his mouth shut."

Dibs leans in close to me. "I would have kept mine shut for a whole lot less," he says. "We only owe Mr. Funk two hundred."

"Did you hear about Mr. Lord?" I ask Mrs. Manuela. "Did they let him go, too?"

"Mordecai Lord?" Mrs. Manuela says. "Oh, that poor, dear man. Tsk tsk tsk." She clicks her tongue. "So much tragedy in his life. Losing both his wife and his son like that? He just gave up, the poor man."

"Did he really kill them?" Dibs asks.

"What? Of course not! Where did you hear something like that?" Mrs. Manuela holds her hand to her chest.

"I—I . . . Diego told me. I mean, um . . . the others said that—" Dibs starts.

"They were hit by a drunk driver out here on Highway Fifty-Four," she says.

I hear a swallow croak down Dibs's skinny neck.

"Such a tragedy," she goes on. "Killed instantly. He was

devastated . . . just devastated. Well, we all were, of course. Mrs. Lord was part of our Roswell Women's Club, which organized the library in Roswell. And she played a mean game of pinochle, too." She smiles, looking off in the distance as she watches her memories.

I see Momma doing that sometimes. Staring and smiling, and I know she's watching her memories of Obie.

"They took him, Mrs. Manuela," Dibs tells her. "They took Mr. Lord and busted up his house something awful."

She nods.

She already knows.

"He was a two-star general on his way to becoming a four-star until they let him go all those years ago. It's none of my concern, mind you."

"Do they still have him or did they bring him home, too?" I ask again.

"Well." She leans in close to me. "I heard from Maryanne Lennon that Lorraine and Joe Taylor saw them dropping him off this morning. Still in his bathrobe. Tsk tsk tsk, the poor man."

I let out all the air I was holding inside me and look over at Dibs.

Mr. Lord is home.

"You know if there's any more of that reward money to be had?" Dibs asks her.

"I didn't say Mac Brazel got any reward money." Mrs. Manuela fans her hanky. "I'm just saying a brand-new truck for a ranch hand in these hard times is very curious, is all. Very, very curious."

"Mrs. Manuela," Mrs. Delgado says. "It's all nonsense. Pure nonsense. It's all been cleared up. It was in the newspaper. It was a weather balloon."

"Oh, yes, I read the paper. But if it was just another one of their weather balloons, why are they running around Corona taking men in the middle of the night and searching homes for the pieces?"

"The Army Air Force is . . . well, they're thorough, is all," Mrs. Delgado says.

"Oh, they're thorough, all right." Mrs. Manuela snorts. "A seven-truck convoy went through the center of town to haul away torn-up pieces of tinfoil and balsa wood? Jake Rooney said that when one of the flatbeds hit a pothole out front here, the tarp flew up just enough that he could see something in there, and I'll tell you this . . . it wasn't any weather balloon. But that's all I'm saying about it. You can ask him yourself."

"Mrs. Manuela," Gracie says softly. "Did they find anything . . . *alive* out there?" Gracie's eyes meet mine.

"Graciela Maria!" Mrs. Delgado exclaims. "What a question!"

"All I know," Mrs. Manuela says, "is that they called up the Ballard Funeral Home in Roswell, looking for caskets. Four of them, to be exact." She holds up four fingers. "But before Mac Brazel stopped talking, he said there were *five* of them. But I'm not saying anything. Not one single thing about it. It's just curious, is all."

We all meet out behind the store.

Me, Dibs, Gracie, Diego, and Spuds.

Gracie comes prepared, removing her notebook from her cloth purse and laying it flat on top of the trash bin. On two full pages is a hand-drawn map of the 509th Bomb Group base in Roswell, and at the top it reads:

MOONTIAN RESCUE AND RETURN MISSION

"This is a map of the entire installation," Gracie tells us.

The rest of us stand in a circle around her, studying the drawing.

"How do you know all this—" Dibs starts.

"I told you, sometimes I go with Daddy on the weekends," she says. "I've been playing at the base since before I could walk. There are only a few special places that hold secrets— the places I wasn't allowed to see, but I know exactly which spots those are. I figure one of them must be where they're keeping J. Moon."

"J. Moon?" I ask.

"Oh, yeah." She looks up. "I named him J. Moon after Jupiter's Moon. Good, right?"

I smile. "Yeah," I tell her. "Real good."

"See here?" She points to a large square drawing labeled HANGAR 18. "This is Hangar Eighteen. I'm not allowed anywhere near there. I'm thinking this is where they brought the ship. The paper said the ship is being sent to Wright Field. So we have to hurry."

"How can you be so sure it's in Hangar Eighteen?" Diego asks. "Just because you aren't allowed in there?"

She looks up at him. "Because I'm pretty sure it's where they've brought the ones before this."

No one says anything while we take it all in.

"*Before?*" I whisper.

She nods. "This may be the first time something crashed in Corona, but not in New Mexico," she says. "And certainly not on Earth. It's been happening for a long time. But I'm not supposed to tell anyone that, so you all need to keep your mouths shut about it." She points to each one of us. "Promise?"

"How do you know that?" I ask her.

"I've seen papers I'm not supposed to see," she says. "And believe me, this isn't the first time it's happened. But you all have to promise you won't tell another solitary soul what I've told you." She points again.

We all nod.

"Now, see this?" She points to a large square with a big red cross on it. "This is the base infirmary. That's where I think they would have brought him. And . . . the other bodies. The whole thing isn't off-limits, but there is a special hallway with a locked door and a sign that says 'Authorized Personnel Only.'"

"What's in there?" Spuds asks.

Gracie shrugs. "It's need-to-know," she says, flipping over the paper to show us a map of the interior hallways of the infirmary on the reverse side. "Here is the hospital. There are regular rooms"—she points to small squares in a line— "examining rooms, and offices, too. Here is Major Williams's office and Lieutenant Bosco's and Major Lewis's. Here is where the secretary sits, Miss Tawney. And here . . . here is the hall that is off-limits."

"But how will we get into a hallway if we aren't need-to-know?" Diego asks.

"That's the question," she says. "Each door has a code on it instead of a regular key."

"A code?"

"Yeah, there's this panel on the wall next to the door with numbers on it and you have to type in the correct code or the handle won't turn, get it?"

"A lock with no key?" I ask her.

"Yep," she says.

"So how do we get the codes?" Diego asks.

She sighs. "That's where I'm stuck," she says. "I don't know the codes. You need top security clearance for that."

"Who has top security clearance?" I ask her.

"Anyone with a need to know," she says. "Brigadiers and up."

"What does that mean?" Dibs asks.

"The generals," she says. "One star is brigadier, two stars is major, three stars is lieutenant, and four stars is the top. That's a full general. There's a five-star one, too, but that's pretty rare."

Dibs sticks his chin in the air and puts his hands on his hips.

"*Tune in tomorrow,*" Dibs says in his radio announcer voice, "*same time, same station, for the conclusion of the adventures of Mylo Affinito and his trusty sidekick, the Mighty Dibson Tiberius Butte, as they send the Moontians back home to Jupiter's Moon, Europa!*" He points a skinny finger to the sky.

Diego laughs this time, rolling his eyes. "Butte," he says.

"What?" I can see Dibs fold his tiny dukes at his side, waiting for Diego's dig.

Instead, Diego jumps into his own superhero pose, his hands on his waist and his chin pointed to the sky. "You forgot Diego the Great."

Dibs laughs.

"And me too," Spuds pipes up. "I want a superhero name, too."

"The Mighty Potato?" Diego says.

Spuds poses. "I prefer the Mighty Jokester," he announces. *"Funnier than a speeding knock-knock joke, more hilarious than a sidesplitting comedy radio program, able to get a laugh with every joke he tells."*

Diego elbows Dibs. "We think the potato one fits better." He smiles down at him. "Right?"

Dibs nods real big and smiles, too.

Bang. Bang. Bang.

My fist hits the door.

"Mr. Lord," I call through the ripped screen. "Mr. Lord!"

The smell of strong coffee fills my nose while heavy footsteps pound the floorboards inside, until he's standing in front of us with his coffee mug in his hand.

"Don't you boys get it yet?" he says. "I'm trying to protect—"

He stops.

The screen door opens and he stands there staring down at us.

Dibs and me.

And her too.

Moon Shadow, back in her tan flight suit with the purple symbols down the sleeve and her gold headband secure around her watermelon head.

Ready for her journey home.

"Mr. Lord," I say. "I'd like you to meet our friend . . . Moon Shadow."

"H-hello," Moon Shadow says, peering up at him with her large black eyes.

"We need you," I tell him. "She needs to get her brother back to Europa. You know that he's sick and they're planning the transfer tomorrow. It needs to happen now, Mr. Lord. Will you help us do that?"

He doesn't say a single word.

Not one single word for a real long time while he takes her in.

When he finally opens his mouth, nothing comes out. Like maybe his tongue forgot what it wanted to say. He just stands there, not blinking or breathing or speaking or anything.

"Sir?" I say after a good long while.

I watch as he slowly kneels down in front of us, until he is eye to eye with Moon Shadow.

"Hello," he says to her, the corners of his mouth turning up. "It's so nice to meet you." He holds out his hand to shake hers.

I raise my eyebrows at Dibs. "He's in."

32

KRYPTON'S HEAVENLY STARS

July 10, 1947—11:30 p.m.

"**Y**ou're sure you want to do this?" I whisper to Dibs while he waves me in through his screen door.

"Will you shut up?" Dibs hisses with one finger over his lips. "My dad's going to wake up. If I don't take them and I'm not here to stop him, he might drive somewhere when he shouldn't be driving nowhere. He finished the whole bottle and started another right after supper. With all that in him he probably won't even be up to slop the pigs in the morning, but better safe than sorry."

"Isn't he going to be mad?"

Dibs shrugs. "Won't be the first time and it won't be the last."

"Still," I say. "Be careful."

He nods and points to the davenport in the living room. "He's sleeping on the couch," he mouths.

Together we creep through the messy kitchen with dishes stacked high in the sink, on the counters, and on the tables, too. There are flies swirling around on the hunt for old and smelly food morsels. The floor feels tacky under my boots and the whole place stinks like food gone bad and like maybe a pig or two slipped in when no one was looking.

Dibs's daddy is sprawled out on the couch in nothing but his dirty undershirt and even dirtier Fruit of the Looms, his clothes in a heap on the floor next to him. Mr. Butte snorts a loud snore and then burps up something that smells like bad burrito. Dibs grabs his daddy's overalls off the floor, pulls out two keys on a key chain, and turns around to face me.

"Mission accomplished," he whispers.

Another loud snort and we both jump and Dibs almost drops the keys.

"Come on," I whisper back.

"Wait." Dibs hands me the keys and grabs a crocheted afghan from the chair and carefully places it across Mr. Butte. "Okay," he says. "Now I'm ready."

Dibs and I run as fast as we can down his dirt drive, past the black mailbox to Mr. Lord's pickup. I give Dibs ten fingers to help him into the back along with Moon Shadow and then climb up the bumper myself. Up front is Mr. Lord in the driver's seat in his class A uniform with two stars on each epaulet. Daddy's on the passenger side in *his* class A with his ribbons on the front.

After a stop behind Corona General to add Spuds, Gracie, and Diego to the back with us, Mr. Lord puts his boot on the clutch and pulls the gearshift into first and then second and the truck lurches back out onto U.S. Route 285 toward Roswell.

The wind is loud in the back of the pickup so we all stay quiet, busy with our own thoughts as we bump and bumble along the road toward the base. Diego is probably thinking about his lip hairs. Spuds is probably trying to think up another joke for later. Dibs is probably thinking about Martian mind control and phasers. And Gracie is probably thinking about . . . actually, I'm not real sure what she's thinking about. I've never seen that expression on her face before as she stares up at the stars, loose hair swinging around her cheeks. Whatever it is, it's probably more profound than the rest of the bunch.

As for me?

I'm thinking about you.

With my head leaning back on my arms, I stare out at your sky. The stars sparkle and light up a million different journeys to a million different places.

But tonight it's different.

Tonight, I feel you closer.

You're here.

And now I know it.

I feel it, just like you promised. I also know you're here because you wouldn't miss this for the world.

Dibs gives me a poke. "Hey, Mylo," he says, jutting a chin toward the sky.

"The mighty Krypton explodes into millions of glowing fragments. Glittering stars that will remain forever in the heavenly sky," he tells me in his radio announcer voice.

That makes me smile all the way down to my noxious toes because I know that Dibs feels Obie here with us just as much as me.

33

STEALING
OUR THUNDER

July 11, 1947—12:45 a.m.

When we finally make it to Roswell, Mr. Lord stops the truck out in front of the post office and he and Daddy stretch a long tarp over us.

"Once we get past the gate and to the infirmary building, we'll guide you to a safe place on the base," Daddy says. "Everyone still doing okay?"

We all nod and Moon Shadow gives an A-OK sign.

"I taught him that." Dibs smiles big, pointing a thumb to his chest. "Me, I taught him that."

"Hey, Mr. Affinito," Spuds says. "Where would a Martian park his spaceship?"

"Anyone who wants to stay in the truck once we get there is welcome to do so," Daddy tells us, tugging at the end of the tarp.

"At a parking meteor! Get it? A parking meteor? It's supposed to be *meter* but I said *meteor*." Spuds slaps his knee and nearly busts a gut.

"*Meteor* and it's supposed to be *meter*," Moon Shadow says, then slaps her knee and makes the same sound Spuds did when he laughed.

Then we all laugh, and so does Daddy.

"What did the Moontian say to the Earthling?" Moon Shadow says.

I turn to face her.

"What?" Gracie asks, her lips slowly stretching over her teeth into a wide smile.

"Where can I get a bowl of Chocolate Swirl? Get it? It's supposed to be Peppermint Bonbon."

Spuds looks at Diego and Dibs and Gracie, all with furrowed brows, while me and Moon Shadow yuk it up.

"You had to be there," I tell the rest of them. "Believe me . . . it's *funny*."

"It's funny because the Chocolate Swirl was on sale but everyone knows Peppermint Bonbon is better," Moon Shadow explains. "Get it?"

The truck lurches and then jerks to a stop at the Roswell base. The 509th Bomb Group entrance.

"Can I help you gentlemen?" the guard asks Mr. Lord.

"Yes," Mr. Lord says. "I'm Major General Mordecai Lord. I'm contracted with the Army Air Force to analyze the communication devices of the flying disk and head the engineering group to learn how this thing works. This is Lieutenant Colonel Affinito, who is contracted to arrange the shipping of the parts out to Wright Field later today."

We hear papers shuffling on a clipboard.

"I—I'm sorry, General Lord," the guard stutters. "I—I don't see any orders listed here, and I haven't been briefed on any contractors."

More shuffling.

"I apologize, but I'm going to have to call General Delgado at home for confirmation of these orders before I can let you on base, sir."

"Oh, sure," Mr. Lord says. "I'm certain there won't be any disciplinary action ordered after you wake up the general because of someone's incompetence. Please," he says. "Be my guest. We can wait." Mr. Lord stomps on the clutch and pushes the gearshift into neutral and throws on the brake.

Shuffling and then a crash as the guard drops the clipboard on the ground. "W-well, it's just that I don't have anything written on my, ah, on my list here," he says.

"Right, you go on ahead, then," Mr. Lord says. "I'm sure this mistake won't stand in the way of any promotions you were hoping for."

"I—I'm sorry, sir," the guard says. "I'm sure your orders are correct. I apologize for questioning you."

The gate swings open.

"Good man," Mr. Lord tells the guard, shifting the truck back into gear. "I'll put in a good word for you."

And even though I can't see him do it, I just know he gives the guard a nod like he really means it.

When Mr. Lord stops the truck again, I pull back the tarp and we all climb out for a final huddle to go over the plan once more.

"You all wait here, and when Mordecai and I are ready, we will come out for Moon Shadow," Daddy directs us.

"But, Daddy," I say, "I want to help."

"Me too, Mr. Affinito," Dibs says.

Daddy shakes his head. "This is too dangerous. I don't want any of you kids in there. It's been a difficult enough decision even to allow you to come along. You wait here with Moon Shadow."

"But, Daddy—" I start.

"Mylo, your mother would skin me six ways to Sunday if she knew I let you in there," he says. "Stay right here so that when we find J. Moon we will know where to find you."

We watch Mr. Lord and Daddy slink around the back of the infirmary and through a back door, using a key from Mr. Lord's pocket.

"This is so unfair," Dibs complains. "It was *our* plan to begin with. They're totally stealing our thunder. Gracie, you must be able to do something to get us in there."

Gracie smiles. "I might have an idea," she says. "Follow me."

34

THE
MOTHER SHIP

July 11, 1947—1:45 a.m.

Gracie leads us to a spot outside the cinder-block building Daddy and Mr. Lord just went into, under an open window.

"What's this?" I ask her.

"Daddy's office," she says. "He always forgets to close his window before he leaves for the day. I figured there was a pretty good chance he did it again."

I give Gracie ten fingers to hoist her up.

"Wait," Dibs says. "We need a warning signal . . . you know, in case someone is coming."

I nod.

"How about a whistle?" Diego offers.

"I think it should be a word," Gracie says.

"*Cracker Jacks?*" Dibs says.

"*Shortstop,*" I say.

Dibs smiles. "Yeah, *Shortstop.*"

Gracie nods and takes a poll. "That okay with everyone? If someone's coming, we call out *Shortstop,* right?"

We all nod.

"Everyone ready?" I ask.

"Holy cheese and jalapeños!" Dibs hisses, pointing up in the sky.

Above us, hanging low in the sky, is a gigantic flying craft hovering without a single sound, only this one is almost the size of an entire football field and in the shape of the letter V. The thing is spit-shine black, but also clear at the same time, and we can see the stars through it as it floats above us. Along the bottom of the spaceship are two long lines of deep amber-colored light. Smaller disk-shaped beams shoot off from the large craft in every direction, like tiny ships taking off from a floating runway.

"It's the mother ship!" Dibs whispers. "It's just like I dreamed it."

Moon Shadow puts her hand on my arm. She points with her other hand.

"They're here for us," she tells me.

"Yes." I take her hand. "You and J. Moon are going home tonight. We're rescuing him. Your ending will be the way it should be. I promise you that."

Gracie grabs Moon Shadow's other hand, and then we're all standing with our fingers intertwined.

"Moon Shadow," Diego says. "It's been neat to know you, and I hope you come back to visit again soon."

"Me too," Spuds tells her. "Except you have to work on your jokes."

"Thank you for showing me that girls can be whatever they want to be," Gracie says, sniffing back her tears. "Even here on Earth. I will really miss you."

"Moon Shadow," Dibs says. "Thank you for not using your phasers on me and for showing me things I would have never learned about without you. Please come back and visit us again."

"You helped me find something inside me," I tell Moon Shadow, feeling tears prickling behind my eyes, "that I didn't even know was there. I will never forget you."

One by one, we hoist each other up and through the window of General Delgado's office. It's mostly dark in there, with one small lamp left on at the corner of his desk. Gracie starts to open desk drawers.

"What are you looking for?" I whisper.

"Papers," she tells me. "Anything that looks official like."

I nod and pull a drawer open on the other side of the desk while Dibs pulls one open below me.

"Look!" Dibs holds a paper out for her to see. "Some need-to-knows are in here!"

She takes it from his hand. As she reads, we lean over her shoulders.

OFFICE MEMORANDUM
UNITED STATES GOVERNMENT

Analyzing flying disk.

Concern to national security.

Witness questioned and silenced.

One thing is clear enough. On the top of each page is a big black stamp.

Gracie puts her ear to the door and listens to the hallway outside. "Sounds quiet," she says. "Come on."

She turns the silver door handle and pushes the door open a crack, slipping out into the hall. We all follow her. Me, then Moon Shadow, Dibs, Diego, and Spuds.

The cinder-block walls are the color of coffee with too much cream in it. The way Mrs. Manuela likes her coffee when she and the other Roswell Women's Club ladies come for coffee and pinochle.

Momma likes hers black with two scoops of sugar.

"Left just up here," Gracie whispers over her shoulder.

Voices.

The clicking of a doorknob.

Boots shuffling.

"Abort mission!" Gracie hisses, spinning around.

In a panic, we bounce and bumble into each other like bumper cars at a carnival.

"That's my foot!" Spuds exclaims.

"Cracker Jacks," Dibs whispers frantically. "I mean Sh-shortstop! Shortstop!"

We scramble back to General Delgado's office. I hold the door as Gracie, Moon Shadow, Spuds, and Diego slip inside, and just as I'm about to close the door, large hands grab me by my overall straps, lifting me clear off the floor.

"How did you get in here?" a very large man demands while my toes hover over the gleaming hall tiles.

He's wearing a tan Army Air Force uniform shirt with his tie tucked in just under the third button.

He slams the general's office door.

"What are you doing in this office? How did you get in here? Who are you?"

More noisy boots shuffle and squeak against the sparkling tiled floor. Screeching and pounding as tan-suited officers grab and push me down the hallway.

When I turn the corner, I find myself face to face with my nemesis, Lex Luthor himself.

So we meet again, the superhero part of me wants to sneer at him.

He stares down at me with that same ugly scowl on his face.

The *real* ugly one.

"How did you get in here?" he demands.

I don't say anything.

"Answer me, boy!" he explodes.

I don't blink.

He shakes his head. "Put him in the holding cell," he tells the men. "A few nights there and you'll be singing a different tune."

35

OUT OF TIME

July 11, 1947—3:02 a.m.

There's one cot with a dark wool blanket pulled over the mattress, a single silver toilet with a sink attached to the wall, and not one single bar of Ivory soap anywhere to be found.

Momma's gonna be as mad as a wet hen when she hears that one.

I lie flat against the mattress on my back, my head on my arms, staring at the ceiling. There are peg holes up there, twenty-two per ceiling tile.

A sharp voice interrupts me while I'm counting how many tiles per row.

Angry voices.

I sit up and hold my ear to the wall next to the bed.

"The president is furious!" someone yells, slamming something on a table with a loud bang. "I had to come all the way out here from Washington to clean up your mess.

First someone gives a press statement letting the world know we have the disk without proper authority. Now we have to mop up and make everyone think we made a big mistake? We look like fools! Like we aren't in charge of our own skies. The American public counts on us to be in control. To provide safety. You could have caused a mass panic!"

"I disagree," a deep voice says.

I know that voice.

It's Mordecai Lord.

"People are smart," he says. "They are caring. They are loving. And this Martian civilization wants to do us no harm. We already know this from the other visitations. From the other crash survivors. We can build a relationship with these people of benefit to everyone. They're communicating with this boy. I believe you should have the president form a government group to work on relations with this population. And it's only fair for the public to be informed that we are not alone in our universe and that we are not in any danger. The Martians come here in peace."

Silence.

"Where are the bodies?" Mordecai Lord asks.

"We've autopsied the bodies, and they will be preserved and sent to Wright Field in Ohio today."

"And the lone survivor?"

"He—he's ill."

Silence.

"My best bet . . . he won't make it until morning."

I hear a key turn in the holding cell door and it flies open.

It's Gracie.

I bound off the bed and race toward her.

"Mylo, I—"

"We're running out of time!" I say, grabbing both her arms. "Where's Moon Shadow? We have to get her to J. Moon right now!"

36

THAT
HORRIBLE DAY

May 27, 1946—2:13 p.m.

Obie's eyes didn't want to stay open on that horrible day.

His breathing was wet and soggy with weak coughs that couldn't muster the energy to hack away at whatever was keeping him from breathing right.

I didn't leave his side.

And neither did Shortstop.

Not for the endless parade of casseroles and baked goods brought by neighbors or others who came by with positive prayers and a friendly howdy. I didn't even go to the bathroom. I held it all day.

I just read.

Starting with Volume One of the Affinito Brothers' Superhero Duo series, I kept reading without once stopping, even though sometimes I knew he wasn't awake to hear it. I kept reading anyhow.

Momma was in with a new cool washcloth for his head

every few minutes. Dr. Shaw was there and Father Kevin, too, in and out of the room, checking on him. But I didn't want to look at them. Their faces were long and I knew what that meant.

But I just kept reading.

I prayed, too.

I prayed over and over.

I begged and pleaded with God to make him better.

Everyone said God would make him better as long as I prayed on it. So I did that. I prayed night and day on it, just in case God might have missed one of the messages.

On that horrible day, Obie woke up just after two o'clock, his eyes parting only a crack.

"Obie," I said. "Obie, are you okay? I'm reading our comic books. Did you hear it?"

He nodded, the edges of his mouth curling.

"I haven't finished my latest one yet," I told him. "But I will, and it will be a good one, too. The way endings are supposed to be."

"Promise you'll finish it?" he asked me, his voice rough.

"Yes, I promise," I told him. "And I promise you that you'll get better. I promise you on a spit shake."

He didn't say anything.

"You have to promise me something, too," I told him. "You have to promise me you'll always be here for me." I wiped at the tears finding their way out of the corners of my eyes. "Because I need my big brother here with me . . . I need *you.*"

"Promise," he whispered.

He had been too weak to lift his hand, so I spit in the middle of my palm for both of us and touched it against his.

There's nothing more binding than a spit shake, but I don't think either one of us really believed that what we were saying was true.

I watched his eyes close again.

I didn't know that it would be the very last time.

Momma, Daddy, and me sat next to his bed for a long while as Father Kevin prayed over us.

We were broken in so many pieces on that day, I thought we'd never be whole again. Even Momma didn't have the words to make it right.

It wasn't the way it was supposed to be.

What came next, after an ending like that?

We didn't know.

37

GOOD-BYE

July 11, 1947—3:03 a.m.

My heart feels like it could explode with every beat inside my chest as Gracie and I sneak out of the holding cell and run to General Delgado's office to fetch Moon Shadow and the others.

"Mylo!" Dibs calls out when I pull open General Delgado's office door.

"Shhh!" I hiss.

"Yeah, but you're okay." He wraps his bony arms tight around me.

"Come on," I tell him. "We have to get to J. Moon, and we have to do it right now."

He nods and pulls his Buck Rogers Atomic Disintegrator Pistol from his back pocket. "Roger that," he says, darting out the door first.

Once we all make it out of the office, Gracie leads the way through the maze of cinder-block halls.

Left, and then right.

Right, then right again.

I know you're here with me now, Obie.

I feel it.

I'm sorry I couldn't find you before. You really did keep your promise, just like you said you would. And I know it's you who will help me get Moon Shadow and J. Moon home.

You.

My brother.

"Here!" Gracie calls, stopping at a door with a large sign: AUTHORIZED PERSONNEL ONLY.

Gracie pushes four buttons on the wall and the door buzzes.

"Well?" I ask. "Turn the knob."

"It rejected the code."

"What do you mean? I thought you said you knew it."

"I—I did, but it must be different now."

"We have to get to him," I say. "We have to do it now."

"I don't know what to say." Gracie's eyes well up. "I—I don't know. Let me try again." She pushes the same four numbers and the door buzzes again, only this time it sounds an alarm that rings loud through the hallways.

Spuds covers his ears with his palms.

I grab Moon Shadow's hand. "Moon Shadow!" I say. "Can you help us?"

She blinks at me and then places her other hand flat on the buttons and closes her eyes.

Clicks.

Beeps.

Boots squeak and shuffle in the next corridor. Voices.

"They're coming!" Diego exclaims.

The alarm goes silent and the door pops open.

"Let's go!" I shout. "We have to hurry!"

Inside the door is the longest hallway I've ever seen. On each side, there are more doors and floor-to-ceiling windows. Through each window, I see what looks like a doctor's examining room. I scramble down the hall, pulling Moon Shadow along with me. I stop at each window, peering inside, looking for J. Moon.

In one room after another, small gray bodies lie still on silver gurneys. They are stripped naked of their flight suits and cut all the way down their bellies and across their chests. Their insides are sitting in clear jars of liquid on the counters. Each time, I look away and scramble on to the next window.

"Don't look in there," I instruct Moon Shadow.

Next window.

Another body cut up.

The next window. Same thing.

I stop looking after that. At least until I get to the very last room.

"He's there!" Moon Shadow exclaims.

I place both palms on the glass and stare in at J. Moon lying on a hospital bed under a white sheet, hooked up to all kinds of wires and machines and a bag of clear liquid.

Alone.

I can't help but think of Obie on that horrible day. He

may have been sick and he may have been dying, but at least he wasn't alone.

And he knew it, too.

Until he didn't.

There's a sign on the door of J. Moon's room:

DO NOT ENTER WITHOUT
PROPER RADIATION PROTECTION ATTIRE

Just then, five men covered from head to toe in white hooded suits with gas masks pulled tightly over their faces bound through the door at the end of the hall.

"Stop!" someone shouts, holding up a gloved hand. "That's a contaminated room! Do not open that door!"

"There's been a breach!" someone else yells into a hand-held radio. "Code White! Code White!"

A screeching alarm sounds through the hallway, a piercing siren that blares and bounces off the cinder blocks.

Angry boots squeak and shuffle.

Men with guns ten times the size of Dibs's Buck Rogers Atomic Disintegrator Pistol dart in our direction. And I'd bet any money they're real ones, too.

I turn the knob on the door of J. Moon's room, pulling Moon Shadow inside with me. "Hurry up!" I call to the rest of them.

They all scramble inside behind us.

Dibs, Gracie, Diego, and Spuds.

I slam the door behind them, locking it from the inside.

Heavy fists pound against the wood as the suited men line the window to the hall.

"Open this door, son. You don't know what you're doing."

"There are two survivors!" another man shouts. "I see another one in there now!"

Mordecai Lord and Daddy push their way to the window, too.

"Mylo!" Daddy calls, his eyes wide and his palms flat against the glass. "What are you doing in here? I told you to wait."

"I couldn't wait. He's dying, Daddy." I stare at him through blurry tears welling fast. "He's dying!"

Daddy holds his lips in a straight line for a moment and then nods at me.

I grab Moon Shadow by the hand and we rush to J. Moon's side while the other kids stand back by the door.

"Just let them be," I can hear Daddy tell the men. "Mylo can help. No one wants them to die, right? Just let them do what they need to do."

"And he will," Mr. Lord says.

The sirens outside the room stop.

The pounding fists quiet.

And the angry voices soften as the men gather at the window to watch Moon Shadow from the hall.

J. Moon's breathing is wet and soggy, just like Obie's on that horrible day.

He's pale and weak.

Still and tired.

Moon Shadow takes his hand, and J. Moon opens his eyes.

They speak in beeps and clicks just like the radio transmission I heard in the flying disk.

"What are you waiting for?" I tell her. "Please save him. Send him home. Do what you have to do and do it fast. I made a promise. *A promise.*"

I can't breathe.

Tears roll down my cheeks and I let them.

It can't happen again. Not again.

Moon Shadow closes her eyes and raises her chin to the ceiling, her headband tight against her watermelon head, her fingers curled around her brother's. I watch her refuel in the moon's energy, and as she breathes it in, it transfers through her to J. Moon. Before my eyes, the color of his skin changes from chalk white to gray, and its texture goes from dry to moist. His eyes change from milky and tired to glassy black.

Moon Shadow stops for a moment, facing me then, her eyes drinking me in as if it is the last time she will see me. "You are my brother now, too," she says to me. "You are family . . . *my family.*"

I turn to look at Daddy in the window, and then at Dibs and Gracie and Spuds and Diego standing close behind. I think of Momma at home and Baby Kay.

And I think of Obie.

"You are our family, too," I tell Moon Shadow. "Always. I don't want to say good-bye. I don't like good-byes."

I reach out and hug her tiny Moontian body tightly against mine. Dibs, Gracie, Spuds, and Diego huddle in, too.

Our Corona family.

I don't want to let her go, but I know I have to because it's time for her to go.

Home where she belongs.

I watch as she pulls off her headband and hands it to me. I hold it tightly in my hand and know that this is not the good-bye I thought it would be. It's not a good-bye at all. It's the beginning of something instead.

A friendship through the stars and to a very special place far, far away.

For all of us.

She steps back toward the bed, and then slowly pulls herself on top of the mattress and stands tall just like she did on the fence post. This time with one hand pointed straight in the air and the other holding her brother's hand.

She closes her eyes.

We watch her large black eyeballs move quickly back and forth underneath her lids.

A beam of green light penetrates through the ceiling from the powerful mother ship hovering high above us, ready to take them home. It's a light so bright, it shines like a sun.

We shield our eyes.

"Krypton burns like a green star in the endless heavens," Dibs says again, still standing next to me.

The electrical energy washes over the room like an ocean wave.

"What is that?" I hear muffled voices behind the glass.

"It feels like a magnet trying to pull our insides out," someone answers.

"Should have used tinfoil instead of the gas masks!" Dibs hollers to the men through the glass. "Anti-Martian-mind-control skullcaps." He points to the foil under his Yankees hat. "Martians will suck your brains out your ears as soon as look at you."

The suited men take a step back from the window.

I smile and shake my head at him. "What are you doing?"

He smiles back. "Don't tell me they didn't have that coming."

We watch the green light blaze, glowing low and then bright, low and then bright, as we watch Moon Shadow and her brother J. Moon slowly fade away.

Little by little they disappear, until even the green beam is gone. We watch until there is nothing left to see but an empty bed with a single white sheet.

"*Good-bye*," I whisper, clutching the gold headband tightly in my fist.

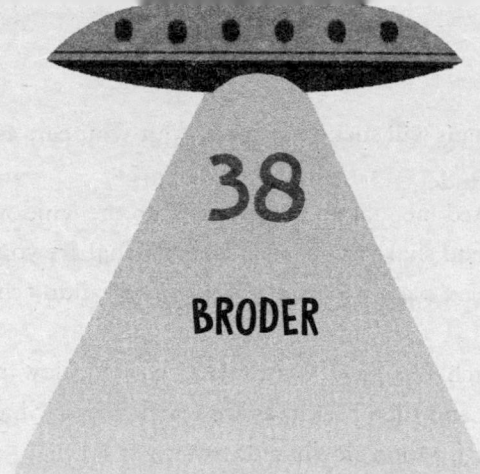

38

BRODER

July 13, 1947—7:40 a.m.

The morning before church, while Momma and Daddy are still getting ready, me and Baby Kay rock on the porch swing. She's in her Sunday best dress and I'm in my tie and nice Brylcreemed hair with the straight part down the front.

I'm holding a photo album on my lap and showing her pictures of Obie.

Our brother.

And even though she's too little to remember him, I don't ever want her to forget he was here.

"See this one, Baby Kay?" I point. "This one is from the Bronx in New York City. It was a real hot day and we ran through the fire hydrant in the street. Momma let us get Popsicles at the corner store, too."

"Pops?"

"That's right. And you want to know what else? Obie knew everything there was to know about history," I tell her.

"He could list every single president and even recite the Declaration of Independence, word for word."

"Wod?"

I nod. "He could catch a baseball even if someone threw it all the way from center field to home plate. And he never missed it, either. Not once," I tell her.

"Frow?" she repeats.

"Yep. And he held you when you were born, too," I say. "Did you know that, Baby Kay? He held you and said you would be a perfect third baseman in just a few years." I laugh to myself. "Do you remember that? Your brother held you. Obie is your brother."

"Obeee?" she repeats. "Broder?"

"That's right. You think you'll play baseball with us, Baby? Momma's only okay on third, but don't tell her I said so. Best to put her in right field. She's a good hitter, though. Daddy plays first, second, and shortstop all at once. That's how quick he is. So we definitely need a third baseman. You think you'll want to do that?"

"Tird," she says.

"Dibs is a good catcher," I tell her. "Not as good as Obie, but pretty darn good."

"Bibby Boo!" Baby Kay exclaims.

"Yep."

"Broder?"

I turn to face her.

She's looking at me with her warm chestnut eyes and a wide smile.

"Dibby Boo," she says again. "Broder?"

"Yes," I say. "Yes, he is."

The screen door creaks and I turn to see Momma with Daddy behind her, his large palms resting on her shoulders, both of them watching us. Momma dabs her eyes with a flowery hanky and pushes open the door.

"Hey, Baby." She reaches for Baby Kay, squeezing her tight.

Then she puts one arm around me, and Daddy joins in with his long, strong arms around all of us in one giant family hug.

Someone very important is missing.

And it's not just Obie this time.

Dibs is missing, too.

I haven't seen him since the base rescue.

Two whole days, to be exact.

I went looking for him at his house, but his daddy told me to *get* and said Dibs was sick. Momma even called over yesterday, asking if she could make some chicken soup and bring it by. Mr. Butte told her he wasn't a charity case and hung up the phone.

Now that it's finally Sunday, we go pick Dibs up for church. But he doesn't come out for that, either. Daddy finally gives up, making his way back to the truck as red eyes peer out at us through the screen door. Then I watch Mr. Butte push open the door so hard it slams all the way to the other side against the house.

"That's right! Get out of here!" he says, slurring his words at Daddy, stumbling across the porch.

When Daddy pulls himself in behind the wheel, he exchanges a look with Momma.

"Well?" I demand. "Where is he?"

"Mr. Butte says he's still sick," Daddy tells me, shifting the truck into reverse, throwing his arm across the back of the seat, and backing us out of the drive.

"He's lying," I say, putting a hand on Daddy's arm. "Why are you leaving?"

Mr. Butte is still shouting sloppy words at us from the porch steps.

"Daddy," I say. "Please try again."

"We can only do what we can do, Mylo." Momma's voice cracks as she wrestles with Baby Kay's flyaways.

"Broder?" Baby Kay says again.

"Yes, Baby," I tell her.

After Daddy makes it to the end of the drive, he stops to look both ways for church traffic, his white knuckles curled around the steering wheel. I turn and stare back at the house through the rear window.

I see him.

Upstairs at the window of his room.

It's too far away now to see him clear enough, but just seeing him up there watching us leave him makes my bones ache so much, I feel like I need a body cast to sit up straight.

Daddy pushes the gas pedal and the truck lurches forward, turning onto State Highway 247 toward church.

I watch Dibs until I can't see him anymore, and then I remember something real important.

The true courage is in facing danger when you are afraid.

I think hard about that on our way and decide it's a good thing to talk to God about. It was courage that helped to get Moon Shadow home, and now it's Dibs's turn to come home.

Home where he belongs.

At church we go to the fifth row like always, behind Gracie Delgado and her family. Except there's someone already there.

Mordecai Lord.

Mr. Lord, with his white hair slicked back with so much Brylcreem it looks like he came in from a rainstorm, a straight part pulled down the middle of his head. He has on a clean suit with a red striped tie. Like maybe the gray has finally let him go.

I guess he found his courage part, too.

"Where's Dibs?" Mr. Lord takes a handkerchief from his front pocket and wipes at the sweat beading up on his forehead.

"Mr. Butte wouldn't let him come today," I tell him.

He holds his lips tight and nods. "I brought something for him." He hands me a small brown bear.

"This?" I take the bear in my hands.

"Yes," he says. "Seems he needs it more than me. Will you give it to him?"

"Yes, sir," I tell him. "He's really going to like having this."

Momma smiles real big at Mr. Lord as she and Daddy slide into the pew next to me. "Mr. Lord." She reaches her hand out to him. "Real good to see you here this Sunday morning."

"Ma'am." He grabs her hand.

Mrs. Meadows starts to play the large organ, while we all stand to sing and watch the procession start up the aisle. Diego and Spuds lead the way in their altar boy gowns, and Father Kevin follows closely, making his way to the altar, where he will give us the messages that God wants us to know today.

He shares a passage about God holding your right hand when you need Him most.

I look down at my palm and smile.

And today, for the first time in a long time, when we all get down on our knees to pray, I pray, too.

God? I start. *It's me, Mylo Affinito . . . I don't know if you're listening but I want to let you know that I think I found my courage part. Sorry I blamed you for leaving it out. I guess it wasn't gone . . . it was just lost. And not to be disrespectful, but I'm still not seeing anything on my upper lip yet. Anyway, I'm sorry I've been mad at you, too. Truth be told, I might still be a little mad, but you probably already know that 'cause you're God and everything.*

I peek an eye open.

Everyone is still, with heads bowed and lips moving.

Mrs. Meadows starts playing on the organ to let us know to wrap it up because God only has so much time. When Mrs. Manuela starts to sing, we all must sign off and say amen.

So anyway . . . I want to thank you, God, for giving me Obie and letting him be my brother. And for letting Moon Shadow and

J. Moon become a part of our family, too. But I have to ask you for your help with Dibs. He needs our help, God. I'm just not sure how to go about it.

Mrs. Manuela's voice rings through the nave.

Amen.

I cross myself, but this time the proper way with the Father, the Son, and the Holy Ghost, the way we're supposed to.

I watch Mordecai Lord cross himself, too, and wonder what he prayed about today.

And then it comes to me.

The ending.

The ending to the unfinished homemade comic book that's been sitting in the top drawer between our beds.

THE DEFEAT OF THE MARTIAN SUPERVIRUS
Volume Sixteen of
THE AFFINITO BROTHERS' SUPERHERO DUO
COMIC BOOK SERIES

It's an ending that isn't really an ending at all.

I cup my hands and peer through the screen. There's low church music playing on the radio somewhere inside and I hear crying.

It's Dibs.

I know it is.

I touch the door handle and it creaks when I pull on it.

"Mylo!" Dibs whispers, peeking out from around the side of the house. "What are you doing?"

The backyard is full of rusted-out machinery, old engines, and pieces of crumbling wood. I watch Dibs slip back down behind an old tractor and sections of broken-up fencing.

"Dibs!" I hiss. "Where have you been? What are you doing back there?"

His head pops back up again. He looks so small behind all that junk, like he's drowning in all the brokenness. "Over here!" he calls in a whisper, waving his hand over his head.

I find him barefoot in the dirt, his back leaned up against a pile of warped wood, with a stack of comic books and a fat lip with a cut across the center.

"What are you doing out here?" I sit down next to him.

He doesn't even look up from his Planet Comics book. "He doesn't want me in there today," he tells me matter-of-factly, like I just asked him about the weather.

"What do you mean? It's your house."

"I'm not allowed back inside." He shrugs, turning back to his comic book. "It happens sometimes. On the days I can't do nothing right."

"Like what things?"

He shrugs again without looking up from his comic. "Like every single solitary thing I do."

"Your lip looks real bad," I tell him. "Maybe Momma should tend to it."

He turns a page and shrugs. "It doesn't hurt."

I stare at him while my bones ache deep inside.

Dibs shuts his comic book. "I've been thinking about Moon Shadow a lot," he tells me. "I miss her already."

"Me too," I say.

"Yeah, but you can talk to her all you want with the head-band she left for you, right?"

I shrug. "I guess. But it's not the same. I still miss her. Like trying to teach her to eat ice cream before I knew she didn't eat ice cream."

"And teaching her to speak English from Superman comic books," Dibs says.

"She could even tell a better knock-knock joke than Spuds," I say.

Dibs laughs. "That's not so hard to do."

"I guess not."

"So, have you learned anything new since she's been gone? You know . . . new and *important* kinds of stuff."

I roll my eyes. "You mean, like the bathroom?"

"Well? It's *important*," he insists.

"I'm too embarrassed to ask her that. But I did learn one thing. She's coming back."

He breathes in. "When?"

I shrug. "Don't know yet. But she promised me it would be real soon."

"Guess we can ask her about the whole bathroom thing then," he says.

"*You* can," I tell him.

I pick up a rock from the dirt and examine it while Dibs shakes his head real slow and blows air out his mouth. "Man alive," he says. "You have an actual friend on Europa. It doesn't get any neater than that."

"*We* do," I correct him.

"Yeah," he says, smiling with his big beaver teeth at me. "*We* do.

"Lots of them, actually," I say.

I can feel Dibs's eyes on me while I dig out another rock from the ground. "They probably see you as some kind of hero, too, huh?" he asks.

I shrug. "Nah," I say.

"I bet they do."

I take a deep breath. "So . . . you missed church today," I tell him.

He goes back to reading.

I wipe sweat off my temple.

"Where were you?" I ask.

"He wouldn't let me out of my room."

"He locked you in?"

He turns the page without saying a word.

"I heard crying in there just now," I tell him. "I thought maybe it was you."

He shrugs again. "He does that sometimes," he says without looking up. "He doesn't know I know that, so don't tell him."

"I won't," I promise.

I pull a long weed from the dirt and start to rip it into tiny pieces.

"Mordecai Lord was there today," I say, pulling up another weed.

Dibs smiles real big. "In church?" he asks. "Nah, you're lying."

"In a suit and everything." I smile.

"Nuh-uh," he says.

"Yep."

"Brylcreem?"

"So much he looked like he came in from the rain." I laugh.

Dibs does, too. "Attic bat breath?"

"Nope," I say. "He sat right next to me and all I smelled was Aqua Velva."

Dibs goes back to his book. "I would have liked to see that," he says.

"Here." I pull the bear out from under the bib of my overalls. "He said to give it to you."

"*Me?*"

"Yeah, it's the bear from his son's room, remember?"

He takes it from my hand and gazes at it. "He didn't really say it was for *me*, did he?"

"Yep," I say. "He said, 'Give this to Dibs.'"

"He said that?"

"He said it just like that."

He gazes at the bear again, and then hugs it close to his chest. "That was real nice."

"Yeah," I agree. "Did you eat today?"

He doesn't answer me.

I hand him a flattened lemon square, wrapped in a paper napkin. An extra that I snuck when Mrs. Meadows was too busy cleaning her cat-eyed glasses during church cake-and-coffee fellowship to notice.

"Oh, man, thanks." Dibs grabs it from my hand and eats it in two bites, leaving a white powdered-sugar ring around his mouth.

"Should have brought more," I say. "Sorry."

"That's okay." He smiles. "Thanks for that one."

"Well," I tell him, standing up. "I better go."

"Thanks for saving me a lemon square . . . and the bear."

"Why don't you just come on home with me now? Momma can make you a summer sausage sandwich with extra butter, just like you like it."

"Nah," he says. "It'll just make him madder. I've got to do what he says, and then he'll cool down soon enough. He's got another half a bottle to finish, and then I'll run in and find something to eat."

My bones ache again. Sharp this time. Pulsing.

"I brought you something else," I say, pulling my homemade comic book out of my back pocket.

He takes it. "You finally finished the ending?" he asks.

"Yep."

"How'd you come up with it?"

I can tell he's already started reading because his lips move while he scans the word bubbles.

"Let me know when you're done with it," I tell him, resting my back against an old engine. "The ending has to do with you."

His eyes meet mine. "Me?" he asks.

I nod.

"You put *me* in your book?"

"Why are you so surprised?" I ask.

He shrugs. "I don't feel important enough to be in any book."

"You're important to me," I tell him. "You're like my brother."

He stares at me for a long time, powdered sugar still all around his mouth like a clown's makeup and big round tears sitting on his lower lashes. "Really?"

"Yep," I tell him.

"Like Obie?"

I nod.

Then I watch the big tears perched on his bottom lashes push their way down his face in two straight lines.

39

A CHAMPION FOR THE UNDERDOG

July 14, 1947—9:10 a.m.

I don't tell Momma about the headband Moon Shadow gave me just in case she makes me wash my forehead to Z, too. It's under my pillow next to Shortstop for safekeeping.

Last night after lights out, all I could do was worry about Dibs. It's been a few days now since we've been toes to nose, and truth be told, I miss his noxious feet in my face. I even pulled the headband over my head last night, hoping to get the answers I was looking for.

But the headband stayed silent.

I guess it's an answer I need to find on my own.

After chores the next morning, I find Momma out in the side-yard garden. She's on her hands and knees in the dirt, weeding around the beet plants that she'll pick for canning in the fall. She's in her blue jeans and a button-down shirt, her hair tied back with a flowery scarf. I sit down on the ground and watch her. She's singing. It's the first time I've heard her do that since Obie got sick.

I like hearing it.

"Momma?"

"Yes?" she asks without looking up.

"My bones are hurting me," I tell her.

She sits back on her heels and blows an unruly clump of hair from her face.

"Your bones?"

"Yes, ma'am," I say. "Deep inside, they're aching me."

"Come over here, let me feel your head."

"My bones don't ache for me," I say. "They ache for Dibs. And you know who else? For Mr. Butte. Even though sometimes I get real mad at him. My bones still ache for him, too."

"Ahh," she sighs, standing up.

She steps carefully over sprouting lettuce and Brussels sprouts and takes a seat next to me on the grass at the edge of the garden.

"Why can't we do more?" I ask her. "Mr. Butte hurts him and Dibs doesn't deserve that, but he won't leave because he has to run the ranch or his daddy will lose the whole thing and Dibs thinks it will be his fault. And he won't leave because he thinks his momma is going to come back, when we all know she's not. Someone needs to do something. And I think that someone should be us."

Momma is bobbing her head up and down like she's thinking real hard about all I'm saying to her. When she thinks of exactly the right words to say, she stops bobbing.

"You're right," she says.

"I am?"

"Yes. I've been lying up at nights wondering just what to do about it, too."

"Did you know that he didn't eat nothing at all yesterday except the lemon square I brought for him from church? And you want to know what else? Mr. Butte made him stay outside in the hot sun all day."

"Oh, Lord," she whispers.

"He's just plain awful," I go on. "I don't know why my bones would ever waste their time aching for a man like that." I put my chin in my hand and pull blades of grass out of the ground one by one.

"Mr. Butte isn't an awful man," Momma starts. "He's just . . . broken is all. And he doesn't know how to fix himself. That's why you ache for him. Because of your heart."

I think about that.

"Well, who does know how to fix him? Because he needs to be fixed quick. Dibs is skinny enough as it is. He needs to eat, Momma, you know that. That kid would eat ten times a day if you let him."

She smiles.

"Can I tell you a secret?"

"Of course," she says.

"I used to *hate* Mr. Butte," I tell her, knowing full well that I owe the penny swear jar a whole dime for that one 'cause Momma thinks *hate* is the worst of all the swears. "For what he does to Dibs. But then there's the whole aching bones thing. So I guess I don't really know how I'm supposed to feel about him. I'm all mixed up about it."

"Oh, honey, no one is all good or all bad. We all have some of both in us. We just have to remember to make the right choices even when they are harder to make than the wrong ones. And that's real tough to do sometimes."

"You mean like his drinking?" I ask her.

"That's definitely one of them." She nods.

"Momma?" I say. "Do you ever feel like the gray is sucking you in? You know, after Obie died and all?"

"The gray?"

"Yeah, like a dark cloud that chases you. Like the one that caught up with Mr. Lord. And that's what I think has Mr. Butte, too."

She takes a deep breath and blows the wisp of hair up in the air again while she considers her answer. "I guess I hadn't thought of it that way," she says, then nods again. "Yes, I suppose it can feel like that sometimes."

"It's dark," I say.

"It is," she agrees.

"And scary."

"Yes."

"And it got Mr. Lord."

"No," she says. "Maybe for a time he let it in, but I think he's finding his way out of it now." She pats my knee. "And I think maybe you had something to do with that."

"It's got Mr. Butte, though."

"I suppose so."

"We have to do something about that for Dibs," I tell her. "You said it yourself, he's our family."

She looks off in the direction of Butte Rise and Shine Pig

and Poultry. "You really have a lot of courage, Mylo," she says. "Do you know that?"

I twist my neck to face her. "Me?" I point to myself.

"Yes."

"I always thought it was Obie who was the brave one."

"He was," Momma tells me. "But you are, too. You are so much like him."

I smile big. "I am?"

"You don't agree?"

I think about it.

"I didn't," I start. "But I'm beginning to find my courage part again. I think that maybe I've had it all along, but I just misplaced it for a time."

"Well, I'm glad you found it again," she says.

I pick more blades of grass while she swats at a fly buzzing around her head.

"Momma?" I say. "Can we help Mr. Butte with his gray? I think he's having trouble seeing his way out of it. And if he loses the farm, what will happen to Dibs and him? Where will they live?"

"You have a good heart, Mylo," she tells me. "It's the very best part of you."

"What about the courage part? 'Cause you said *courage* earlier . . . remember? You said it."

She laughs and throws an arm around my shoulder. "Yes, definitely the courage part, too. Let's talk to your daddy and see what we can do," she says. "Maybe he has some ideas about how he can help with Mr. Funk at the bank. Maybe some others from church would be willing to pitch in as well."

I smile up at her. "Thanks, Momma."

"Mylo?" she asks.

"Yeah?"

"How did you get so smart?"

"Well," I say. "I know this sounds weird and all, but it kind of started with a box of Cracker Jacks, and that was only because Dibs's tongue was tired of chocolate Neccos."

40

NEW BEGINNINGS

October 6, 1947—6:15 a.m.

Jor-El McRoostershire the Third is belting out his morning wake-up song.

Chickens cluck.

Horses neigh.

Clark Kent is barking from the front porch steps.

A whole lot of nothing.

Until there's something.

Something new to the Affinito Ranch morning ensemble. Well, not exactly new, but newer.

And it starts with a word.

Just one word.

But this time, it's not a whisper or a scream.

It's Dibson Tiberius Butte.

"Mylo," he whispers. "You up?"

My eyes open when I hear it.

He's smiling at me with his big beaver teeth. But not at the end of my bed sleeping toes to nose. He's snuggled up under the blue quilt that's usually pulled straight and tight without any wrinkles in it. Except today the quilt's not pulled straight *or* tight; it's in a lump with Dibs underneath just the way Momma tucked him up under it last night.

He's holding a very special bear. Dibs named him Jupiter B. Bear. The B for Brooks.

"Mylo?" he whispers again.

I pull myself up and rub one knuckle over my eye.

"This is your best one yet," he says, holding up my latest comic book series:

MOONTIANS AREN'T GREEN, AND THEY DON'T HARVEST YOUR BRAINS, EITHER
Volume One of
The Galactic Exploits of Mylo, Dibs & Gracie
By Mylo Affinito and Graciela Maria Delgado

"You think so?"

"You bet I do. I can't believe you put me in it." He smiles even wider. "In the title and everything. And not even just a Jimmy Olsen. I'm a real live superhero. Just like you."

"And Gracie."

"Yeah, her too. I mean, like I'm really someone."

"What do you mean, *someone*?"

"Well, I mean most of the time I'm no one. And to be someone in here . . ." He lifts up the book. "Well, it's pretty neat, is all I'm saying."

"Boys!" Momma calls. "The others are here and we're almost ready to leave for Mr. Butte's farm. You better hurry up if you want breakfast first!"

I stretch my neck to see past Grammy Hildago's curtains. The dirt drive below is filling up fast. Mr. Lord's pickup is parked out front next to Mr. Butte's rusted Chevy, with Diego's Lupe, Spuds's Bazooka, and Gracie's Betsy Bobbin tied to the porch post. Mr. and Mrs. Delgado's Chevrolet Fleetmaster is off to the side, and Mac Brazel's shiny new truck sits in the open pasture.

"Good morning!" Mrs. Manuela calls, ringing the bell on her bicycle as she pedals up the drive.

"Good morning, Mrs. Manuela!" Momma calls back through the screen door.

I lie back on my pillow and smile.

"What if they made this story into a movie on the big screen in Roswell?" Dibs says to me, pulling the covers back. "It'd be even better than *Flash Gordon Conquers the Universe*. Because it'd be me and you saving humankind and Moontiankind, too . . . together. *Pledging Strength, Courage, and Justice*. Just like Superman does for the city of Metropolis. We'll be the ones to do it for the town of Corona."

"Yeah, but Flash Gordon and Superman really *are* superheroes. I only write about 'em."

"You do more than that, and you've even got the card to prove it, too," he says. "And I'm your trusty sidekick. You said it yourself."

"Dibs, anyone could have gotten that card," I tell him. "Even you if I had taken the marbles and you got the prize at the bottom."

"Yeah, but that's not the way it happened," he says. "Things happen for a reason, Mylo. That's the way the universe works. And it anointed *you*, not me or anyone else. And yes, it was through a Cracker Jack box, but still, it means something. The universe doesn't make mistakes about anything."

"Who says?"

"People," he tells me. "And they don't make that kind of thing up."

I laugh.

"Hey." He sniffs the air just like Clark Kent does when he smells a rabbit hiding in the brush. "You get a whiff of that?" He flips the quilt back and comes to sit on the edge of my bed in a bright white, brand-new pair of Fruit of the Looms Momma got him from the Montgomery Ward's in Roswell, which are still two sizes too big. "I think I smell chorizo and eggs this morning."

I push my covers back, too. "Yeah, I smell it."

"Ready?"

I grab my jeans from the floor and dust the dirt from yesterday's chores off the knees.

The Superhero Club Membership Card falls out of the back pocket, and Dibs reaches down to pick it up.

"See?" He examines it. "Here it is again. It keeps coming back to remind you."

I smile. "You think?"

"For sure," he says. "No matter what you say, I know you have the power."

"Yeah, but technically, I didn't save anyone," I say, pulling one leg on and then the other. "Moon Shadow did all the work, really."

He stays quiet then while he pulls a long-sleeve T-shirt over his head.

"You sure did too save someone," he mumbles.

"Who?" I ask, pulling on a plaid button-down.

He hesitates again.

"*Me*," he whispers.

I stop messing with my buttons then and stare at him.

"And Daddy too," he adds.

Skinny Dibs with teeth ten times the size of his mouth standing like a skeleton with the skin still on half naked in gigantic underwear that he has to give a good yank to once in a while to keep it from slipping off his hips.

"What?"

He grabs his overalls from the floor, too.

"Maybe you can't be everyone's hero," he says softly, pulling the legs on and buckling up at the shoulders. "But you're mine."

I stand there blinking at him until he's finally done with the buckles. When he looks up, I can see two big drops balanced right on his bottom lashes. They make two perfect lines down his cheeks, along his neck, and down the front of the bib on his overalls. Then my eyes feel like they're going to start, and the last thing I want is to let Dibson Tiberius Butte see two perfect lines down me. So I punch him in the arm instead, and he almost falls right over.

"Boys!" Momma calls again.

"Come on," I say. "If we get all the chores done, we'll have time to play a game out back before lunch."

"Gracie sure is shaping up to be a good third baseman, huh?"

"Yep," I say.

"Better than your momma." He giggles behind his hand.

I roll my eyes to the ceiling. "Way better," I say. "But don't tell her I said that. With your daddy in left field and mine on first base, we're getting mighty close to having a full team."

"Still need a center fielder."

I nod.

"How about Eunice Snodgrass?"

"No way," I tell him.

He laughs. "Daddy's taking me to watch game seven of the World Series on the televisions in the window of the True Value in Roswell later this afternoon."

"Maybe you can use this when we play today," I say, pulling up the mattress and grabbing Obie's glove out from under it.

"That . . ." Dibs points. "*That's* the lump I've been sleeping on all this time?"

I toss it to him, and he catches it with the tips of his fingers. "You're going to let me use it?" he asks, staring at it with wide eyes and caressing the smooth leather.

"Nope," I tell him. "It's for keeps."

"No way!"

"Yep."

"For real?" he asks, wiping his nose with the back of his hand.

"For real," I tell him.

"Boys!" Momma calls again from the kitchen. "Breakfast!"

I watch him slip his fingers into the glove and smack the center of it with one tiny duke. A fine mist of red dirt glistens in the sun streaming through the dusty lace curtains that slow dance to the cool fall breeze blowing in the window.

"I won't miss one catch with this!"

Dibs darts out of the room and down the stairs, hollering for Momma. "Mrs. Affinito! Mrs. Affinito!" he calls. "Look what Mylo gave me!"

There's really only one very important thing to know about Dibson Tiberius Butte and nothing else really matters:

1. He's my very best friend in the whole entire universe.

I pull Shortstop out from under my pillow and breathe him in at the top of his head, smelling the oil from your leather catcher's mitt and the dirt from the pitcher's mound that we built together out back . . .

And I remember when Moon Shadow put her headband in my hand and how it felt between my fingers and how I learned about new beginnings. There were a lot of those this summer.

Good ones, too.

I peer at the boy in the mirror above the dresser.

He's different somehow.

I hold my arms up like a saguaro cactus. Still not much happening there, but I have counted four wisps on my lip. Not exactly enough for a comb, but at least there's hope.

I set Shortstop down against the pillow on the bed. He looks back at me with his one good eye while the other hangs by a thread.

Just the way you left him.

I learned a lot about new beginings this past summer, Obie, but also about endings.

And the truth is there really isn't any such thing as endings.

I know now that your story will never have a true end.

Because you're my brother.

And you always will be.

No new beginning will ever change that.

AUTHOR'S NOTE

ROSWELL DECLASSIFIED

Do you enjoy the mystery of cryptozoology, the study of unknown creatures, as much as I do? Well, fellow crypto-zoologists, *The Truth About Martians* is based on facts and eyewitness reports of one very special UFO (unidentified flying object) sighting that happened in 1947. Let's explore the mystery together.

I was so excited to travel to New Mexico to personally investigate the story of a mysterious crash that happened in the dark of night in Corona, a small desert town just north of Roswell, during the summer of 1947. Whatever it was that fell to Earth is still being debated even today, both in Roswell and around the world. One of the reasons so many people continue to talk about this particular sighting is that it was the first and only time in history that the U.S. government reported they had captured a flying saucer. The story was on the front page of many newspapers, and at the time, this report shocked the entire world. The Roswell radio station and the military base were flooded with calls from around the globe demanding more information about the extraterrestrial spacecraft found in the desert.

Soon after, the U.S. government changed their story and reported that the materials found in the field were really just a part of a simple military weather balloon, a device used to measure atmospheric conditions. They said it had all been a big mistake.

The story died. The phone calls stopped.

It would be the last time an official would speak of the incident.

Until they did.

Years later, the world began to take an interest again in whatever crashed out on the Foster ranch. It started in 1978 when one very important witness, Major Jesse Marcel, the Head Information Officer and the first man from the Army Air Force Base in Roswell assigned to investigate the crash back in 1947, broke his silence and shared his truth with the world. He first began to tell close friends, and then later the media, that the pieces he gathered in the desert that day were not pieces of a downed weather balloon at all, but a kind of metal he had never seen before.

During my time in Corona and Roswell, I met a lot of wonderful people. Some believed that what crashed in the desert was a real flying disk, while others thought it was just a story. Whether you believe it or not, these are the facts:

A man named Mac Brazel, a ranch hand working at the Foster ranch in Corona, New Mexico, found hundreds of strange metal pieces spread across his field one summer morning. The mysterious pieces were of a strange material, some of them engraved with odd purple symbols, similar to Egyptian hieroglyphics. Mac wasn't sure what to do about the mess in his field. After calling out both the Roswell sheriff and the Roswell fire department, they agreed that Mac should call the Roswell Army Air Force base to look at the pieces and decide what to do with them. Mac called the base, and Major Jesse Marcel was sent to investigate. The major drove out to the Foster ranch, gathered some of the pieces, and brought them back to the base.

After the military examined the strange metal, the base commander ordered a press release, stating that the U.S. government had captured a flying disk. As Major Marcel tells it, the military soon changed its mind about what the public should know about the discovered extraterrestrial materials. They said it was all a big mistake—it had only been a broken-up weather balloon found in the field that day. Immediately after, hundreds of military men surrounded the crash site and removed every piece of debris they could find, including what some say was a crashed disk. In the following days, Major Marcel was asked to pose for photos holding up flimsy material from a broken weather balloon for the newspaper, to prove the first story about a flying saucer was an error. Major Marcel would later say the materials he was photographed holding were not what he had recovered in the debris field.

Some of the children in Corona and Roswell also came forward to say that they had seen the strange metal with purple markings. Frankie Rowe, the daughter of the fire chief in Roswell, and Jesse Marcel Jr., Major Marcel's son, both said they had touched the mysterious pieces. They also told stories about the people in town being pressured by the military not to speak of the incident as a matter of national security. Other witnesses claimed to have seen the actual disk, and a few even said they saw the mysterious creatures themselves. There have been retired military officers who have come forward years later to say that some of the creatures actually survived and were brought to a secure base to be studied.

Back in 1947, there seemed to be a lot of UFO sightings, both before and after the Roswell crash. Some believe it was because of the nuclear bomb detonation that was happening on Earth at the time. In fact, the 509th Bomb Group in Roswell was the base responsible for the two bombs dropped in Japan at the end of World War II, and they had also done a lot of bomb testing in the desert. At the time, the government didn't believe the nuclear materials would harm our planet or the planets in our solar system, but we now know that's not true. It's believed by some people that advanced beings from other worlds may have understood the damage we were causing the universe and traveled to Earth to see what we were up to.

President Truman was the first president to have to deal with UFOs publicly. During his presidency, many government agencies were formed, including the CIA and the NIA, to control what they thought should be secret information. Additional government projects were formed to investigate what was happening in our skies, including Project Sign (1947), Project Grudge (1949), and Project Blue Book (1952). In the 1950s, a top-secret air force base called Area 51 was formed to create and test secret new aircraft. Some say that this is where the military brought the Roswell disk to study it and learn about their advanced technology. It is the opinion of a select few that this may have been how we learned to create the technology that we use today.

And we know that the government continues to search our skies, after the U.S. Department of Defense revealed a long-secret government program in 2017 called the Advanced Aerospace Threat Identification Program. This project, which cost $22 million, ran from 2007 to 2012 and investigated UFO sightings. The Department of Defense also shared a video of one secret sighting, as U.S. military pilots attempted to identify it.

They couldn't.

Stories of strange creatures, advanced flying disks, and the possibility of life on other planets continue to intrigue and excite us—including the mysterious crash that happened in Corona, New Mexico, during the summer of 1947. Whatever it was made a big impact on the world, and yet still remains a mystery. Was it a downed weather balloon property of the U.S. military? Was it a spaceship filled with small beings from another world?

You'll have to decide for yourself.

If you want to learn more about the Roswell incident, you can find additional details, witness interviews, government documents, and the original newspaper articles by visiting the International UFO Museum and Research Center in Roswell at roswellufomuseum.com/incident.html or the National Archives at archives.gov/research/military/air-force/ufos.html.

To learn more about our history of using atomic weapons, visit the National Museum of Nuclear Science and History at nuclearmuseum.org.

And if you're interested in more extraterrestrial adventures, there are many wonderful fictional stories based on the Roswell incident. Some of my favorites include the television show *Roswell* and Steven Spielberg's miniseries *Taken*, and J. J. Abrams's movie *Super 8* has a reference to the Roswell crash.

ACKNOWLEDGMENTS

I am so grateful to have been given the opportunity to write with Crown Books for Young Readers. I have met so many amazing people and learned so much along this journey. Thank you to you all, including the dedicated teachers, the enthusiastic librarians, the passionate booksellers, and especially the kids I have had the privilege to meet. I've loved the opportunity to connect with each of you to talk about the amazing power of story. This has been a dream come true for me, and I am thankful to everyone who has been a part of the adventure.

Laurie McLean, superagent with Fuse Literary. Many thanks for your patience and guidance and for always being just a phone call away.

Emily Easton, Samantha Gentry, Kathy Dunn, and all the wonderful people at Penguin Random House. Thank you for your support, enthusiasm, dedication, and commitment to sharing my stories with so many. It's such a privilege for me to be a part of your team.

Kelly Easton, author, teacher, friend. Thank you for sharing your expertise, guidance, and encouragement. You have been an incredible mentor for me along this journey.

My family and friends, it has meant the world to me to see your excitement, love, and support as I pursue this new writerly life. Thank you for your kindness.

And last, Tobin, my very own little superhero. You continue to shape and inspire me to find the courage to reach in directions I never thought I would. You are what I'm most grateful for every single day.

1

BANANA FAMOUS

Words may seem innocent enough, but I'm here to tell you that they're a way bigger deal than most people know.

They are *so* powerful, in fact, that they can change you in a single, solitary second.

Words can propel you so high that you could fly straight up to the sky blue. Or can seem so heavy on your shoulders that you think you'll never stand straight again. And there's one reason for that.

Words make us *feel*.

And feelings are everything. They control who we are and how we live and every single choice we make.

My name is Adelaide Ru Fitzhugh.

Ada Ru for short.

Ru for even shorter.

I've been writing since I was born so I know words real good. One day I plan to write words so important that lots of people are going to want to read the way I put them together. And they'll feel something while they read them too.

I'm talking about a legit, big-time writer.

And by that, of course, I mean super famous. Like go-to-the-grocery-store-for-bananas-in-a-limo kind of famous. Just like J. K. Rowling probably does. I mean, if you're as famous as her, you certainly don't go shopping in a plain old white Prius named Patty that has a SAVE THE TREES bumper sticker on it like we have.

In my Kreative Kids writing class in Denver, I learned another real important thing about words. If you want to write a really good story, I mean, a really super-good one, you should write what you know.

So I decided to think long and hard about what I know. Unfortunately, I got bubkes. And bubkes is a big problem for a serious writer. My life is actually pretty boring. Not that I'm complaining about that. I mean, I love my life on Tennyson Street just outside the city of Denver.

It's predictable.

And that's me.

But predictable isn't exactly exciting or interesting and it certainly doesn't make you *feel*. There's no *pop* to predictable, and as a writer, if you don't have pop, you've got zip. I mean, where does a girl like me find pop when I've never been kidnapped by pirates on the high seas or raised by wolves? I've never known one single animal that could talk and I've certainly never been abducted by aliens . . . at least as far as I know.

I just finished sixth grade at Skinner Middle School, I'm the president of the Tennyson Street Beyoncé Beyhive Fan

Club, and a champion cupcake eater. I refuse to swim in any public pool (because of the pee) and I have an award-winning collection of ceramic kittens.

See what I mean?

That's bubkes big-time.

This year Mom even helped me start my very own podcast. It's called *Words with Ru*. The problem is, it's very hard to find something with pop in it to talk about on your very own podcast when nothing interesting has really happened to you yet. That's probably why I only have two subscribers to date.

Nan and Granddad Fitzhugh.

But if I had pop, who knows how many people I'd get.

I've been waiting all this year for something cool to happen to me.

And now, the summer after sixth grade . . . *it does*.

Dun, dun . . . *dun*.

Spoiler alert: there may or may not be an actual real live lake monster involved, but that's all I'm going to say about that.

For now, anyway.

And it all started with a Friday Family Fitzhugh meeting.

2

WHAT'S SO WRONG
WITH DISNEY WORLD?

"Hear ye, hear ye," I call out, banging my fist like a gavel on the kitchen table. "Let the Friday Fitzhugh Family Meeting come to order."

It's my job to bring the meeting to order every week. I don't wear a judge's robe or anything *that* official, but it's still a pretty big deal.

"Mom." I nod in her direction. "First order of business."

Her job is agendas and refreshments. Tonight's snack is a plastic bowl full of Jelly Belly jelly beans.

Side note: I only eat the Buttered Popcorn ones.

It's because I totally love them. It's like if I was forced to live on a desert island and could only bring two things with me for my survival, it would be Buttered Popcorn jelly beans and an endless supply of soda.

Which is the exact reason why I'm digging through the plastic bowl as Mom announces the first order of business.

"First up . . . chores and cleanliness."

I sneak a covert eye roll and keep on digging through the beans.

Other than the *hear ye* part and an occasional *order in the court*, the meetings are pretty dullsville. They *always* start exactly the same.

Who's been slacking on their chores? (Me)

Who isn't keeping their room clean enough? (Me)

Who's not making their bed in the mornings? (Yep, me again)

Who's not mowing the lawn? (That one . . . has Dad's name written all over it)

For the spring meetings we sometimes have an additional category on the agenda.

The Fitzhugh summer vacation destination.

That's also when someone inevitably brings up the subject of Disney World and why we can't ever go there (that's me too if you didn't already guess it).

Can someone please tell me what's so wrong with Disney World?

My best friend, Britney B, went two summers ago and said it *really is* where dreams come true. It even said so on the Disney souvenir book she brought home with her.

Me and Britney B have been best friends since first grade when her family moved two doors down from us. We like all the same movies, we both agree that adding vegetables will ruin a perfectly good pizza every time and we look just alike, with plain brown hair and skinny bodies with ugly knobby knees that we both detest. Last month, in an extremely-bad-idea best-friend pact, we both chopped our hair in bobs at the chin. I hate mine, but she loves hers. Probably because she looks way better in it than I do.

I know everything there is to know about her and she knows the same about me. That's the way real best friends are. For instance, I know that right this second, she's waiting on me to come over so we can watch *Taken Souls* on the Syfy channel. We watch it together every single Friday after the Fitzhugh Family Meetings.

When Mom is finished with her chore slacking list, she nods to me.

I pound on the table three more times. "Next on the agenda," I announce.

Mom looks at Dad. "Summer plans," she announces.

Wait . . . what? This is way earlier than usual and I haven't even planted all my Disney World hints yet.

I sit straight up and cross two sets of fingers on each hand. I close my eyes tight and wait for it.

Come on, Disney World.

Come on, Disney World.

Come on, Disney World.

"Dad's going to talk about summer plans this year," Mom says.

I peek one eye open.

Dad never leads any agenda item and he's certainly never led the summer plans one. It's unprecedented. Maybe that's a good sign.

Or maybe not.

I close my eyes tight again and wait for it.

He clears his throat.

I hold my breath. Magic Kingdom, here I come!

And then . . . he says it.

He lays a bomb on me that changes my entire life. With just one line, and believe me, it's got nothing to do with dreams coming true either.

"We are spending the entire summer in Scotland."

No warning.

No doomsday prep.

No *You had better sit down for this one.*

It has to be a joke. I give him a good long stare while I wait for the punch line.

Except there isn't one.

"Order in the court. Order in the court." I pound my fist gavel on the table, then stare at Dad. "Are you seriously kidding me right now?" I ask him. "Because it's so not funny."

He gives me his *extra-wide* grin. The one that shows all his straight white teeth and the getting-old crinkles right at the corners of his eyes, and he says, "Nope. We are going for the whole summer. We'll get to see Uncle Clive and Aunt Isla and your cousin Briony. It's been six years since we've gotten a chance to visit."

Suddenly, all the Buttered Popcorns aren't sitting so well inside my belly.

"Adelaide Ru," Mom says, grabbing my wrist and pulling my hand out of the bowl of beans.

Mom's the only one who never calls me anything short. She uses my whole name every single time. She says it's because it's too beautiful a name to go short. Even though she goes short on hers all the time because her real name is Elizabeth and everyone calls her Libby.

Right this minute she's frowning hard at me. "You know I don't like it when you dig around in there with your licked-on fingers. It's gross. One more time and I'm putting the jelly beans away."

"Dad, do we really have to spend the entire summer there?" I ask him.

"We don't *have* to, my little Rutabaga," Dad says. "We *get* to."

Dad never goes short on my name and he doesn't go long either. Basically, he calls me anything with an *r* and *u* in it. *Rutabaga* is one of his favorites.

I sigh and lay my chin in my hand. This can't be happening.

Tennyson Street is my life.

My home.

My world.

I can't live somewhere else for an entire summer.

On our summer vacations, I'm usually homesick by Tuesday and already packed by Wednesday. I mean, unless we were to go to Disney World. That's a whole different story.

It's not that I don't like seeing other places. I just love our Tennyson life and get homesick real easy. The small redbrick house just outside the city is ours and always has been. It's the best house on the best street. The bright white shutters and a matching porch swing that I helped paint. Mom's rosemary shrubs lining the front walk that I helped plant. Tennyson is even where we found our three-legged orange tabby cat, Mr. Mews. He was a stray in the back alley by the garage, snacking on old leftovers from Parisi out of our garbage can. He looked up from his gnarly ravioli and actually smiled at me.

That's when I knew in my heart he was mine.

Side note: Parisi has the best spaghetti carbonara on the *planet*. And I'm not even exaggerating either.

"I'm sorry to inform you but I am unable to move to Scotland for an entire summer at this time," I tell them.

Mom raises her eyebrows at that one. "Oh?" she says.

"What about my Sunday-afternoon Bookworm Club at the BookBar? Or . . . or our Italian Wednesdays at Parisi? Or Mexican Tuesdays at El Chingon when we order our *cena y bebidas* completely in Spanish? Not to mention we just painted my room cornflower blue and put up the new curtains too. Oh, and what about my podcast? I can't let my audience down."

"I'm sure Nan and Granddad Fitzhugh won't mind missing a few episodes."

"I have more subscribers than Nan and Granddad Fitzhugh," I inform her.

"Who else?" she asks.

Silence.

"This isn't about subscribers," I tell her.

"Ru Ru Bugaboo," my dad says with that same wide smile. "We'll be back in September."

September? This is a nightmare.

"It's good news," he goes on.

"Ah, *wrong*," I inform him. "Good news would be a week at the Magic Kingdom. This is the opposite of good news. This is . . . it's . . . well, it's *bad news* is what it is."

The Buttered Popcorns are now sending a critical warning that they might want back out.

Mom chimes in. "Wait until you see where we're staying this time. It's called the Highland Club, and it's inside a Benedictine abbey. It's one of the oldest buildings in the town of

Fort Augustus and was originally built in 1876 as an abbey, but they've renovated it into modern apartments. Doesn't that sound fun?"

"Not especially," I say.

She ignores me.

"What an adventure," she goes on, popping in a green Jelly Belly.

Maybe a Sunkist Lime or Watermelon.

"I'm the number one reviewer in the Bookworm group. I need to keep up my quota because you just *know* that Emmanuelle Penney is chomping at the bit to take my top spot. She's only two away." I hold up two fingers to show them both. "*Two . . . away.*"

"This is going to be wonderful," Mom goes on. "Do you remember how much fun you and your cousin Briony had last time?"

"*Remember?* How could I forget? She shaved my Malibu Barbie doll."

"Oh . . ." Mom waves a hand. "You've long outgrown Barbies, anyway."

"Barbie was bald, Mom. *Bald.*"

"I'm sure Briony's grown up just like you have," Dad chimes in.

"Did I not mention that she also still sucked her thumb at *six*? And she smelled . . . shall we say *questionable*?"

Mom isn't listening. "I think it's an amazing opportunity to get to visit family we hardly ever see," she goes on.

"Uh . . . try crazy time," I mumble. "I mean, who spends an entire summer in a whole other country? People go for a week, maybe two. Not three months. That's nuts."

Dad cocks his head to the side the exact same way that Britney B's beagle, Cheez Whiz, does when you talk to her because she only understands certain words, like *park*, *ball* and *pizza delivery*. For all the rest of the words she just turns her head sideways, trying real hard to figure out what you're saying. Me and Britney B call that look a Cheez Whiz. And it's Dad's Cheez Whiz that makes my heart start beating even harder because I realize that this situation is just like with Disney World.

I don't get a say.

"Dad got a position at the University of the Highlands and Islands in Inverness," Mom says. "To teach an advanced photography class for the summer term. We will be renting out our house at the end of the month to a lovely family. The Morgensterns. They have a five-year-old daughter named Delilah."

Some random girl rolling down Tennyson on *my* Razor scooter with the pink trim?

Eating *my* raspberry-filled Funfetti cupcakes at Valhalla?

Sleeping under *my* poster of Beyoncé—the *I AM . . . Sasha Fierce* album.

It's a complete and total nightmare is what it is.

"What about Mr. Mews?" I demand. "He's not going to like this one bit."

"The Morgensterns have graciously agreed to take care of him for the summer while they're here," Mom says. "They said their little Delilah loves cats."

"He's not a *cat*," I remind her. "He's part of the family, and he's not going to want to sleep with some random girl. Not to mention, he's very particular about the way his whiskers are stroked. He'll be very lonely without me here. Maybe one of us should stay home. Me and Mr. Mews could stay with Britney B. Her mom won't care."

That's when my mom's head starts with the slow nod and I know exactly what's coming.

I give her a straight pointer finger and say, "Don't even."

But she goes and does it anyway.

"How does it make you feel, honey?" she says with . . . *the voice.*

The smooth-as-silk one.

Mom's a child psychologist and teaches at the university and for her, feeling words are *huge.* It's always feelings this and feelings that, and this isn't any different.

I cross my arms tight over my chest in protest. "Frankly," I tell her, "I think it stinks."

"That's a *thinking* word, honey, not a *feeling* word," she reminds me. "Try again."

"Fine," I say. "I *feel* . . . like it stinks."

She sighs at that one and pops a red jelly bean into her mouth.

A Cinnamon or maybe a Very Cherry.

"Why can't Dad just go without us?" I ask. "Like he does when he goes to New York."

Dad's a big-time photographer. And by big-time, of course I mean famous. Not limo famous because Mom and Dad share Prius Patty, but still. His pictures have been in some of the most popular newspapers in the world, like the *New York Times*, and well-known magazines like *Smithsonian* and *National Geographic* and even in some photography museums in Los Angeles and New York. He's been asked to speak at some colleges on the East Coast, but never to teach full-time. Never for a whole entire summer.

"Because it's for a whole summer this time," Mom explains. "And you're out of school and . . . we're a family and, well, we stick together. Anyway, we'll be back by the time school starts."

"What about *your* job?" I ask her. "Who's going to teach your summer classes?"

"I'm taking a three-month sabbatical to research and write a journal article."

I don't even have to ask what her article is going to be about.

Feeling Words and the People Who Love Them

By Dr. Libby Fitzhugh, Phd (a lover of feelings)

So just like that, the Fitzhugh family summer vacation is decided and I don't get a say.

Again.

It's so unfair.

Seriously, can someone please tell me, what is so wrong with Disney World?

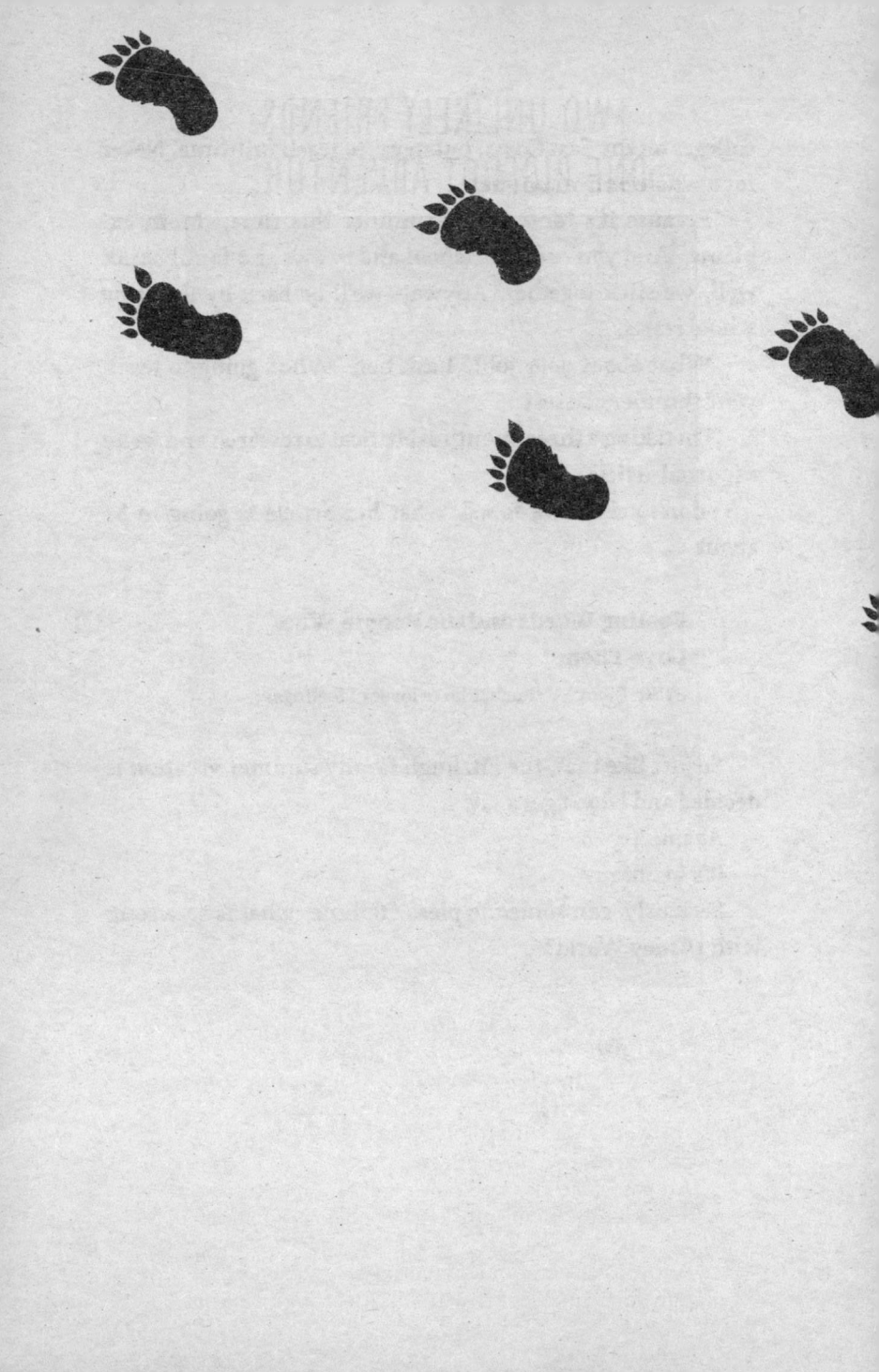

TWO UNLIKELY FRIENDS.
ONE BIGFOOT ADVENTURE.

"Lemons will steal your heart."—KAREN CUSHMAN,
Newbery Medalist for *The Midwife's Apprentice*

MELISSA SAVAGE

LEMONS

HER SEARCH FOR
BIGFOOT MIGHT
LEAD HER HOME . . .

BIGFOOT DETECTIVES INC.

A KIDS' INDIE NEXT LIST SELECTION

"Packed with humor, mystery, friendship, family secrets,
and even Bigfoot!" —Karen Cushman,
Newbery Medalist for *The Midwife's Apprentice*

"An enjoyable and welcome exploration of sorrow,
healing, and friendship." —*School Library Journal*

"A joyous celebration of cryptozoology, friendship,
family love, and coping with loss." —*Kirkus Reviews*